A GOD COMES ALIVE

Laojiu sat in his room at the Consulate. The exhibit was a great success. But every few days, the brutal murder of another young girl was discovered. All of them had visited the exhibit before their deaths. Could it be that . . . ? Laojiu pushed such irrational thoughts from his mind.

Suddenly he heard a shriek from his daughter's room. He found her covered with cuts, her pajamas almost torn off. "The Madjan," she gasped. "It was he who did this to me . . ."

THE MADJAN

JEFF ROVIN

CHARTER BOOKS, NEW YORK

All characters in this book are fictitious.
Any resemblance to actual persons, living or dead,
is purely coincidental.

THE MADJAN

A Charter Book / published by arrangement with
the author

PRINTING HISTORY
Charter Original / April 1984

All rights reserved.
Copyright © 1984 by Jeff Rovin
This book may not be reproduced in whole
or in part, by mimeograph or any other means,
without permission. For information address:
The Berkley Publishing Group, 200 Madison Avenue,
New York, New York 10016

ISBN: 0-441-51602-5

Charter Books are published by The Berkley Publishing Group,
200 Madison Avenue, New York, N.Y. 10016.
PRINTED IN THE UNITED STATES OF AMERICA

PROLOGUE

IT WAS A PLEASURE to be able to hate them again.

Kuo stared from his tower aerie atop the rim of the dry Turpan Basin. He studied with resignation the personality of a city impatient for nightfall; the giddy contagion was everywhere, in exaggerated smiles and spirited steps. The merry idle clustered about the palace gate, and Kuo could not begrudge them this. The only time they were permitted to leave the fields was to celebrate the triumphs of Emperor Ch'en.

The soldiers were a different matter. Brightly colored monoliths, they were uncrowned royalty, from General Jiang to the lowliest foot soldier. Darkness would make their god the almighty god of Ch'en-shimm in honor of Jiang's victory over Xiqing. The same darkness that filled the heavens with wonder would see the earth given over to the purveyors of blood and infamy.

It was good to be able to hate them with his eyes as he had with his heart. To be able to fasten his loathing on a piggish face here or a lumpish figure there. It was a rare, almost narcotic delight. He savored that enmity because it reminded him of how superior he was to them.

The astrologer gazed from his observatory, allowing his yellow eyes to linger a moment longer on the obscene tableau. He could understand how these savage, sweaty husks were like sons to the Emperor. The aging ruler had himself been a warrior, a fine one, Kuo's father had once mentioned. But Ch'en had been a king eleven years, and his devotion should extend to all his subjects.

Or if not his love, at least his generosity, thought Kuo.

The thick queue of fighting men twined from the palace to the temple, along a walkway that had been finished only that afternoon. To Kuo, the row of warriors was neither a conquering army nor the hierarchy of a new order. It was a mass of cattle feeding on the royal treasury. Every soldier was a research aide he could not have, every sword a much-needed sighting tube; the hammers and picks that had beat designs into bronze shields should have been used to raise dots on the surface of celestial globes. As if hating these human oxen were not distracting enough, Kuo drifted into despondency, dwelling upon the relative importance to Ch'en of their brawn as compared to his mind.

A pair of red-robed youths walked slowly from a door in the palace gate and began to light the torches that lined the cobbled path. Kuo's tired eyes rose with grateful purpose to the Mountain of Flames on the horizon. Beyond its tawny slopes, the sun offered up its last light; it flickered as it seemed to snag on a peak, and then the day was gone. It was time for his final observation in the matter of the Madjan.

Kuo turned from the low rock wall that rounded his private peak, the tall, cylindrical observatory. Bent beneath a black silk frock decorated with crescent moons and dragons, he mounted a raised platform and clasped a bony hand around the broad central band of an armillary sphere, a heavenly yardstick composed of five bronze hoops and supported by a quartet of miniature warriors. He peered into the twilight skies.

"Red. Ch'en asks, 'What does this mean?' If I tell him in truth, 'My lord, I do not know why the moon is red,' I am disgraced, and my own son does not become astrologer. The proud legacy of seven generations ends with me. If I augur wrongly, I am executed and my family exiled. Yet," he lamented aloud, "how can I understand such a phenomenon without a pigmented glass and color chart? Just so, the great dragon pursues its own forked tail."

He sighed, unspooling a scroll that lay on a marble writing pedestal beside the sphere. "Seldom has one who has an emperor's ear wielded so little power," he murmured, then glanced out again at the temple. A frail cackle bubbled briefly in his throat. "I suspect that Emperor Ch'en fears me. Knowledge is a power which transcends physical might. He recognizes this and sees in me one who would use him as a dray horse to pull the wagon of state so I could commune more intelligently with the gods. Ch'en will never give me what I need. No," he wagged a bony finger at the sky, "whatever I achieve, it must be on my own."

A soft, warm breeze stirred the parchment, and his eyes turned to the scroll. "Until then, I must sanctify this repugnant ceremony. Red . . . red. Blood is red, yet the moon does not live, and so it cannot bleed. The sun is often red, but that is because it is fire; the moon is ice. As the two do not share the sky this night, the one cannot borrow light from the other. If only I had more time, let alone the tools to conduct a proper study—"

Kuo tapped a long, spindly nail against the cold marble. "Perhaps I am pursuing the answer in the wrong manner. Perhaps the stars do not hold the solution. Yes. Yes, I have taken a wrong fork. The moon reflects our world and the blush on its face may spring from something it has seen among mortal endeavors."

He depressed a pin protruding from the lip of the marble slab. A complex series of counterweights slid the platform aside. Within the column was a library of tightly wound scrolls, over three dozen of them, end up. The document Kuo sought was bound with orange and black ribbons, with the ends tucked into the mouth of the scroll.

"A treatise on the climate," the astrologer muttered as he unwound the ancient parchment. "My great grandfather's lasting work of scholarship." He lifted a lantern from its perch atop the armillary and hung it on a pole beside the pedestal. He turned his aching eyes to the faded writing, which was barely visible in the flickering light. His perpetual scowl pinched about the edges into something resembling a smile. "For once, my ancestor, your tendency to overexplain is precisely what I need. Let me see. 'The leaves die red, and the waning sun sinks in a sea of red. The dragon exhales red, while men perish into a flood of red. Red are the fruits made from the flesh of evil ancestors, and red is the face of the lustful or truthless. The gods created red to signify death.' "

Kuo started. "Not death," he implored, looking over his shoulder at the burning moon. "In two years of war, we have had *enough* of death." He returned to the writing. " 'There can be no good omen in the presence of red, for it opposes the blue of hope and calm.' " The astrologer's frown returned as he scanned the document. "A bad sign," he concurred, "yet a combination of red and the moon's ice may presage a different—"

Kuo's bloodshot eyes locked on one entry beside an illuminated rendering of a dragon bellowing beneath the plane of the world. "Now, this is interesting," he murmured. "He attributes this to the explorer Chi-pin, who lived a generation before him. Chi-pin wrote, 'I have seen the earth spit red sand into the air. I have seen this sand bury a village and color the skies for days.' " Kuo considered this as his eyes wandered to the drawing. "The earth dragon on whose back we rest could cause this to happen. Was I not awakened this morning by utter quiet? No animals stirred, and now—" he looked around "—only the barest wind crosses the basin. It could be . . . let me think."

The astrologer turned again to the red face of the full moon as it climbed high in the darkening sky. Then he glanced at the temple, the magnificent edifice that Emperor Ch'en would dedicate to the Madjan in honor of his great victory. "The earth's inhabitants are all still for fear of disturbing the dragon coiled beneath our feet. Yes, it must be that he has been awakened—but by what? Is the moon a clue? Red? Red . . . the seeping blood of war's dead!" He tapped his temple with a crooked finger. "Yes, the dragon has been roused by spilled blood and with a snort of his nostrils blew it skyward, to color the moon, to warn us that we are disturbing him. Which means if any more blood is shed—"

Clutched by a sudden, raw fear, the astrologer nodded with understanding. He made a few additional calculations to see if the heavens predicted a stirring of the earth dragon. The stars painted a grim picture: the Hunter's bow was poised, the Warrior's ax was raised, and the Jackal had fled. They knew. Even now, it might be too late.

His robe swirling behind him, the astrologer spun toward the steps that sloped steeply around the conical tower. Reaching the stone floor, he hurried to the great brick wall that protected the palace of Emperor Ch'en from mortal enemies.

Seventy warriors formed two rows from the throne of Ch'en to the massive double doors that fronted the palace's Great Chamber of the Emperor. The soldiers, one for every week of the campaign, stood in the regalia of imperial review: green skirts, plated chest armor with massive shoulder guards, sword, dagger, and a small shield, this lashed to their leather girdles. Every man held his battle-ax before him, gleaming edge out, each of the metal blades carved with a monstrous face intended to intimidate a foe. The fighting men stood neat and proud, from their intricately braided hair to their sandals topped with puttees. The sight of them was a remarkable contrast to what it had been a week before. Then each man was covered with the blood of an enemy, with the emptied life of those who dared serve a rebellious lord.

The Emperor regarded his troops with kingly severity. But his critical regard was softened by pride. His subjects saw the indulgence in his eyes, in the uncharacteristic way they seemed to caress rather than judge. It was the only aspect of the Emperor that was irresolute; seated in his massive ivory throne, he was set apart from it by his innate majesty, by the powerful limbs of a one-time warrior, by his royal robes of brightly colored brocade and the somber strength of his weather-beaten face.

When the priest poised by the window signaled that all the torches had been lighted, Ch'en nodded slightly, his lengthy gray queue barely moving. At his signal, the gold bas-relief doors opened outward.

Kneeling in the corridor was General Jiang, his head bowed. An old but vicious scar stared jaggedly from beneath both rims of his chin-tied helmet. He was dressed in the red blouse and skirt of the battlefield, with a yellow scarf of victory draped between his shoulder plates. In his hand was the spear with which he'd executed his counterpart in the recent strife, its tip still caked with the man's blood.

The gray eyes of the Emperor dwelt on the spear, and his smile was renewed. He motioned casually for his friend and devoted subject to rise, and as Jiang did so, his men bowed their heads in tribute.

The hall was silent. His smile waning, Emperor Ch'en

leaned toward a bald-headed old man trembling beside him in a short blue robe.

"Steward, we await Kuo."

"I—I am certain he will be here momentarily."

"We do not wait. Fetch him."

"My lord," the senior minister said, "the heavens are not always willing partners in prophecy. Perhaps Kuo has discov—"

"I *suspect* what Kuo has discovered is some worthless intellectual curiosity which means more to him than our royal pleasure." More angrily he said, "Our astrologer insults the court and insults Jiang. Unless he wishes to end up as his father did, I will have him here *at once!*"

The steward bowed and turned. However, before he could step from beside the throne, the court herald appeared in the doorway and announced Kuo. The blue-robed man relaxed visibly as, pale and slightly breathless, the astrologer scurried toward the throne.

Before he could be bidden to speak in accordance with protocol, the astrologer approached the Emperor. "Great Ch'en," he panted, waving the scroll before him, "it is the will of the gods that this dedication be postponed."

The singular gasp of the royal party, soldiers and ministers alike, was like the rush of a sharp winter wind. Ch'en looked past Kuo to the open doors. "Steward, take this scholar from among us."

"*Emperor*," Kuo insisted, "this is no delusion. There is grave danger!"

The steward glided to his side, gently taking Kuo about the shoulders. "Come, you've been stricken by the full moon."

"The full moon, the *red* moon threatens more than my sanity. I implore you, my lord, hear what I have to say! Before morning, Ch'en-shimm itself will fall!"

A fresh outburst rolled through the hall. This time it was a medley of laughter and anger at the pronouncement. Only Ch'en was not amused. He lowered his gaze to the wan astrologer.

"It is my city whose destruction you predict. *My* city. I will have your evidence and then your tongue. Our downfall," he snickered mirthlessly. "We haven't an enemy within a year's travel. Who will work this disaster? Who?"

"The havoc I see will not be by mortal hand."

"The gods favor us. The Madjan has shepherded our armies to glory."

"The victory," said Kuo, "was against men."

"Man or god, there is none as powerful as the Madjan. He will reign supreme in our land after the consecration of his temple. As for you, astrologer, you have—"

"There will be no temple if the earth dragon awakens."

Emperor Ch'en exploded to his feet. "Impudence! You hasten your death with lies about ours. Go from here, astrologer, before we spill your wife's blood upon the Madjan's altar. The gods have confused you, sent you this ill omen to try my courage once again. My faith is absolute! And if, as you predict, there is a struggle to be waged, then we shall wage it, not flee!" Throwing himself back on the throne, the Emperor motioned for a pair of royal guards to leave their post at the door and remove the astrologer.

Kuo's eyes dulled with surrender, his cheeks draining chalky white with dread. He bowed and remained suppliant as he backed from the throne into the arms of the approaching guards. They escorted the astrologer from the palace compound, heaving him into a crowd of loitering vassals. The peasants fell silent as Kuo stumbled to keep his footing, no one extending a hand, no one doing anything but staring.

When the astrologer had pushed from their midst, he hurried toward the stone stairway laid in the basin rim that led to his tower. He would send his wife and son away and then turn to the scroll of the Madjan. If there were a prayer or rite to strengthen the deity, he must learn it. Once the sacrificial blood was spilled, the Madjan would be their only hope.

Tall and muscular, General Jiang fully commanded the open archway in which he stood. It was his responsibility to restore an air of triumph to the proceedings. With a flamboyant gesture, he clapped loudly for his orderly. The youth, his long black braid wagging, stepped smartly from the corridor that surrounded the Great Hall on three sides. He carried a lidless bronze vessel. Its large body was etched with fantastic animals, each of whose outsized eyes was inlaid with malachite, the claws with darker copper. Within the four-legged vessel were a thousand and one small jades.

The victorious general moved forward now, passing between a pair of tall, gold-inlaid censers whose smoke curled slowly toward the ceiling. Reaching the throne, he motioned for his orderly to set the prize on the mosaic floor at the Emperor's feet.

Ch'en studied the boy's movements, more fluid and assured than he was accustomed to seeing in those who were not yet men. "What is your name?" he asked.

"Ronbgiao, my lord."

"You carry yourself well."

"The honor is Jiang's."

"Nonetheless," the Emperor replied, smiling benignly and trying to regain his own spirit of celebration, "we are pleased."

The youth snapped his head in obeisance, rose, and backed into the corridor to await Jiang's command.

"I bear tribute from Lord Kezhen," the general announced, "along with a prize jade as a token of my own great love for Emperor Ch'en. You shall receive an equal treasure once each year while the people of Ch'en-shimm feast upon half of the foodstuffs collected by the lord as taxes from his people."

"You have seen to it that Lord Kezhen is *disinclined* toward future rebellion?"

"We have returned with his daughter as a royal concubine, to be offered to the Madjan at any sign of insurrection." The officer drew a scroll from his red sash and laid it on the floor beside the vessel. "The terms of surrender, signed with the blood of General Xiqing." Jiang knelt again and placed the spear across all, its tip pointing to the east and the conquered city.

A surge of pride broadened the smile on the face of the Emperor. "You have brought us another victory, Jiang. Steward, the proclamation."

The gangly man trembled forward, not yet recovered from Kuo's display. He unspooled a crisp scroll, though he recited from memory. " 'Eleven years ago, when our glorious Ch'en ascended to the throne of his beloved father, the temple of the Madjan was begun. The first stones were mortared with the blood of an enemy warrior, carried from the battlefield where it had been spilled over farmlands disputed by a forgotten noble. Today, that temple is completed. Today, all wars are ended. Today, the Madjan shall be honored as supreme. Today, he drinks the blood of peace, for the blood of combat is no longer shed.' " The herald's eyes did not rise from the floor as he slithered back to await the will of his master.

The ruler ran a finger along his pointed chin. After peering past the assemblage, his narrow eyes settled on Jiang. "Do you, General, fear the proclamation of our esteemed astrologer?"

The general looked faintly surprised. "I fear nothing save your displeasure, my lord."

"Yet Kuo's line has correctly predicted critical events in the past."

"His father was executed at your command for treason."

"His father hadn't the courage to tell us the truth of what the stars foretold about Kezhen's ambitions." Ch'en's manner was no longer critical but pensive. "Long before they occurred, Kuo spoke of your victories, your nearly fatal wound at Shaanxi, the famine in the northeast which drove other nobles to join Kezhen. Steward—" he turned to the quivering fellow "—what do you say?"

"My lord Emperor." He took a step backward, wishing he were rid of this affair. "The wise ruler weighs the counsel of his advisers. When they oppose, as do those of Kuo and the general, it is best—" his eyes rolled toward Jiang "—forgive me, General, but it is best to side with the gods."

"General Jiang," Ch'en queried, "are you swayed by the will of the gods?"

"Only as it does not interfere with the will of my lord, Emperor Ch'en."

The potentate allowed his head to rest on the pillowed peak of the throne, his eyes casting toward the domed ceiling and its mural of the gods in their realm. "Is that loyalty, I wonder, or sacrilege?"

"It cannot be sacrilege," Jiang insisted. "Not Kuo but the royal presence is the emissary of the gods on this world. If anyone is misled by them, it is not my Emperor."

Ch'en considered Jiang's testimony and then smiled again. "The way of the gods is often curious. Yet they do not disdain being honored. Kuo's reading must be false."

"Pardon, lord," the steward all but whispered, "but the fiery sea on which the earth dragon floats is not within the dominion of any deity."

"The earth dragon!" Jiang sneered. "I have never seen him! But I have witnessed the strong hand of the Madjan in the valiant carriage of my armies. One is real, one is legend. Which shall we obey?"

"Legend," said Ch'en. "Is not Jiang legend in the remotest ends of our domain?"

The general inclined his head. "You honor me. Yet I honor the Madjan, and my faith in him is not so weak as that of your steward. I trust in him to protect us against some mythical demon."

Ch'en's gaze rolled to his steward. "Do you dispute what Jiang has said?"

The gangly fellow drew himself erect. "N-no, lord. I . . . I merely felt obliged to represent Kuo in his absence."

"Of course," the monarch noted. "Then go before me, steward, and bid the herald announce to all of Ch'en-shimm what we are about to do. Let the dedication begin."

"As the Emperor wills," he answered, bowing and hastening from the Great Hall, chased by Jiang's sinister glower.

Ch'en rose regally and walked toward the door, with the general following close behind. As the Emperor passed, the ax of each warrior snapped toward the throne, toward Ch'en's flank, symbolically protecting him. When the two men reached the double door, the soldiers closed ranks and followed them single file down the large empty corridor into the palace courtyard.

The corridor was decorated with a delicately inked mural, showing Vermilion Herbs twined with gold fish in a pale blue sea. The vision signified a beauty remote to Ch'en's flat, dry province. Although he usually paused to enjoy the art, tonight he was annoyingly distracted by Kuo's proclamation, and he was aware—or did he but imagine it?—of an uncustomary calm in the warm air. There were no insects astir, no horses neighing in their stalls; he listened carefully for the snorting of livestock at the rear of the compound and heard only the soft echo of his own footsteps.

There is a reason for the stillness, he told himself, *something which Kuo in all his wisdom has not understood. The eyes and ears of the gods and of my ancestors are upon us. They have sent this quiet because they will not only* watch *how I honor them, they will also* listen.

When Ch'en appeared beside one of the four stone lions that crouched at the portal of his palace, a sea of many thousand heads bowed in unison. Farmers, poets, craftsmen, soldiers—all the men of his province. In their hands a thousand torches burned, sending their smoke to the west as though bearing away the twilight sun so the ceremony could begin. Emperor Ch'en raised his hands and descended the great stone steps. As he walked along a path left by the crowd, his iron voice invoked a blessing for peace that also assured all of readiness in the event of war.

When he approached the massive wall of the compound, the iron gate was pulled open, revealing two rows of four hundred green-clad archers each, reaching from the wall to the temple of the Madjan. Behind them were clustered the women and children of Ch'en-shimm. Arms aloft, Ch'en passed through the ranks of fighters toward the imposing edifice. He was oblivious to each head dipping in turn; as the temple loomed ever closer, his eyes caressed each of its five tiers, enjoying the sight of the yellow-robed soldiers standing there, his elite force of experts in weaponless combat.

The doubt Ch'en had experienced following the audience with Kuo began to dissipate. *The gods will be pleased*, he was certain, *and will keep us from misfortune.*

Illuminated by torchlight along the walk and by fires on each level, the circular temple was at once somber and glorious. Framing each gray stone of its structure was a casement of highly burnished bronze; inset on every face was a porcelain hilt and gleaming ivory blade. Ten thousand swords pointed in every direction from the temple, floating in the night sky against the nearly invisible stone. In the balustrades of each balcony were arched shelves a pace apart, each of which held an iron dragon whose mouth was filled with fire. The flames cast shadows of the beasts on the posterior wall of each shelf, making the figures seem alive.

At either side of the golden doors was a white-robed priest. The holy man to the left held a gold vase filled with oil; the priest to the right bore a leather quiver filled with golden arrows. Ch'en and his general paused at the threshold, and the priests entered before them.

There was only one light inside the temple, fire that spit from the upturned mouth of a dragon altar. The interior of the temple took most of its ruddy glow from the fires that burned on the balconies.

Ch'en had not come to the temple in the many years during which it was raised. He'd wanted to be a part of what was taking place but could not mingle with the common builders lest he lower himself in the eyes of his people and, more importantly, in the eyes of the gods. He had seen only the carefully sketched plans and drawings of the interior and of the statues.

For the first time, Ch'en observed the rows of clay warriors that filled the temple. He could but dimly discern those toward the rear of the army, cavalrymen seated on horses draped in bronze bridles and jewel-encrusted reins. In the center, more plainly visible, were crossbowmen whose weapons pointed ominously toward the door. At the front were the foot soldiers and officers. Each figure had been built from coils of rough gray clay, hollow inside to enable them to fill with the breath of the gods. A coat of finer clay provided the lifelike details of whiskers and the texture of fabric for their dress. The realism was heightened by the bright paint with which the figures were adorned.

Several heads larger than life, the one hundred fifty-eight soldiers filled Ch'en with a feeling of power and confidence, of certainty that his was a kingdom that would last a millennium. Yet no emotion, no welling of strength or satisfaction could match what the leader felt as he turned his eyes ahead toward the supreme warrior of the land, toward the new chief deity of his people.

"The life of the Madjan is blood," muttered the two priests together. "The warrior is strengthened when the god is sated."

The idol stood behind its lighted brazier, the bronze dragon whose open mouth formed the Madjan's flaming ceremonial dish. While one priest fed the perpetual fire with oil from the vase, the other continued the liturgy.

"May the spirit of the Madjan infuse those who worship him. May none usurp that loyalty, god nor demon. May those who dishonor the Madjan be punished for their wayward beliefs."

The surging pillar of fire threw stark, riotous shadows on the Madjan, a figure that chilled the Emperor to gaze on it.

The brawny legs of the demigod were spread slightly, his studded boots rising to just inside a flap of silver-leaf-coated armor plates. Several red gems were inset in the hem of the statue's armor. Strung from a carefully textured sash above the skirt was a solid gold dagger and a leather bladder; his chest was draped in clay plates that bore a meticulously sculpted dragon. His torso was topped with clay armor contoured to his massive shoulders; his arms were covered with clay molded to resemble folds of silk, painted yellow to rival the brilliance of the sun. The statue wore a square, raised helmet ornamented with horns that jutted from the front above the stylized features of a bull. Huge flaps ending in feline claws fell along the side of the head over the Madjan's ears and framed his ominous features. A long braid of clay hair ran down his back, knotted up and down its entire length with a sculpted serpent.

The Madjan's arms were bent at the elbow, his hands fisted. Into these, the two priests slid a golden sword and ax. As they did so, Ch'en imagined that he saw the Madjan's hooded eyes widen. The sensation seemed stronger still when the golden arrows were fitted into the bows of two clay crossbowmen positioned behind the idol.

Those are the eyes of the Madjan himself, Ch'en thought. *They gaze upon the earth through this surrogate. We are* indeed *a people blessed.*

Kuo painted his characters feverishly, recording in precise brush strokes the time and placement of the heavens and then describing the events that had transpired even to the tart, musty scent that now rose from the east. His mouth was dry from the night's unusual heat, compounded by the fever of his note taking.

"So it will end," he wrote. "All the pettiness and caprice, the tragic misdirection of an entire people."

Convinced that this would be the final entry in his private log, the astrologer hurried into a passage about the titanic struggle he'd predicted. The scroll crinkled in the breeze that brushed the tower top; Kuo's splayed fingers pinned the onionskin to the surface of the pedestal as he continued to write. Although his hand cramped and his columns became increasingly less ordered, his thoughts remained clear.

The astrologer didn't know why he wrote, why he hadn't fled with his family. He had no obligation to posterity, if indeed another mortal soul should ever find and decipher his log. Filled with bitterness about Ch'en and unorthodox reflections about the heliocentric nature of the cosmos, the diary had been kept in the obscure tongue of the mystics of Dzenglu, where he'd studied before being summoned to replace his father. As a seer, he was trained to evaluate events and ideas in terms of the future. If the future had any characteristic, it was a god-ordered irony. Thousands of men had died so that Ch'en could triumph, only to have the heart of his kingdom wiped from the earth in a terrible instant. Kuo wrote on; a year, a generation, an eon hence, who knew but that his words might be the guideline for some leader's benevolent rule. Perhaps history had been fated from Jiang's victory to Ch'en's stubbornness to the astrologer's frantic documentation, designed for that grand purpose. A scientist's compulsive nature fired by a philosopher's bold conceit kept Kuo hunched over his diary, dabbing ink to paper even as the wind died completely and the ground rumbled beneath him.

He looked up. There was a gray cloud on the horizon, blooming faintly against the evening black. The cataclysm witnessed by Chi-pin was renewing itself as the earth dragon wriggled awake within the bowels of its mountain lair.

The worshipers felt the floor crawl for a moment, and the entire structure swayed before easing still. Ch'en let his eyes drag slowly across the dark interior of the temple. He noticed Jiang and the priests doing the same.

"Holy men," the Emperor growled, "be done with the words of tribute. Have the Woman of Peace brought forth."

The priests had been shaken by the rolling of the temple and were only too happy to comply. At a word from the priest who had poured oil into the brazier, everyone knelt, heads bowed toward the Madjan. The other priest spoke: "Great Madjan, who grants us victory and who looks after and is served by the spirits of our dead; great god of war and protector of the realm; great deity, hear our prayer of thanks for the honor you have allowed us to bring to your holy name."

When the four kneeling figures rose, a pair of fighters belonging to Ch'en's elite guard came forward, leading a girl to the dragon brazier.

She was a tall maiden who, though she wore no clothing, was far from naked. She carried the dignity of her office like a robe of gemstones. Her hair hung straight in layers of long braids that reached to just beyond her waist and were wound through with threads of gold. Her skin, even in the amber glow of the temple, was exceedingly white, made so by the lifelong diet special to women of her caste.

There was not a trace of red on her. The woman's eyes were

lined and shaded with yellow powder, her lips dulled with blue translucence. The nails of her hands and feet were dyed a soft violet. Each tint of her makeup represented the color of a division of Jiang's army.

The warriors left her and strode from the temple while she lay belly down on the flat back of the dragon, between its twining neck and the spiked tail. Her head, by virtue of this position, was bowed toward the Madjan.

The priest continued, "We have brought this daughter of our village, the Woman of Peace, to celebrate the might of the Madjan, for the warrior does not spill his blood except in battle."

As the priest droned on, the woman became aware of the faint scent of incense wafting from the palace, borne with dust from the basin over the balconies, like the breath of the gods. She no longer heard the priest, only the thumping of her heart and her own heavy breathing—until a faint ringing seemed to come from nowhere yet everywhere at once.

The clang of swords, the Peace Mother had told her to expect first. The dead who form the advance guard of the Madjan.

"Below," wrote Kuo, "they make ready their barbaric ritual in the shadow of disaster. The people trust Ch'en, precious faith which shall kill them. His god will prove pitifully insufficient, and if there is any justice in this impending holocaust, it is that while sinew will perish tonight, the thoughts I record may survive. I am driven, though hardly, I admit, consoled by that realization."

As he recorded this final confession, Kuo saw the red of the moon deepen and the stars themselves seem to twinkle with blood. The tip of his brush shook out a crooked line; he looked at it with involuntary horror, aware from the fresh trembling that this was not the result of an unsteady hand.

The astrologer was unable to step from the platform before the tremor became a roar; his tower shifted, and the floor split along its entire length. Jerked from its base, the armillary rolled toward the rim of the observatory, spilling over it and seeming to drag the entire structure behind it. Kuo was just able to slide his diary into the column of the pedestal before his world turned over, the tower collapsing as the lip of the Turpan Basin crumbled before the volcanic earthquake. The astrologer's last mortal thought was unabashed joy over the deaths of Ch'en and his brawny, ignorant kind.

Ch'en, Jiang, and the priests stood still among the silent clay army of the Madjan, looking anxiously about.

"The thunder of enemy mounts," shouted Jiang at last. He reached for his sword.

Ch'en stayed the general's hand and then turned toward the west. "No," he said softly, "this is no mortal enemy which approaches."

"Then—"

The Emperor looked at the Madjan. "It is the earth dragon, for the confrontation Kuo foretold."

Scowling, Jiang hurried to where the Woman of Peace lay prostrate. The priest backed away, and the general drew his weapon. "My lord, the Madjan will need strength."

Ch'en looked at the woman. Her breath was sibilant, as though it were being forced from her chest; her eyes were shut, and her mouth was drawn tightly at either side. A trickle of blood had begun to flow from between her legs, along the channel formed by the spines on the dragon's tail. The Madjan was near but not near enough.

"Quickly," the Emperor commanded, "be done with it. We have little time."

The general put his blade to the girl's belly and slid it in. She died with a shudder, her blood coursing from the wound into a receptacle formed by the forked tip of the serpent's tail.

One of the priests hurried to the idol and removed the leather sack from its girdle. But before he could reach the red flow, a jagged fracture split the floor of the temple from door to altar, throwing the men from their feet. Flames coiled upward in small, plumed columns, the rush of heat causing several of the statues to shatter. From outside the temple, the men could hear screams amid the shattering of clay walls and the snapping of timbers as the ground heaved under and around the subjects of Ch'en-shimm.

Unable to stand on the buckling floor of the temple, the Emperor dropped to his hands and knees. "Great Madjan," he implored, "protect us from this demon. Slay the earth dragon who dares to rear its head against your devoted war—"

A monstrous bellowing rattled the temple as a funnel of

scalding wind spun from the earth's core. The force of the cyclone tossed Ch'en's warriors from the balconies even as the earthquake brought the parapets tumbling to the ground. Moments later, the temple itself folded into the earth as though an awesome maw had opened and swallowed it whole. Blocks from the walls of the structure blew and twisted through the air as though they were weightless, falling heavily into the whirlpool that sucked the Emperor and his party to oblivion. Downward too flushed the clay warriors, mute and defenseless against the onslaught.

All the while, the wide eyes of the Madjan stared helplessly at the decimation of his proud guard.

They had not been mighty enough.

They had not drunk at the fountain of the Woman of Peace.

But they would be ready for the next encounter with the earth dragon or any foe...

CHAPTER ONE

THE NIGHT'S CONSTANT WINDS swarmed across the Turpan Basin, spinning sand and heat in a wide, low column on the dead expanse. The hot gust stirred a cloud of freshly excavated dirt from the rim of the pit, spilling particles into the cracked pedestal chamber and dusting the partially unearthed scroll. The bony man patiently blew them away and then crouched lower to the writing to shield it from the wind.

"Bring the lantern closer," he urged his daughter as he tilted his spectacles back on his nose to sharpen the parchment's faded characters.

" 'I cite this about Chi-pin because so much of his life and bold travels are veiled in legend, fables that obscure the fact that his methods were hardly scientific and his writing often inarticulate. Yet in his century-old Kholan tablets, translated by my great-grandfather, he speaks of a mountain which spat red earth and colored the sky with blood. If this account is true, I fear it is the same mountain which reddens our heavens tonight. In my too many years at Ch'en-shimm, I have never seen such a phenomenon. No one has seen it. Fittingly, no one *will* see it. Below, they make ready their barbaric ritual in—' "

The frail Chinese stood up, his delicate, bent shoulders barely reaching the top of the excavation. His eyes lingered on the brittle document. "I thank you, Kuo, for waiting."

Her own soft face aglow, Yu regarded her father's long, wrinkled features. "It fits your fragment exactly."

"Yes. Yes, it does." Although he stood as one transfixed, Wang Laojiu's voice was rich with feeling. He recited, " 'Below, they make ready their barbaric ritual in the shadow of disaster. The people trust Ch'en, precious faith which has killed them.' So long," he said. "It has been so very long. Yet the well was dug only yesterday, it seems."

The girl rose, setting the lantern on the edge of the oblong pit. Beyond the light's ruddy glow lay a field of sparse yellow grasses and aged trees, all within the moon-spun halo surrounding the Mountain of Flames. Beyond the basin lay fertile ravines that had been trodden for centuries only by the grape and melon farmers who worked them. Somewhere in that distance a farmer shouted at the crops spilling from his two-wheel cart as they returned with the day's harvest.

"You've not been from the pit since last night," Yu said gently, tugging her father's slender hand. "We'll cover the scroll and finish here in the morning. Rested, we will be better fit to return to Beijing with word of your great find."

The archaeologist withdrew his hand and bent again beside the curl of scroll that protruded from the dry earth. "No," he said as he slowly and delicately picked away the broken shards of marble in which the fragile document had been stored and which had protected it from two millennia of erosion. "I cannot leave when the most critical question remains unanswered. Please fetch me the canister."

"But you will be fresher after you've had sleep."

Laojiu's hands remained defiantly busy. "Dear girl, you worry too much about matters which are inconsequential. Please, the canister."

The young woman did not protest further. Even in the relatively enlightened days of 1977, the will of adult Chinese was never contested by their children. Besides, although Yu wished that her father would rest, she knew that his sleep would be fitful at best. He had journeyed too long and too far to postpone this moment.

Igniting a second lantern, she climbed the foldable military ladder from the pit and collected the airtight canister and a cashmere sweater from their tent. In one of the compartments of the container was the scrap of writing that Laojiu had discovered at a bookshop over two decades before, the closing lines of the enigmatic history that had started him on his epic search.

When Yu returned, she knelt beside Laojiu and draped the button-down sweater over his shoulders. As she held the lantern for her father, the years of suffering seemed a swiftly fading nightmare. It was as if none of the pain had really happened, the years of loneliness or living in tents or under the chilly heavens, of surviving awful heat and days without food or drink. All she could remember now, vividly painted across her nineteen years of life, was her father never doubting that they would find the entire scroll and, through it, the lost empire of Ch'en-shimm. She looked out into the moonlit basin. Yu was awed to imagine a great city buried beneath their feet. But her greatest satisfaction derived from her father's joy and from the professional recognition that would be his at last. He would be able to rest and write and finally enjoy his life.

The wind spilled anew into the excavation, causing Laojiu's taut queue of silver hair to sway against the sun-baked back of his neck. Yu watched as he plucked away the last fragment of the ancient pedestal with the dexterity of a surgeon and then firmly pushed his spade beneath the exposed scroll. The soil was hard, and it resisted, the secrets of 20 B.C. unyielding to the last. But finally the sod split, and the loosely wound, yellowing paper was worked free. Yu unscrewed the lid of the canister, and her father spaded his find into the lowermost of the container's three compartments.

"Light the tent," he ordered quietly. "Let us read what my colleague has kept to himself these many centuries. Only he can tell us whether we have at last found Ch'en-shimm."

The girl left to do her father's bidding. In her wake, he smiled, not at his daughter but for Kuo. "I wonder what you'd have thought, knowing the upheaval that swallowed your city would make you immortal," he said aloud. Rising, his black balloon pants covered with dirt, Laojiu offered a silent prayer to the gods of his ancestors. He had given up everything to pursue this dream. Although he didn't believe in the gods, Laojiu was a thankful man. He wished to acknowledge that gratitude in a way that seemed both courteous and appropriate.

The red disk of the sun blazed skyward. Laojiu was struggling through Kuo's account of his summoning from the scholars' retreat at Dzeng-lu to serve in the court of Emperor Ch'en. Before beginning the Ch'en-shimm portion of his diary, Kuo had taken a moment to contrast his isolated mountain home with this virtual metropolis. The vista he described from his tower observatory was the same one the archaeologist had known for the past fifteen days.

Breaking from the passage as tears welled beneath his eyes, the archaeologist embraced his daughter. For the first time since his wife's death, Laojiu wept openly.

He had found his sovereign kingdom. Now the most difficult and rewarding part of his work could begin.

Chapter Two

"I've got to be the lousiest diplomat the U.S. has ever sent here. Or if not the lousiest, the least committed to his country's best interests."

Grant Chapman raised his cobalt-blue eyes from the open folder on his lap to the heavy rainfall that drummed on the plastic side window of the jeep. His disgust with himself, with the way he'd handled the assignment, compounded by the bumping of the canvas-topped vehicle, made reading difficult; he pitched the clutch of papers to the dashboard of the compact, Japanese-built transport.

As the rain speared the car, Chapman still found it remarkable that it rained the same here as it did in Manhattan, that the rolling gray clouds could be as dreary, the distant thunder as ominous, the flickering of the window wipers as tiresome, the people as vicious when threatened.

"You are wrong, Mr. Chapman."

"Huh?"

"As I recall, your nation's emissary during the Boxer Rebellion locked himself in his residence for two months, refusing to side against the United States, with the Boxers, or even confer with ambassadors from the other besieged legations." Nieh nodded sagely. "Yes, he was worse."

Chapman smiled. "Thanks for the compliment. I can't tell

you how being merely the second worst diplomat has boosted my spirits."

"By the same token," the young man continued in polished, colloquial English, "other envoys have had to contend with nothing more than royalty and revolutions. You have had to deal with Dr. Laojiu for six days." The youthful driver did not grin, nor did he speak again. He simply stared past the sloshing wipers whose motion cast liquid shadows on his blue frock and cap.

Chapman looked ahead at the storm-drenched ravine. Beyond lay the Turpan Basin and, the American was certain, the chilliest reception awaiting any man since Hitler had marched through Paris. He considered how closely the damp, somber view matched the way he felt.

The jeep bucked along the rutted dirt road into the mouth of the gorge and through the small village of Tahnsien. Chapman considered Nieh's blunt assessment and found it insufficient reason to feel good about taking a man from his life's passion. "Well," the American sighed at last, "politics and science have always been unwilling partners. I suppose I shouldn't take this mess personally. Tell me," he prodded the driver, "you've been with me since this deal was struck. You heard the orders I've had to give him by phone. Don't you feel bad for the old man?"

"I'm only sorry that your most delicate diplomacy has not been appreciated by Laojiu. I have known him for three years, ever since my office agreed to finance the Turpan dig. Not once in that time has any argument swayed Laojiu from a path he'd selected. I tell you in confidence, Mr. Chapman, that after our first month of underwriting the excavation of Ch'enshimm, Minister Guo and the professor stopped speaking to each other directly. Until your government's request to exhibit the statues, they'd not communicated for nearly two years."

"Our State Department has personnel who operate like that. Only we call them bureaucrats. They'll do anything they can to postpone making decisions."

"Oh, no, Mr. Chapman," Nieh said with uncharacteristic urgency. "The Department of Cultural Heritage is concerned with one mission above all, and that is to show the world the best that China has to offer, our industry and our art. There is no tangle of red tape between Beijing and the Turpan Basin.

There is simply a sharp conflict of personalities: Laojiu versus everyone in the department."

"In one of my phone conversations with Laojiu, he said there was a twenty-year period when he couldn't raise a grant to finance his efforts. Is that true?"

"Yes. But consider the facts in context, Mr. Chapman. Would anyone in your government provide money to a scientist who absolutely refused to reveal what he was searching for?"

"You aren't serious?"

Nieh nodded.

"Odd. He didn't seem like an egotistical guy."

"Nor is he. Laojiu feared pillaging and haphazard excavation by others more interested in riches and fame than in archaeology. He and his daughter spent months at the site. Only when the scope of the task had become apparent did they come to us."

"Well, you certainly can't fault the guy's integrity." Nieh offered no opinion, so Chapman continued, "I'll bet he wishes now that he'd never involved the government."

"One can't have it both ways," the driver said curtly. His concise rhetoric reminded Chapman that this was, after all, a communist society and Laojiu a barely tolerable eccentric. The irony of it all was that while Chapman hadn't met the archaeologist or been to the dig, after nearly a week in Beijing his sympathy had drifted from the government to the scientist. It was not a matter of wrong or right, since both sides were motivated by selfish desires; it was a question of the strong overwhelming the weak. It was a circumstance that Chapman himself had experienced and one that tore at his insides.

Despite the rain, the road was not muddy. Wayne Teres at the American embassy in Beijing had correctly described it as fossilized. Thin, long puddles were everywhere, and on those occasions when they had to pull over to make way for an ox cart, the bordering grasses provided a welcome respite.

Chapman tried to ignore the cramped discomfort he'd endured for over three hours. He played briefly with the notion of returning to Deputy Ambassador Teres's report, which actually consisted of his own comments on this cultural loan translated into what Teres had referred to as "officialese." Chapman decided that there'd be time to read it on the long flight home, and he continued to peer through the rain.

The farming commune of Tahnsien was like everywhere in China that wasn't Beijing or Shanghai or some other populous city. It consisted of a central square stocked with wooden carts, surrounded by commodious clay huts and tool sheds. Beyond the small village were the melon fields. It looked to Chapman as though the twentieth century had never happened here; the American suspected that Tahnsien was little changed from what it had been thousands of years before.

It took less than two minutes to travel through the silent village, whose croplands were unworked in the driving storm. Through the open door of one hut the American glimpsed a group of men hunched over a table, playing the ancient card game of *p'ai-fen*. Their eyes rolled up as he passed, eyes that were wary and suggested both wonder at the automobile and suspicion of outsiders. Teres had mentioned that the commune dwellers were like his Polish grandfather, unwilling to trust even those from a neighboring village. Nieh drove past bicycles and pedicabs herded beneath a thatched shelter at the end of the square and then pushed on through the ravine to the basin beyond.

The two large structures rose slowly from behind the sloping horizon. Chapman's first impression was one of surprise at the awesome size of the shelters; this was followed by an awareness of how incongruous their cinder block walls and domed glass ceilings were in this agrarian setting. Although Minister Guo had shown him photographs of the site, the twin hangars reminded Chapman of a vision from *War of the Worlds*—the sleek, anachronistic Martian war machines crouched in the midst of the English countryside.

"Invaders from another world," he said under his breath. Nieh, smiling politely, swung the car from the cart path, crossing the boggy sands to the cavernous Pit One. As they approached, Chapman caught a glimpse of the fleet of trucks around back. His stomach roiled as he considered the pain their arrival this morning must have caused Laojiu.

Nieh braked and pointed to a small placard above the nearest door, a sign decorated with black Chinese characters.

"Each building has six entrances for convenient access to any area of the dig. According to this sign, we can reach Laojiu's laboratory through here."

Chapman raised the collar of his trenchcoat and followed

Nieh from the car. His shoulders hunched, the American ran through the warm, slashing rains. Nieh walked more slowly and, reaching the door, had to tug twice on the bell string before anyone came to admit them. While Chapman reminded himself that the Chinese were not a petty people, he couldn't help wondering if the delay was intentional.

The two new arrivals swept past the doorman, a dispassionate young man in a white lab coat. Once inside, Chapman shook off his wetness, feeling more canine than human. He brushed the clinging beads of rain from his curly black hair and then raised his eyes to look around. For a long moment, he was literally dumbstruck.

Noticing his fascination, Nieh remarked, "It is large."

Chapman numbly agreed, though the vastness itself was not what impressed the New Yorker. The artificial cavern was an assault on the senses. The smell was musty and ancient, a blend of dead, dry earth and dust stirred from the remote past. The resonant sloshing of the rain on the glass roof contained and heightened the quiet within as the thirty-eight archaeologists, all of them young Chinese, worked silently and busily with clinking picks in the pit at the center of the structure. It was warm and humid, somewhat like a greenhouse, although death and not life was what flourished within.

"What patience." Chapman shook his head as he watched the crew work on the most staggering sight of all, the remains of Ch'en-shimm. He could see now why Laojiu was unwilling to leave. After three years of digging with spade and whisk broom, a city was beginning to emerge. The earthquake had swallowed everything, snuffing out life while bestowing immortality. Here and there a roof or wall poked through the floor of the pit, hinting at the tantalizing treasures that lay below. The burned-out buildings had all but monopolized the scientists' attention. Nieh had explained earlier that ashes from the holocaust would have preserved almost intact whatever lay within. Rubble from structures that had collapsed but had not burned was everywhere, along with pieces of buckled roadway, smashed mosaics, bronzes, and vases, the torn and twisted frames of chariots, and the bones of those who had not been consumed by fire or pulverized by the shifting earth.

Remotely aware of the warmth, Chapman removed his coat and threw it over his shoulder. "Come on," he growled at Nieh, "let's get this damned caravan rolling." Chapman absently straightened his tie and with Nieh in tow headed toward a cinder block cubicle that seemed grown from the wall at the near end of the pit.

"You are still not comfortable with this undertaking," Nieh observed rather than asked.

"Less and less with each passing second."

The Chinese gestured toward the pit as they traversed its eight-meter-wide brim. "There are more than enough caretakers; science will not suffer."

"What about Laojiu?"

"Yes, one man, one self-possessed, insensitive man will suffer. Why do you dwell so on him? Can't you think of the pleasure of many, of those who will see and enjoy the exhibit in your country?"

"I've been trying to do that all week, but there's a limit to what I can milk from that bromide."

"Is this because you perceive Laojiu as an underdog, a figure which Americans seem to—"

"I care because he *hurts*," Chapman snapped, "and because my job is to pour salt in the wound." They reached the cubicle, and Chapman knocked.

"It is not an ideal world," Nieh agreed, "and there are priorities which unfortunately preclude appeasement, sometimes make even common courtesy impossible." As if to illustrate his point, Nieh pressed past Chapman and threw open the door. "After you, please."

"Thanks, but I'll wait to be asked."

"You won't be," Nieh assured him, stepping inside.

The room's sole occupant was Laojiu's aide. Seated on a high stool and examining a frayed square of flowered silk, the archaeologist turned from his magnifying glass when Nieh entered.

Nieh looked around the room. "The professor knew we were coming."

"He is in the tunnel," said the archaeologist in precise Chinese. "He has been there since late last evening."

The official was unimpressed. "Will you call him."

"I'm sorry, but one of your men caught a dolly on the phone line and severed it."

"Did you report it?"

"As I have said, there is no telephone."

Chapman edged into the room. "I'll have Einar fix it when

he's through with the crating. Let's just get down there and see that everything's on schedule and Laojiu's satisfied with the job they're doing."

Nieh nodded, pinning the scientist with an icy glance before leading Chapman to a broad plank at the corner of the pit.

The walkway was used by the researchers to ferry dirt and relics from below and to bring in supplies. Although the facility had a generator for night lighting, no electric tools were used on the dig itself. Laojiu feared that the vibration of mechanical equipment might shake the more delicate articles apart.

Chapman strode down behind Nieh. Their arrival at the floor of the pit was ignored by a group of workers, who were busy swathing their arms to the elbows in soft bandages to prevent accidental abrasion of the artifacts. The vistors walked to a canvas flap that hung from halfway up the far wall. Nieh drew it aside, and Chapman ducked in.

The two men had to crouch within the tunnel, and it took a moment before Chapman adjusted to the thick, hot air. He looked ahead. The tunnel was utter blackness except for two thin phosphorescent strips that had been laid on the ground to prevent researchers from stumbling into holes and the shielded lamp whose yellow radiance fell on a small excavation at the far end of the tunnel. Three people knelt behind the lamp, their attention fastened on the shallow hole. They spoke in low tones as if they feared rousing someone from a light sleep.

"The jackal and serpent were his symbol," came a dark gray voice which Chapman recognized immediately as belonging to Laojiu. "This must be the royal party. Yet this skull is scarred, and we know that Ch'en was never wounded in battle. What do you make of it, Deng?"

"Scarred as though cleaved, but not fatally." A stubby finger dipped into the pit. "You can see here how the bone mended over the ears."

A third voice, that of a woman, said, "Nor would it have been Ch'en's custom to wear a helmet. He knew how proud the generals were, and would not have usurped their sovereignty."

"Very good, Yu," her father remarked.

"Then," offered Deng, "what we have discovered must be the remains of Jiang, the general spoken of in the astrologer's text."

"So it would seem," echoed Laojiu, his voice tired but intense.

Worming closer, Chapman gazed into the oval pit. In it was a helmeted skull from which the mandible had been wrenched. This lay chin up, partially embedded in the earth. A gold sword protruded horizontally from the wall of the pit behind Deng, and beneath it lay the disordered bones of a hand. The top of another skull, much smaller, was clearly visible. In a tiny plastic dish lay several strands of black hair, which Chapman presumed had been discovered near one of the skulls.

The American crouched beside the professor. "Have you found something significant?"

The professor continued to study the skull as he said in gravelly English, "You are Chapman?"

"Yes, sir."

"Your men are at work in Pit Two."

Chapman had taken more pointed rebukes in his thirty-two years, several of them, in fact, from Laojiu himself. This one did not sting as much as it challenged. "Is that a polite way of telling me I'm not wanted around here?"

"As you can see, we have work to do, work on those relics which our government has kindly allowed me to keep. And my time, as you are aware, is suddenly very precious."

"Yes, I know. As I told you over the telephone, I sympathize with you enti—"

"That is most gratifying," Laojiu finally faced the American. The archaeologist's features were cold in the dim light. "For centuries, Chapman, the earth possessed Ch'en-shimm, and no one cared. Now the city breathes again, and the vulture Guo cannot wait to feed upon the carcass." His eyes swung toward Nieh, dimly lit in the entrance to the tunnel. "The vulture and his nestling. Both were boys when I began my search. They have no right to Ch'en-shimm. No right."

Nieh looked away as Chapman asked, "Sir, doesn't it flatter you that people in my country want to see the statues you have found?"

Laojiu returned to the skull. "I searched for this city across the breadth of the continent, dug for it until my hands trembled and my palms bled. My wife died assisting me, Chapman, perished from pneumonia in the northern wilderness. After all the years of lonely effort, the one favor I ask is for the world to continue to leave me alone."

The archaeologist's words were less bitter than resigned, his resistance less fervent than it had been on the phone.

"Well, sir." Chapman hunched closer. "I used to be a lawyer, an expert at debating ethics—even when I was wrong. But my job now is not to incite or browbeat or even to argue. I'm supposed to mollify, make your life as pleasant as possible in New York. I don't blame you for being indignant, and regardless of what you think of me, I *understand* what it's like to have something dear taken from you." Laojiu continued to stare at the skull. Chapman concluded more passionately, "Look, all I'm asking is that we trust one another. These two months will pass much faster if we do."

The archaeologist sat back. Removing his spectacles, he began to rub them with the hem of his lab jacket. "Your good manners are welcome, but they are merely the eye that comforts in the midst of the storm. There was a tale recorded some two thousand years ago by the statesman-poet Qu Yuan about the ogres of Mount Xiang. Qu wrote that each night these red-furred creatures would come from the peaks and raid the fields of local farmers, stealing armfuls of crops. They never harmed anyone, nor did the farmers blame them for seeking sustenance. But that did not ease the pain of the many villagers who died from shortages of food. Like those peasants, I am starving inside and have been so for over twenty years." He spread his spindly arms. "At last a feast lies before me. I can see it, smell it, have even begun to taste it. Now I must leave it for two long months so that I may sit on display with my statues."

"To answer peoples' questions—" the American corrected.

"A cage is a cage. Your kindest efforts cannot change that. Now," he went on, formal once more, "if you'll excuse me, my time here is limited, and there is much to do. I suggest you see to your men as, upon my life, I cannot bring myself to watch."

"I will go with him," Yu volunteered.

Chapman apologized once again, then watched as the girl unwound her legs from beneath her and moved sinuously to the passage that opened into Pit Two. The American and Nieh padded behind.

The serpentine impression created by Yu vanished once they had left the dark, constricting tunnel. Her flesh grew rosy, her loose-fitting white blouse and red skirt unfurling as she stood fully erect. What had seemed a snake's hood disappeared in the light, becoming a blue and white checkered scarf into which her black hair had been tucked.

Putting from his mind Nieh's description of the girl as being "worse than her father," Chapman jogged up beside her.

"We were relieved when your father allowed us to bring in the equipment to protect the statues. You know, if Jiang had had those vibration sensors, he could have detected an enemy army miles away."

"The general would have found your technology needlessly extravagant, as I do."

"Oh?"

"There were other ways, such as putting one's ear to the ground, watching the skies for dust stirred by approaching warriors, sighting a false sun glinting in their armor."

"I believe the American Indians used to employ tactics like that. Maybe we have taken a few steps backward." There was uncomfortable silence for a moment, then Chapman beamed. "By the way, your English is excellent. Your father taught you, didn't he?"

"He felt it would be useful. He is right about many things, you will find."

"And he learned it—"

"In India. He studied there, and worked on a great many digs with British scientists." She shook her head. "And he thought he was through with masters."

Chapman said nothing as they continued through the maze of Pit Two, which was a network of trenches rather than an open excavation. The household and daily life artifacts that had littered Pit One were not to be found here. Jutting from the floor and walls were large, dirt-encrusted statues. Workers were diligently unearthing them, a brush stroke at a time, being especially careful not to dislodge any flecks of paint that still clung to the figures. This once was a temple, Chapman had been told, hallowed to the people of Ch'en-shimm. To see these modern Chinese treating it as nothing more than an object of archaeological interest prompted him to imagine a New Yorker of the thirty-fifth century patiently working a stone Madonna from the rubble of St. Patrick's Cathedral.

Chapman dropped back beside Nieh. "So where are the fangs you promised?"

"You're feeling good about this now?"

"Better. Hell, there isn't a job on earth where you don't have to coddle someone, and God knows, I've had to take crap from worse than these two."

"So far, so good," Nieh admitted. "But I still do not trust her."

Chapman chose not to be distracted by the official's pessimism. Instead, he fastened his attention on the high walls of the trench and the clay figures that were everywhere within them. When they finally reached the large, open area at the end of the pit, Chapman had managed to forget entirely about Nieh and his veiled warnings.

Before them was an imposing array of cleaned and restored clay figures. The photographs he'd seen in Beijing had not done them justice; seeing them here, Chapman began to understand more fully what the archaeologist was giving up to be with the exhibit in New York.

Taken as a whole, the vision was a dreary one. The flakes of color that still clung to the statues only hinted at the grandeur of the original hues. Yet, though all that remained was the dead gray clay, it was remarkably detailed and lifelike, even to the bulging of the eyeballs against the lids and the intricate weaving of the braids of hair. Here and there, the trio stepped around clear plastic tents that had been raised to protect the more perishable fragments that still were buried. *Oxygen tents for stone men*, Chapman noted.

Men and crates were everywhere, clustered primarily about some of the lesser statues: the archers and unarmed warriors. But for Chapman, everything in the pit faded to insignificance once his eyes came to rest on the Madjan.

The god was not only larger than the rest of the figures, it loomed over all by virtue of the feral promise etched in its face and in its regal posture. Above all, from its massive, clenched hands to its unforgiving eyes to its dead scowl, it was humid with horror. Chapman could only wonder at the nature of a people who would worship such a thing.

Over her shoulder, Yu said, "I observed the crating of the first statue, then left the rest to the care of your foreman. We have had to rely upon your assurances that Mr. Björkman's expertise in this area is beyond reproach."

Snapping from the nearly hypnotic presence of the Madjan, Chapman assured her that the figures would be safe. "Einar and ten men moved a fifty-ton meteor intact from Alaska to the Hayden Planetarium in New York some twenty years ago. Six years ago, he personally supervised the transfer of the Liberty Bell, our symbol of independence, from—"

"A rock and a metal bell are not one dozen fragile clay statues," Yu reminded him. She stepped to one side. After watching a half dozen Chinese and Americans lay out the lumber for the Madjan's crate, she tightened the kerchief on her head. "Here you are, Chapman. Your men. The army which conquered an aging scientist. Enjoy the spoils."

The charge caught Chapman, and by the time he'd recovered, Yu was gone. Nieh approached while Chapman watched the girl vanish back into the trenches.

"One thing you will learn about Yu is that she always has the final word. I'm glad, Mr. Chapman, that she doesn't offend you."

"Only *idiots* offend me," Chapman rejoined, shifting his gaze to Nieh. Calming, he said, "I'd expect nothing less than familial loyalty from Yu." Returning his attention to the matter of crating statues, Chapman continued to the rear of the pit.

As the American approached, a broad-shouldered man waved, his long arm a flannel mast. "Grant!" his voice rumbled through the pit. He handed a wire stripper and a length of coaxial cable to a black man at his side and then lumbered away from the crate being assembled for the Madjan. Wiping his palms on his jeans, he extended a hand to Chapman.

"Fancy meetin' you here. How're things in Peking?" His eyes darted playfully toward Nieh. "I mean Beijing, or whatever they're callin' the bloody place nowadays."

"The paperwork's all done, if that's what you mean. Thought I'd come out and see how you're doing." Chapman took a moment to introduce Nieh to Einar Björkman. "I gather you've already met Laojiu."

"Yeah, Teres introduced us. Cold sort of fish." Einar's bushy red eyebrows arched. "Anyway, Grant, you're lucky. That's all I can say. Some patron saint must be watchin' over you."

"How so?"

"How so? Who's that, some other Chinaman? Never mind. The plane didn't land till six on account of the weather, and

Teres had us here four hours later, which was an hour more than it should have been. But my guys skipped breakfast and ate lunch on their feet, then kicked some of the dumber coolies they gave us here off the project, so we're actually runnin' a little ahead of schedule."

"What was wrong with the Chinese workers?"

"Some of 'em wouldn't go within spittin' distance of the big guy."

"You mean the Madjan?" Chapman faced Nieh. "These people come from the city. They aren't supposed to be superstitious."

Einar snorted. "Tell that to them! One guy said the statue smells foul. Me? I can't tell the difference. This whole pit stinks like a barn, the whole country, in fact."

"It's blood," Nieh said indignantly. "The power of suggestion. The laborers must have overheard someone talking about the flecks of blood which were found at the feet of the Madjan, preserved from a sacrifice offered at the time of the earthquake."

"A sacrifice?" Einar boomed from behind his outthrust jaw. "Some poor chicken or dog was cut to pieces for the blessin' of some clay soldier?"

"Not an animal, Mr. Björkman. A human sacrifice."

"A person? Sick ancestors you had."

"Their values were different from ours."

"It still sounds sick to me."

Chapman cleared his throat and glanced at his watch. "You'd better get back to work, Einar. I've known you to get hung up on glitches."

The burly Swede shrugged. "Sometimes the best takes a little longer."

"Right. Just keep in mind what will happen to us both if those statues are late."

Einar clasped Chapman's wrist and jabbed a thick middle finger on the face of his watch. "Eight hours, fella. The plane doesn't leave till 9 P.M. We'll be there."

"NASAT says the rain's going to keep up through the night."

"We'll be there, at the airport, on the cargo plane, in time!" He jerked a thumb toward a clutch of archaeologists huddled near the Madjan. "I'd get done even faster if you'd tell those zombies to stop hovering over us like mother hens.

Even the head zombie doesn't do that. Teres told me he trusts us."

Chapman nodded, recalling how Teres was wont to lie to him as well. "All right, Einar, Nieh will have a chat with the scientists. In the meantime—"

"I'm goin'," the engineer grumbled. "I'm sorry I ever came the hell over. I'm even more sorry I didn't go back to the embassy with Teres. The guy's more fun than the lot of you put together!"

Chapman grinned as Einar stormed off, his leather boots kicking up small clouds of fury.

"He's an interesting man," offered Nieh. "I have never seen anyone quite so large."

Chapman directed Nieh to the four archaeologists loitering near the Madjan and the official hastened to disperse them. The American watched as Einar finished baring the lead wires of a small oscilloscope and began helping the black man, Renny, prepare the Madjan for crating.

To move the Ch'en-shimm statues, the Swede had designed a neat, protective binding that had impressed even the unflappable Minister Guo. Metallically reinforced latex balloons were being slipped tirelike around the waists of the nine standing warriors and around the necks and rumps of the two cavalry mounts. The balloons fit into leather sleeves to which metal hooks were fastened; cables would be run from these clasps to the walls of each wooden crate. The cables were tightened to ensure maximum support without any danger of shattering the figures, and their pressure, translated into sound waves, was monitored with the same sensor system Einar had used to make certain the Liberty Bell crack wasn't strained during its Bicentennial transport. The statues then were packed with sprayed foam that was both fire-retardant and moisture-resistant, and the crates, when sealed, were swathed in mylar sheets to keep the temperature constant.

Two of the thirteen figures had already been moved into the trucks, and Einar wanted to do the largest of the group, the Madjan, while the crew still had the energy. As Einar, Renny, and two other Americans assembled the crate and arranged the internal monitors, three Chinese moved the blocks and tackles into position at the rim of the pit. The binational mix of the group handling each statue was a diplomatic arrangement engineered by Chapman; it meant that the blame for breaking or chipping any figure would be shared. It was one of those silly details he had learned to be wary of in matters of international diplomacy.

Since it would be at least a half hour before the Madjan was moved, Chapman decided to take a look at the Turpan Basin, which sprawled beyond Pit Two. His hands jammed into his pockets, he headed for the ramp, with Nieh hurrying alongside.

Outside, Chapman and his companion were drenched quickly by the continuing downpour. They backed up against the nearest of the canvasback trucks, with the American looking dolefully across the expanse of mucky sand.

"I'll tell you this much, Nieh. If Laojiu is as antisocial as he claims, I can see why he's reluctant to leave. This place is truly desolate, a misanthrope's paradise."

"People who have no business here do not come—yet that is also true of other communes throughout China."

"No, I've seen some of your outlying villages, Nieh. Daqing, Shaanzi, Yunnan. No matter how far off the beaten track they were, there was—I guess you'd call it a bit of the gypsy in them. There was a smile or a fire, something alive. This place is a wasteland that's more than just isolated. It's bleak."

"Like the back of a water buffalo," Nieh observed.

Chapman looked over at his associate. "All right, I'll play straight man. You care to explain that somewhat elusive metaphor?"

"I've felt this way since the first time I drove out here." He pointed back toward the village. "The basin is the buffalo's back, the ravine his shaggy hump, and Tahnsien the frail bird which nests upon it."

"You see life, and I see death. Maybe I'm just morbid."

"Not necessarily. The two are not so different as you might think. I grew up in a farming village much like Tahnsien. Think, as I did in my youth, of the dead buried underfoot. Do they not decompose and nourish the crops and sustain new life in that fashion? My grandfather used to tell me of bodies left naked in the fields to enrich the soil, before anyone understood that disease was also bred in this manner. Beneath our feet lie thousands of ancient bodies, victims of the fall of Ch'en-shimm. If their spiritual presence has heightened your sense of death, dispel it by considering the life they have perpetuated. Nothing is ever one way or the other. There are always two sides."

"Spiritual presence? Do you believe in that sort of thing?"

"As I have said, there are always two sides. Do you not put trust in an eternal life, in the undying soul?"

"I don't believe in anything I can't see."

"Then you deny the existence of honor and integrity?"

Chapman laughed. "Touché, Nieh. No, I believe in them deeply. As a matter of fact, I've taken a few beatings for that faith. But as far as religion is concerned, I started to doubt Catholicism when I was twelve. God didn't hear me begging for my mother's life, and nothing since then has convinced me He's listening."

"He saved her soul."

"That wasn't what I'd ordered." Chapman felt his throat getting raw, unaccustomed to so much moisture. "Anyway, you've got me at a disadvantage. If you're right and we are immortal in some way, you'll have the last laugh in the hereafter. But if *I'm* right—nothing. Let's go." He turned toward the door. "My mortal self is getting soaked."

As the mud sloshed underfoot, Chapman looked down, wondering which motes, which atoms had once belonged to living bodies. He shivered, chilled by the rain, and was glad to get back inside the hangar.

The instant Nieh had pulled shut the aluminum sliding door, there was a loud snapping sound from below. Chapman hurried to the rim of the pit and stood dripping wet and staring at the sight of the Chinese and Americans rushing to aid the four men who had been framing the Madjan's crate. As Chapman ran toward the ramp, he saw that the block and tackle they'd been using to raise the crate had snapped, leaving the considerable weight of the statue entirely on the shoulders of Einar, Renny, and two other Americans. Amid Einar's relentless yelling, his crew managed to keep the crate upright while Laojiu and Yu watched helplessly from the entrance of the tunnel.

Chapman joined the others, and together the thirteen men were able to distribute the weight among themselves and right the statue.

Perspiring as much from fear as from exertion, Chapman backed away. Through the blur of sweat streaming from his brow, he thought he saw the Madjan's head in a new position, tilted slightly to one side, toward the tunnel. He blinked and dragged a sleeve across his forehead, and the statue was as it had always been.

Einar, standing nearby, was busy shouting at his men. "Good save, boys, but I'll have the bloody balls of whoever rigged that hoist! Fix it and fix it right, or I'll feed your guts to the pigs in Tahnsien!" Exhausted, he leaned against the wall of the pit, shaking his head. "I don't know, Grant. Maybe it's been too damn long a haul from New York. But I checked that damn riggin' myself, and it looked fine."

"Maybe you need glasses."

"What I need," he replied, throwing the toe of his boot toward the tunnel, "is to get those zombies off my back!"

"You can't blame Laojiu, Einar, or his daughter. They haven't said a word to you."

"They don't have to. They've got slanty little eyes that see through walls. I can feel their stinkin' attitude."

"Baloney. I think this place has us all a little on edge. Just finish up so we can all get the hell out of here, okay?"

"Sure, sure, I'd like that. I only took this bloody deal so I'd get to see China, which has amounted to a quick look at the airport, the inside of a friggin' truck, a bathroom, and this lousy pit!"

"Calm down," Chapman insisted, "or you'll drop another statue."

"No chance of that. My pride's on the line now!" Grunting out the exclamation point, the Swede stalked off, muttering to himself.

Nieh and Chapman headed back up the ramp for some air. Chapman noticed Laojiu's eyes on him. He did not acknowledge the scientist. *What would I tell him, that the men will be more careful? He wouldn't believe that so why waste my breath?* He paused. Shit, *because I owe it to him, that's why.*

Chapman started toward the tunnel. As director of cultural exchange for the State Department, he had been to more nations in two years than most people knew existed, having toured with a jazz troupe through Bulgaria, brought comic book art to Somalia, hosted a six-city tour through the southern states of primitive art from New Guinea. And he was convinced that no people on earth were as humorless and thankless as the Chinese. They were leaping from the Stone

Age to the future with no thought of the present, and Chapman found it difficult keeping himself, Laojiu, and the statues from being run over by the impatient machine of state.

He'd have to remember to ask Teres how he stood it here. Then he'd curse his friend out for having helped get him the State Department job in the first place.

Laojiu had gone back inside the tunnel. Leaving Nieh outside, Chapman threw aside the canvas flap and crept toward the archaeologist's party. He and Laojiu might well be working to opposite ends, but Chapman was convinced of one thing: He was the only Chinese who actually listened to what other people had to say before rejecting it.

CHAPTER THREE

IT WAS TWILIGHT when the trucks rumbled through Tahnsien. The card-playing peasants looked up, more amused than impressed by the vehicles; human thunder remained dull and slow compared with nature's heaven-rattling drum beats. Civilization seemed to them a silly, pointless complexity. When the distraction passed, they returned to their game.

The rains had dwindled to a drizzle, and Chapman's sense of melodrama faded with them. His feelings were more practical now. He had chased away the bulk of his melancholy by reminding himself that though there was history here, progress crawled along from day to day. It was a sluggishness that had to frustrate the Chinese leaders and feed their disregard for the feelings of a Laojiu. *After all*, Chapman reminded himself, *one gift panda or a touring Madjan can get you an American breeder reactor faster than the research of a thousand archaeologists.*

The jeep brought up the tail end of the convoy. Chapman unsnapped his window. The muggy night air clung to the hard earth in clouds of mist, swirling around the jeep as it plied the rutted path. But there was more than the damp night's fog rolling from the ravine. Chapman had a sensation of being cut off from reality and enveloped by something clammy, something surreal. The evening was not cold, but Chapman shivered.

"Stop the car," he ordered Nieh, and the vehicle rolled to a lopsided halt as the caravan moved onward. "The engine— shut it off, please."

Nieh twisted the key, and the motor coughed to silence. There was no sound but the chirping of a few stray locusts and the mewing of a cat. Chapman looked out at the cardplayers, who once again had stopped their game and were staring back.

"Is something wrong, Mr. Chapman?"

"Probably." He touched his temple. "Most of it in here, I'm sure. Tell me, Nieh, do these people know about the temple?"

"They have seen the cars passing through."

"Yes, but do they know what happened here? Did they know about it before Laojiu arrived?"

Nieh looked at Chapman in the rearview mirror. "Who can say? These villages have their own customs. They rarely confide in outsiders."

"Even Chinese outsiders?"

"To most of these people, China is something thrust upon them by others. For them, there is only the village. It was thus with my own people. We had rituals, homage through prayer and fasting."

"And just who were you honoring with these traditions?"

"Not who, Mr. Chapman, what." He frowned. "These matters are difficult to simplify, nor was I a farmer long enough to see them with adult eyes."

"Try," Chapman urged. His eyes slid back to the unwavering stare of the peasants. "I can't believe they don't feel the same thing I do."

"Which is?"

"That this place is forlorn in a way that gives me goose bumps. If it weren't for the religious overtones, I'd almost describe the basin as forsaken. Look at these people. They make things grow in the fields, yet they themselves look like the living dead."

Nieh thought for a moment. "Every form of worship in our country is tied to the earth. We do not pray for strength as you Christians do. Necessity has always bred the strength we've required. We honor the earth, for our worship is returned to us as nourishment. Your world moves quickly, Mr. Chapman. Their world does not. What you see in them is no thought of self. Do you see what our leaders are up against? What you view as cadaverous is patience."

Chapman studied the men a moment longer. "Yes, you can see it in their eyes. They haven't left the past; I'll wager these people know about the temple, all right, knew about it long before Laojiu ever heard of it. For them, it probably never even fell."

Chapman shut the window and told Nieh to drive on. The jeep and its groaning engine were soon gone from Tahnsien, leaving it once more to the locusts and cats and to the quiet chatter of the men discussing their card game. When the sun finally set, the players disbanded.

A police car was waiting for the convoy at the sentry booth of the Paoting bridge. The officer ran to the jeep and handed over a message.

"Let me guess," Chapman complained as he opened the embassy envelope. "The transport has been hijacked, and Teres wants us to buy tickets for the statues on a commercial flight. Tourist, I'll—" He fell silent as he read the one-line message. "Report to the embassy? What in God's name for?" He leaned toward the policeman. "Is there a telephone here? I want to know why we have to bring the whole damn convoy."

Nieh translated, and the officer's answer left him shaking his head.

"What's wrong?"

"He says there is a telephone, but the rains have washed out the lines. He does not know when they will be repaired. The serviceman, he says, is stranded on his farm."

"Swell." Chapman crumpled the telegram and tossed it to the floor. He checked his watch. "It's seven-ten, and the trip to Beijing will put us at least an hour behind schedule. Jesus, Teres, I'm the one who's going to have to answer for the delay."

Chapman swore. There was no choice but to do as he'd been ordered. Reluctantly, he ran up to the lead truck to inform Einar and his passengers, Laojiu and Yu, that they'd be making for the airport by way of Beijing. Only the Swede grumbled about the detour.

China's capital city was not so much a metropolis as an ancient village that had been elaborated on to its utmost. Nothing new was over five stories tall, and very little of that broke with traditional design. A few of the industrial plants could have been transplanted from anywhere, but all else was well-preserved antiquity: temples from the fifteenth century and roads that were even older. There were telephone poles and trolley buses, taxis, and an occasional neon light. But mostly there was the promise of modernization rather than the fact of it.

The caravan passed slowly through the broad main streets, a quarter lane on each side of the roadway allotted to bicycles. Very few people were about.

The American embassy was a thirty-two-year-old red brick building, less opulent than the Soviet mansion nearby and less heavily guarded. There was a single sentry posted outside the gate. Leaving the jeep, Chapman flashed his ID and ran up the short flower-lined walk to the front door. As he was about to enter, he heard footsteps slapping the wet pavement behind him; turning, he saw Laojiu approach the gate. Chapman waited until the archaeologist had been cleared, and they entered the embassy together.

"Are you supposed to see Teres as well?" Chapman asked.

Laojiu stopped at the mouth of the long corridor. "I beg your pardon . . . Teres?"

"I heard you tell the guard you wanted room 202. That's his office, Deputy Ambassador Wayne Teres."

The old man's features seemed to darken, though he said nothing. Chapman suspected that the scientist knew more about the summons than he'd revealed, but said nothing as they continued along the hallway.

Chapman had gone to Yale with Teres, at least until the army found that the Brooklyn-born student was not officially registered and simply had been hiding from the draft. Teres was sent to postwar Korea, and they'd been together only twice since then, at the airport when Chapman had arrived and, before that, at a cocktail party in Washington after Chapman's legal problems had become a cause célèbre.

"Hey, Grant!" The young man rose behind his desk. Teres's disposition still brightened a room, and although his cheeks were a little fuller since he'd left Washington, at least they were healthfully tanned. Where Teres got a tan like that in Beijing eluded Chapman, although the source of his ever-pleasant demeanor, judging by the roach in his ashtray, did not. The men's hands remained locked far longer than protocol demanded.

"Evening, Wayne. It's almost worth the trip to Beijing to see you."

"Yeah, sorry about that. Apart from baggy eyes you're looking good." He continued shaking his friend's hand. "Jeez, it's too bad you were assigned to Vinnie Papa's office. We could've had some great times here."

"Listen, Wayne, I hate to be rude but we're a little behind—"

"Speaking of rude, where are my manners? Want a hit?" He pushed over the ashtray. "You look like you could use it."

"Thanks, no. If you don't mind, though, I'll take back my hand."

Teres glanced down and saw that he was still pumping. "Ooh, boy. That Cambodian stuff is mighty." The deputy ambassador released his grip and stepped from behind his plain, gunmetal desk. "Okay, gentlemen, down to business." His smile lost its edge of sincerity as he greeted the lanky Chinese. "Dr. Laojiu." He bowed slightly, arms held stiffly at his side. "It's a pleasure to meet you."

"Thank you, Mr. Ambassador."

Teres grinned boyishly. "Thanks, but I'm not Mr. Ambassador. I'm Mr. Deputy Ambassador, or just plain Wayne if you'd like."

The archaeologist's thin, silvery brow arched. "I was told—"

"Yes, I know. I'm the one who told you that Ambassador Hartworth would be here. But he's been called away on other business." To Chapman he said, "Chairman Hua decided to organize an impromptu banquet for three thousand people in the Great Hall."

"The caterer must have loved that." Chapman felt his droll college humor returning, wishing it had never been chased from him.

"No problem, Grant. It was bring your own rice. See, they'd planned fireworks in Tien An Men Square to commemorate National Liberation Day, but with the rain, they decided to have a feast instead." Teres shifted back to Laojiu.

"That's why the ambassador is not with us. However, I give you my personal assurance that he will be briefed fully on this problem you're having."

"Problem?" Chapman swung toward the archaeologist. "What now? I thought we'd reached some kind of understanding."

"I'm sorry, Mr. Chapman, but what you thought is not my concern. I am troubled by more important matters. Today I have seen one of my statues nearly destroyed and have ridden in a truck which bounced like a fornicating animal." Teres hid a giggle behind his hand, but Chapman continued to stare at Laojiu with alarm. "I cannot watch you treat my find with such disrespect." He faced the deputy ambassador, who put on as serious a face as possible. "Only the United States can call off this exhibit. Indeed, as I explained over the telephone—"

"Telephone?" Chapman sneered. "I thought the line had been cut."

"You ordered it repaired. Mr. Teres, I am aware of my own honor being compromised by this request. I have considered that on the ride to Beijing and will gladly take slides to your country, provide lectures, publish articles, do anything you wish. Only leave the statues in China. I can be replaced, but they cannot."

Teres sat on the edge of his desk and folded his hands on his knee. "Professor, your uneasiness is valid, and actually I expected your call. Opening night jitters are not confined to the stage. Of course, I'll bring your concerns to the attention of the ambassador, although frankly, I hesitate to lodge a formal complaint. I'm sure that Grant will double his efforts to safeguard the statues."

"We've done a pretty damn good job, considering everything."

"But," Teres went on, "I repeat what Minister Guo no doubt explained. It is your government that wants the tour and that suggested it. To withdraw our commitment or to imply less than our fullest support would be highly insulting."

"The statues, Mr. Teres. They matter far more than wounded feelings. Surely an intelligent man must recognize that and act accordingly, regardless of the ramifications."

"Yes, but I'm powerless to do anything other than bring your complaint to the attention of the ambassador, who will forward it to the State Department through the proper channels."

Laojiu's eyes were white heat. "Why did you allow me to come here, give me the soul of hope by agreeing to listen to my plea when in fact you had no intention of helping?"

"On the contrary," Teres said soothingly. "Like yourself, sir, I can't answer for what you may have thought we'd accomplish. I asked the two of you over to see if we could perhaps reach some informal solution to your problem."

"Informal? I have not come to discuss manners, nor is this my problem. There is a world at stake, a priceless treasure. Ch'en-shimm is a time machine; it strips away the centuries to reveal the secrets and hopes and mistakes of the past. How can any thinking individual weigh that against a plan which is merely expedient for our leaders, destined for nothing higher than to divert a dull lay public? No, Mr. Teres, I will not accept this verdict."

The deputy ambassador opened his desk drawer and withdrew a pen and a pad of yellow paper. "Very well, Professor. How shall I begin my report to the ambassador? A bold phrase like 'Posterity will hold you responsible for this cultural rape' ought to get their attention in Washington."

"Tell him that the present is insignificant in the scheme of history. The people of Ch'en-shimm had problems which were no less important to them than yours are to you, or Minister Guo's to him. Yet what do they matter today?"

"Then what is it you want from Ch'en-shimm?" Chapman asked sincerely. "If they don't matter and we don't matter, then what does?"

"In mathematics, a single point tells us very little, Chapman. Alone, Ch'en-shimm is also of limited value. But two points define a line, and three a plane. Perspective is what matters. Humanity does not stand on a point or even a line but a plane, parallel planes, solids. Figuratively speaking, these are the foundation of knowledge."

Teres tore a page of hastily scribbled notes from the pad and slid it into the wastebasket. "I'm afraid you're talking over my head, Professor. Like in the stratosphere. Maybe that's why you're a scholar and I'm just a civil servant. If you could dictate that again more slowly."

Laojiu said nothing, and Chapman stepped toward him. "Please, I said before that I don't like this arrangement any better than you do. Maybe less, because it's just not in my blood to be a pirate. But behind all the posturing and repartee, there is one fact which has yet to be mentioned. And that's that we in the diplomatic corps also labor under the belief that we're serving society. It may not be as lofty or farsighted as what you've done, but we pride ourselves for keeping the wheels moving forward. I don't agree that only illiterates will come to see the figures. I don't agree at all, and I hope you'll give us the opportunity to prove you wrong."

Teres applauded lightly. "Well said, Grant." He turned to Laojiu. "You see our position, I think. Or do you still have some questions?" He rested his hand on the telephone receiver. "If there's something else you want to talk about, I'll be glad to ask the transport to wait at the airport." Still staring at Laojiu, he said, "Grant, you have Chinese workers accompanying you to New York?"

"We do."

"And you will instruct your men to be more careful?"

"Einar knows what has to be done."

"Professor?"

Teres's challenge narrowed the archaeologist's eyes to venomous slits. "I hope, Mr. Teres, that one day something will touch you deeply and then fade before you've had a chance to savor it. You will weep and beg for it to return, and you will understand the anguish I endure." His anger unabated, he turned to Chapman. "And you must tell me one thing before we go. You arranged this exhibit. Was the ultimatum also your idea?"

"No," Chapman answered. His stomach knotted with shame, as it had when he'd first heard of the plan. "I didn't know anything about it until I arrived in Beijing. I'm sorry—it taints this whole enterprise."

"Who thought of it?"

"Why do you ask?"

"Why do you not answer? You have it in your hands to help restore some faith in my species. Is it someone from whom I would have expected infidelity?"

Chapman couldn't look at the man, couldn't remain objective before his indignation. He was not used to being on the side of the deaf bureaucracy and didn't have the words to defend or explain it.

"It was one of my countrymen," Laojiu uttered at last.

"No doubt the minister. He is fond of harassing. Did you argue against it, Chapman?"

"I did what any number of people in my bureau would have done. I informed the—the parties responsible that I did not approve of coercing you, of threatening to bar you from the dig if you didn't agree to the display. I argued against it even though I knew my case was hopeless. Having the discoverer of Ch'en-shimm present with his find is the kind of personal touch that goes over very well in the U.S."

With a leer, the archaeologist said, "I do not think I will like your country. But by my soul, this affair has turned me against mine." Bitterness welling within him, he shook a bony fist at Teres. "No one can justify this. No one. There will be a reckoning, I swear it."

"Are you threatening this office?" the diplomat huffed. "Need I remind you that you are on American soil?"

Laojiu pulled himself confidently erect. "Ch'en-shimm fell because its leaders were arrogant like you, Mr. Teres. They believed in the sovereignty of a strong arm. Then the earth rippled, and they perished, their armies and their gods unable to protect them. Put your faith in learning, Mr. Teres, in a strong mind. Nothing else matters." Proudly, as though he had won a great victory, Laojiu spun past the deputy ambassador and made his way down the hallway.

Teres's expression grew impish. "Let me tell you, Grant, you really know how to pick 'em. This banzai makes your pederast pals at Tarlo look like angels."

"Not quite angels. Laojiu may be a hothead, but I don't think he'd ever hurt anyone."

"Did we hear the same lecture? Sounded to me like he was predicting the fall of Western civilization." Teres eased from the desk and stretched. "Well, he's a grouch, but we handled him okay, another crisis averted by the diligent personnel of the United States government. Hey, speaking of crises." He took Chapman by the elbow and led him to the door. "I saw a woman nearly killed today. Slipped from a wet scaffold while she was working on a generator at the electrical station. Broke her back, I hear."

Teres was still gabbing about the mishap when they emerged from the embassy; his voice suddenly cracked, his jaw falling open as he noticed a girl beside the rearmost truck trying to shield herself from the renewed rainfall.

"Shit!"

The deputy ambassador hurried forward, nearly skidding on the slick walk. As he passed through the gate, the girl glowered at him from under her rain-soaked black bangs. "I only came to scream at you," she shouted.

"Christ, I deserve it, I really do. I'm sorry, hon."

"You were supposed to meet me for dinner! I waited an hour, and then this bastard—" she indicated the gum-chewing sentry "—this cud-eating boy wouldn't even put in a call to your office!"

"Sorry again; those were my orders." Teres kissed the tall Chinese girl on her pink, wet cheek. "We had a bit of an international dilemma—uh, Grant, this is Mei Serizawa, a friend of mine."

"Not any more," she hurled her back at him, facing the truck.

Teres slipped his arms around her waist. "Well then, Grant, this is Mei Serizawa, my enemy and prisoner. Mei, Grant Chapman, our government's distinguished cultural exchange director and tattler on toy companies which murder children."

"I'm delighted," Chapman said uncomfortably. "Listen, Wayne, I'd better get this show moving again. I'll let you know when I'm bringing Laojiu back. Maybe we can have dinner then."

"Yeah, great. Good idea." He offered Chapman his hand.

The girl snarled, "He won't be alive to keep the engagement. You're going to pay for that hour, Wayne Teres, or I'll never be home when—"

"Hey, Grant, have a safe trip." Teres quickly released his hand. "And a quiet one. The exhibit will be great, put you right back in the newspapers."

While the diplomat ushered the indignant woman past the sentry, Chapman returned to the jeep. The caravan continued on its journey, the only traffic about in the still Beijing evening.

Tahnsien was quiet, all of the men and most of the women and children having gone to bed once their prayers had been offered.

Three women were still awake, gathered in a hard mud alcove toward the rear of Jen's home. The youngest of the three, Jen, was a child, barely in her teen years. The others, gray-haired and bent from years of labor in the fields, stood on either side of the girl. Silently, they helped her as they had helped countless others over the years. One woman held Jen's hand as she slipped from her simple smock and pants, while the other raised a knife from beside a small dragon brazier. A tin of incense smoked beside the serpent, whose fire was the room's sole source of light.

The woman handed the blade to the girl while she and her counterpart recited a prayer.

"His seed is blood, and the warrior is strengthened by it."

"We serve," chanted Jen, her high voice trembling slightly.

"The women carry the seeds to the fields, the tools with which the men hoe, and the water which is sprinkled upon the earth."

"We serve."

"The women carry the man's seed and return it as a child."

"We serve." The words finally emerged clear and steady.

"The women care for the man's weapons, which protect us from defilement and the stranger's ways."

"We serve."

"The women honor the men by nourishing their god."

At this, the girl slowly put the blade to her palm and, wincing, slashed it.

"The hand too fair for battle," chanted the other two. She cut her arm near the shoulder.

"The limb too weak to lead." She bravely cut her breast above the heart.

"The bosom which flows with milk rather than sinew." She turned the knife toward her genitals and cut them.

"The woman must be as the bloodied man so that the Madjan does not want."

When the ritual was completed, the two women ministered to Jen's wounds, sealing them with balm and bandages. Then the elder women left to allow the Woman of Peace to rest after her ordeal.

As she lay on her straw mattress, she felt the slit in her palm open. After pulling the bandages tighter, she drifted into a satisfied sleep.

The deputy ambassador lay naked on his desk and watched the girl walk to her clothes, which lay heaped on a wing chair. "You know, you're actually worth all the aggravation."

The girl did not respond; she simply pulled a towel from the closet and sprinkled it with amber powder from her purse. She dabbed it under her breasts and between her legs and then ran the towel across her belly, wiping away the sweat. Even her routine movements had flowing sensuality to them; watching her, Teres found himself imbued with renewed vigor.

"Any other embassies on the agenda for tonight?"

"The German ambassador at three."

Teres glanced at the clock on the rear wall of the office. It was a round clock with a white face and black hands, like the one under which he'd stolen his first kiss, from Nancy Joseph in the first grade. "You've got ninety minutes. Can I buy you dinner?"

"I'm no longer hungry."

"Okay, then, can I buy you?"

"Again?" She continued to stand with her back toward him. His eyes fastened on her long neck, followed the gently swaying curves down. She moved with a slow gyration as she reapplied her lip gloss. She tossed the stick to the chair and ran her open hands along her sides. "Get me a drink first. Something tart."

Teres swung from the desk and pulled on his pants. "Wash away the taste? Sure, hon, anything you say." Teres stole a final glance at her smooth, unblemished back; then he slipped on his shirt and hurried from the darkened room to the liquor cabinet in the ambassador's office.

Teres shook his head as he poured her drink. "What an incredible sexual machine, everywhere at once with everything she's got. Hits erogenous zones like a Cruise Missile." He quietly blessed the AP reporter who had turned him on to her; then he hastened back to his office.

He felt it a moment before he turned into the open doorway, an unusual stillness in the air. Even in repose, Mei generated a kind of sexual heat that went straight for the libido. There was none of that—no heat, no chill—just a lack of palpable energy.

"Mei?"

Teres stood in the doorway, peering into the darkened room. "Mei, what is this? Hide and seek? Seek and fuck? Where the hell are you?"

There was no sound. With a disgusted sigh, convinced that

she'd run out on him, he walked toward the lamp on the other side of the room.

His bare foot stepped in something warm and wet. He stopped, dragged his toe along the ground, and found more of the sticky stuff.

"She must've puked. Sure," he hollered, "run to the bathroom and leave yours truly to clean up." Teres doubled back toward the closet for some towels. On the way, he stubbed up against something spongelike. It slid several inches after he'd nudged it, and without looking down, he spun back again toward the standing lamp. He tugged the chain and looked into the room. He could not comprehend what he saw.

Blood was everywhere, on the floors, walls, and furniture. His eyes fell to the floor. Mei was just a memory, at least the Mei he knew. Bits of dead white flesh lay strewn about the room like chunks of meat tossed to an alley cat. Several of the girl's limbs were intact, though in different corners of the office. He saw now that it had been a forearm and hand he'd trodden on; had he continued a few inches beyond, he'd have found what was left of her head. Even in the fleeting glance he allowed himself, he saw that the chin, nose, and one ear were missing. The fine long hair was red with blood; her hazel eyes had rolled into her head, leaving the whites glaring.

"Jesus H. Christ," he swore, and resumed shaking his head. "Jesus H. Mother-of-God Christ."

Slowly, as though in a trance, Teres sloshed through the blood to the telephone and rang for the sentry.

CHAPTER FOUR

THE NEW YORK POST headline was tailored to attract stares and, in their wake, impulse purchases. Screaming in large, vertical type, "CHINESE ARMY INVADES NY!" the tabloid all but flew off the newsstands. It conveniently relegated to page 3 the fact that the warriors were from the second century B.C. and that they were built of fragile clay.

The fifteen-hour flight had been a quiet one, with the American laborers eating, drinking, or sleeping while their Chinese counterparts slept. Einar was busy planning his next undertaking, positioning a large radar unit on a twenty-thousand-foot-high ledge of Mt. K2 in India, while the professor and his daughter sat alone and fleshed out notes they'd taken over the previous few weeks.

Chapman was exhausted by his efforts and by the initial jet lag from which he'd never quite recovered. He napped until roused by subconscious guilt at having not yet read Laojiu's ninety-page treatise on the Turpan dig, his most recent report to his government sponsors. With a groan of resignation, he slid the report from his carry-on bag.

Although he had to reread several of the more technical passages more than once, Chapman found himself wishing that he had gotten to the manuscript sooner. Laojiu's almost poetic description of the statues, particularly the Madjan, told him just how precious they were to the archaeologist. Had he but known, he might have compromised and left the god behind.

The deplaning of the thirteen figures took just over three hours. Einar assured Chapman that everything was well in hand, and when Laojiu's own foreman echoed the appraisal, Chapman ushered the archaeologist and his daughter to the waiting limousine for the forty-minute ride into Manhattan.

Their destination was the Consulate of the People's Republic of China, where the visitors would be staying at their own request. They had been offered a suite of rooms at the Pierre, but Laojiu had insisted upon a more work-conducive environment. It was his intention to study when he was not at the museum, and he had brought along several ancient parchments rolled snugly within a metal cylinder.

It was nearly 9 P.M. in New York, and there was little to see on leaving the airport save for the traffic on the highway, abundant by the standards of the Turpan Basin or even Beijing. Laojiu remarked on it to Yu in Chinese, with Chapman picking up only a few words of the terse exchange. It wasn't until they crossed the Fifty-ninth Street Bridge, the city's lighted towers like frozen flame before them, that Laojiu addressed Chapman.

"It is an impressive view," he said with a hint of childlike enthusiasm, "as majestic to our era as Ch'en-shimm in its time." His suddenly lively eyes moved and dipped with the skyline. "Yes, there may be perspective here, an unanticipated dividend."

Chapman, pleased that this might not be the disaster he'd been anticipating, said, "That's the Empire State Building," as they had a momentary glimpse of the skyscraper between the United Nations Building and the Pan Am facade. "Over twelve hundred feet high without the broadcast tower. Third tallest building in the world." His finger tracked east. "That flat building is the U.N., and the river is the East River."

Yu, sitting on the far side of the car, craned over her father to see. "I've read that the rivers in New York are so dirty that one cannot bathe in them. Why is that permitted?"

Chapman ignored the barb and pointed across the river to

Queens and the factories perched on its shores. "As your people will soon learn, Yu, pollution is the chaff of our agriculture—of any industrial society."

"Of a careless one," the woman returned. She sat back in the velvet seat. "Large and busy and dirty cities do not impress me nearly so much as—"

"As dead ones?" He regretted the rebuke immediately. "That was uncalled for, and I'm sorry. It's been a crowded week, as you know."

"Of course," Laojiu said appeasingly. "It seems that in spite of your speech at the embassy, there is a great deal you regret about your work."

Chapman had quietly turned and stared out the window. Faces in cars along the FDR Drive turned to the limousine as it passed, eyes squinting for a peek inside. Chapman felt anything but privileged and was looking forward to time away from these ascetic intellectuals. What he really needed was a good dose of New York decadence to flush the desolation from his system. He hoped that Linda was free for a late dinner, and he barely resisted scrapping protocol by phoning her from the car.

Thinking of food reminded Chapman. "Incidentally, our ambassador to the United Nations is expecting you for dinner at ten o'clock. The car will wait at—"

"I trust you will thank the ambassador and express our regrets," Laojiu interrupted. "We are very tired after the long flight."

"But you'll want to eat something, I'm sure, and there will be no formalities of state."

"It is pointless to ignore one need for another. We would prefer to rest."

Chapman surrendered willingly. He picked up the telephone hooked to the door of the limousine and called the ambassador at home. Accustomed to reading between the lines, the woman understood fully what Chapman was not quite able to spell out.

"Off the record, Grant, should I bother scheduling him for another night?"

"It'll be the same, I'm sure, but we've got to try."

"You're right, of course. I'll pencil him in for Thursday night. Is he that much of a stiff?"

"Call Wayne if you want a ditto," he said vaguely. "There was a tiff."

The ambassador was silent for a moment. "Wayne? You mean Wayne Teres?"

"Right."

"When did you see him?"

"Oh, about eighteen hours ago. Why?" Chapman felt a fluttering in his stomach.

"After a meeting of the Security Council, I noticed a telex that said they're hustling Wayne home."

"Did it say why?"

"No reason whatsoever. It struck me as odd, but I got tied up with something else before I could look into it."

Chapman groaned. "Damn, I hope they didn't catch him with that woman."

"As I said, I don't know what happened, but I'll let you know if I hear anything. In the meantime, keep me posted about Thursday."

"Will do. See you at the opening tomorrow."

Chapman dropped the phone back into its cradle and gnawed his lower lip as he wondered about Teres. Convinced that it was either the prostitute or drugs, he spent the remainder of the ride rummaging through his mind for the names of good international attorneys.

The passengers ignored one another until they reached the mission. Although he really didn't care to speak with them, their coldness annoyed Chapman. He had been ignored by experts, and that hadn't bothered him: Russia's Gromyko, when he'd been brought to a grounded 747 to defend a defecting ballet dancer; and Richard Nixon, in whose White House he'd worked briefly on the Watergate defense before Tarlo reared its head. But the aloofness of these two rankled him because it was faceless, impersonal, scattered across the political and social spectrum of two continents. He was just a convenient target; yet it was impossible to defend himself to the couple without defending all of civilization.

The Chinese Consulate was located at 54th Street and Eleventh Avenue, and Chapman deposited his passengers with the perfunctory reminder that he'd be back for them at eight o'clock the following morning. After they'd vanished into the darkness of the small foyer, Chapman loosened his tie and slouched in the seat.

Chapman's apartment was on the Upper East Side, in a nine-story, prewar building nestled just off Park Avenue, though he told people it was on Lexington, since that sounded less pretentious. The building was in fact in the throes of becoming a co-op, six rooms with an alley view his to own for the bargain price of $148,500. He'd had to borrow from countless relatives to make the twenty-five percent down payment, generosity for which he was sure to pay dearly whenever they flew into New York and felt entitled to stay with him longer than in previous years.

Maybe I should let Linda move in with me, he told himself as he went through mail his neighbor had collected while he was away, a thick stack of litter that included detailed plans for an upcoming spring visit from two of his patrons. *My family couldn't stand that kind of relationship for more than an hour, and then, only if they were drunk or in the presence of the Pope.*

Tossing the bills, magazines, mail-order catalogues, and lobbyist literature on the sofa, he went to the study and phoned his answering service.

"Hi, Gail. Yes, I'm back. Glad you liked the postal card. Hold on, the pen's out of ink." He fished another from among the papers on his desk. "Okay, shoot. Accountant called about audit—wonderful. My cousin Mary, a personal tour of the White House." *She didn't lend me money, so screw her. She'll take free tickets to the public tour and like it.* "Who's next? My mother . . . my mother . . . the Yale alumni association . . . my mother. That's it?"

That was not it, the girl exclaimed. Linda had called each of the eight days he was away and left erotic messages. Did Grant want to hear them?

"I'll pass, as much as I'd love to hear you utter lewd things into the phone. What? No, you're not past your prime. You're not. My mother came alive when she was forty, kicked my father out the door. You've got two years to wait, and you'll be reborn. I promise. Yes, we can have an affair then even if Jack hasn't left you. All right, talk to you tomorrow. Thanks. Bye."

Chapman hung up and wondered again if Gail was the Nancy Reagan lookalike he imagined.

One day I want to find out for certain, though seeing her

face to face might ruin our otherwise perfect relationship.

He consulted his watch. *Einar will be at the museum in about an hour. That leaves just enough time for a fast shower and a can of chili.*

The hot, forceful water was ecstasy after nearly thirty hours in the same clothes. When the shower was over, Chapman snuggled into his cool, comfortably broken-in jeans and was reborn. After pulling on his panda sweatshirt, a gift from the National Zoo for helping to bring Ling Ling to America, he flopped on the bed and phoned Linda.

The phone was snapped up on the first ring. "Jeans and your Grant's Tomb sweatshirt. Say yes or I'll die, because I haven't been right about a thing all day!"

Chapman considered lying but knew he'd never pull it off. "I'm not wearing my namesake, but I am wearing my lookalike, a big cuddly fella."

"Ling Ling? Never let it be said that you're impressionable. Back from China for an hour or so and right into your panda shirt."

"It was on the top of the pile. As for dying," he said more seriously, "don't do it. I love you. Need you, too."

"Hmmm . . . There's an 'and' in your voice, I can feel it. Out with it, Chapman. Who'd you lay in China?"

"No one, it's nothing like that." He hesitated. "I love you, and also—I might have to borrow you again come May. I've already got three cousins looking for my key under the mat."

He could see her shaking her head. "I'll tell you, Grant, that's a classy segue, planted deep in the conversation so that it wouldn't stick out like a zit. Okay, let's whip the dead horse one more time. This time I move in for good or I don't move in at all."

"Lawfully wed?"

"Forget it."

"It's forgotten."

"So," he pressed on, anxious to leave the topic that had dominated the last six months of their relationship, "what happened while I was away? How's your father?"

"He's coming home tonight. The doctors say there's nothing they can do for Dad except to let him die in his own bed. You may not be an MD, but you called it two weeks before they did. It's spread to his lungs and is inoperable."

"Just like my stepfather. Sorry, Linda."

"Don't be. He's days away from death, and the first thing he said to me this morning was that I'd better be wearing a bra when I come back tonight. Can you believe the balls of the man, right to the end? I hate myself for it, but I swear I'm not going to miss him."

Chapman said he was sorry about that as well. "Did you call that lung specialist I recommended, the one who took care of the shah?"

"We called him in the day after you left," Linda told him. Chapman could see her twirling a lock of curly blond hair, which she did when she was unusually depressed. "He said the same thing that Kahn and Jelkowitz told us, that the cancer was too far gone. Your man was nice, though. He even made a pass at me."

"I asked him to."

"Piss off, you did not. He's smart enough to recognize grade A stuff when he sees it." There was a silence, then Linda exclaimed suddenly, "I recognize this pause, Grant. It's your breaking-off-the-talk pause because you're late. Well, don't do it, don't even look at your watch."

He had been about to, and he didn't.

"To hell with the museum," she said, "and with your punctual self. I'm off to the hospital in a few minutes, but you're going to take a minute to tell me how it went in China. Would I like it there?"

"Probably. There's a lot to please a painter's eye, though the only time I saw any sights was riding from office to office."

"How were the people? On TV they always seem pleasant but formal."

Chapman expressed his general approval of the Chinese and took the opportunity to prepare Linda to meet Laojiu. He decided it was fortuitous that Linda wouldn't be there in the morning, when the archaeologist would have to be consulted about recreating the lighting in the temple. She hadn't the patience for his kind of scientific and personal fastidiousness.

After hearing Chapman's overview, Linda remarked, "Sounds like a classic case of finders keepers. Can't say I'm awfully upset that Tally will be doing the really heavy conceptual stuff, as much as I'd love to have worked on it."

"Don't worry. When Tally's done, you can have that relic from the sixties stuffed and design a hippy display in the Hall of Vanished Cultures."

"Tally will get the job done," Linda pointed out with a trace of indignation. "She's got a good eye for design and will probably do a better job lighting the figures than I'd have. You know I can't envision things; I've got to *see* them."

Chapman knew, just as he knew from that sinking tone of voice what was coming.

She whispered, "I've got to see you too, Grant, and soon, even if you do belong next to Tally as an example of mid-Victorian male puritanism."

There was a buzz on the line signifying an incoming call; Linda heard it and sent Chapman off with a kiss. He felt a tinge of guilt. As deeply as he cared for her, as much as he wanted to be with her, their conversations of late had see-sawed between clever digs and emotional desperation. He missed the carefree middle ground of a year ago. Chapman depressed the cradle and switched wires.

The caller didn't wait for a hello. "Well, Grant, another miracle performed by yours truly!"

Einar's irreverence was a gust of fresh air. "Glad to hear that you and more importantly the statues made it to the museum in one piece."

"Hell, yes! Discountin' the traffic at the airport, it ran as clean as the waterworks, maybe cleaner. Anyhow, since I got you on the phone, do you want us to wait for you before we start unloadin'? Does someone official have to be there?"

Chapman squinted at his watch. "Technically, yes. But go ahead. You'll save the illustrious curator some overtime. I'll be there in about a half hour." He threw out as an afterthought, "Any reporters?"

"A few. Looked to me like the usual stringers. One or two might pick at your scabs, but they're mostly bored-lookin' men with nothin' better to do on a Monday night."

Chapman thanked the Swede for his assessment and then reminded him to be careful. The image of that crate slipping in the pit was still vivid. Hurrying into the kitchen, he decided to skip dinner. Grabbing a cola for the caffeine, he slung a windbreaker over his shoulder and, disdaining the long wait for the elevator, ran down the stairwell.

The darkness and the blood were everpresent, but the vortex was new. It was a wave moving from him, a black vortex ribboned with red and disrupting his sleep. Spinning into the deep pitch of eternity, it created a sense of loss he could not disregard.

They had not abandoned him—it was not in the nature of the beast. Even at the cascading height of the holocaust, with fingers of flame dragging them down, his warriors had fought on. Now, bereft of all but a chosen few, he must rise. Those who had dared assault his ranks would perish.

He sensed a new enemy, alien but powerful. He would deal with it.

For centuries, he had allowed mortals to tend to his needs. But his subjects hadn't acted swiftly enough when the earth dragon stirred, and their descendants were no better prepared.

He willed the red tendrils toward him, and the flush of life coursed through his legs.

He moved, and a pinpoint of light broke upon the vortex...

CHAPTER FIVE

THE FOUR TRUCKS were grouped like a fan at the rear entrance of the museum, radiating from a collection of hoists, floodlights, and reporters. As Chapman emerged from his cab and headed toward the museum, he scanned the assemblage. Not that he'd have turned back; he just wanted to prepare himself psychologically in the event that Tarlo was exhumed.

He walked slowly across the museum's westside park, picking out Koenig from *Newsweek* and Bent from the Washington *Post* and several other people who were probably reporters but who he didn't know. Unfortunately, he recognized Doug Reedy from the *Daily News* a heartbeat after the muckraker had noticed him, too late to avoid an encounter. The syndicated political columnist threw his cigarette aside and ran across the damp grass.

"Now here's someone really worth writing about." Reedy's craggy cheeks billowed before a racking cough. "How's the new life treating you? Good, dull, moral?"

"It's quieter than the old one."

"Better? Richer? More fulfilling to your tortured soul?"

"Less spectacular, Reedy, which is how I prefer it."

"You did right, kid," the veteran reporter gushed. "You know how I feel." He reached for a cigarette but let it slide back into its rumpled pack. "I'll wait. See? Even a guy like me, with a lot on his mind, remembers that you don't like smoke, or smokescreens, if you get my drift."

"It's been three years. Why can't you just let it lay?"

"They're still talking about the crucifixion, and that was centuries ago."

Chapman quickened his pace toward the trucks, with Reedy keeping up beside him.

"To tell you the truth, kid, I didn't come here to see those frigging statues. I wanted to talk to you, and since you never return my calls, this seemed the best way. D'you mind?"

"If I say yes, will you leave me alone?"

"Of course not. What I want to know is if you're ever going to write about it."

"No."

"But just think, you'd never have to work again. Admit it, you don't really like slaving for the State Department. Don't! A book will make you *rich*, a sure best-seller."

"I'm not interested." Chapman quickened his approach to the trucks, following the horseshoe-shaped path set in the center of the park.

"What you want doesn't really enter into this, you know." Reedy huffed alongside his quarry as Chapman broke into a jog. "The *public's* still interested. There's a book in it, a movie-of-the-week, maybe even a series. Let it all out, get it off your chest. All the anguish, the wrath and the hatred."

"I get absolution and you get the royalties."

Reedy gulped down a wheezing breath. "Forget me! Keep on being morality's champion, don't let the flame of justice die. And it won't cause you to miss a beat in your day-to-day business, which you'll keep on conducting until the riches roll in. I'll ghost it."

Chapman laughed, too astonished by the bounty hunter to take him seriously. His attitude caused Reedy to try a tougher tack.

"That's the trouble with people who get in the media's eye. They fight to get there and then tell everyone who helped them or who wants to know about them to go screw. No fair, Grant, not only to me, but think of all the people just waiting to be reinspired by your shining example. We don't see too many phoenixes rising from the ashes of a corporate blacklist."

Chapman paused, his brow hooded, his voice a shade darker. "Reedy, in less than two minutes you've managed to convince me of one thing." The reporter's eyes brightened hopefully, but Chapman dimmed them with a sneer. "You're not just a poor journalist, you're a ghoul. I didn't *ask* for any kind of notoriety, and I'm happier without it. I only did what I thought was right. The toys weren't safe, and I said so. The people who designed them were no damn good, and I said that too. My only mistake was saying it all too late, after I'd gotten them off the hook. People don't seem to realize that doesn't make me a hero. It does nothing except make me a tiny bastard and the Tarlo people much bigger bastards. I can live with that, but it doesn't mean I want to resurrect it in detail. And just for your own information—" he turned and started up along the path "—if I ever did sign to do a book, you're the last writer I'd call for help."

The rebuke left Reedy fuming. "You're no saint either, Chapman! You're a selfish man, a real prick. Can't you see that there's more to life than the day-to-day shit you do for Washington? You've got no future without me."

"If it's the future you're interested in," Chapman shouted, "or the past, talk to Laojiu. He can draw you a map."

"But I don't want a map, I want a lousy best-seller." Reedy was screaming now, less at Chapman than at the world, fired by his own frustration. "I need one, 'cause I'm rotting just like you're going to rot. Man, you're just a nowhere government figurehead now, hired by assholes because you're honest; because they were paranoid about Watergate, not because you're any damn good!"

Chapman slammed to a stop and half turned. He stood that way for what seemed an instant frozen in time, his insides smarting, his arms tense with anger. He stood because he knew that if he moved, he'd do what he had never done before—grab a man and beat him to death.

Let it go, he counseled himself. *Just roll with it. This man's opinions have never meant anything to you; he's just another attention-seeking loudmouth. Leave him in the gutter and get on with more important things.* Chapman turned and continued on his way, slowly, covertly wringing his windbreaker.

Chapman was greeted warmly when he reached the museum. Several reporters offered their hands, and Cara Piri Thomas of NBC kissed him on the cheek. He appreciated their courtesy and even managed a half smile as he climbed onto the lip of the one open truck. Inside, Einar was just checking the way the first of the clay warriors had been lashed to a minicrane. He did not tug on the ropes but tapped them with a pencil. The bonds were so taut that it was like drumming a rock.

"Don't you want any give?" Renny asked.

Einar scowled at him. "Use your head, mister! They'll have some bounce once they're carryin' the weight of the statue."

"But we had 'em this tight in the pit, an' you remember what happened there."

"That had nothing to do with the cables. Christ, there's no arguin' the physics. If we lessened the tension any, we'd heave the crate out and it'd drop." He thrust both of his hands palm down toward the floor. "That kind of jerk would snap the ropes, no question."

"Then what happened in China?" Chapman inquired.

Einar shoved his wool cap back on his head and dragged his sleeve across his sweating brow. "Someone screwed up. But don't blame Isaac Newton; he had nothing to do with it. Now, can I get on with this, or do you want to talk overtime?"

Chapman backed against the wall, out of the way.

"Okay." Einar turned to Renny. "Let's get this first guy out."

Renny and another muscular worker, along with two hefty Chinese, steadied the crate while a dolly was slipped beneath it. The fragile parcel was rolled onto the lip as Einar walked beside the men, his eye bolted to the stress monitor mounted on the forecorner slat.

"One thing I noticed about these reporters," Einar said to Chapman, his eyes never leaving the gauge. "They're mostly the ambulance chasers. I overheard some of them talkin'. Christ, they'd love to see us drop one of these, wouldn't they?"

Chapman squinted into the TV lights and popping flashcubes. "It's nothing personal, I'm sure, just their sick sense of priorities. Anyway, I read the press releases Tepper sent out. Nothing but praise for you."

"Great, but what makes you think these beggars can read?"

Chapman admitted that Einar had a point. Suddenly his head jerked round and he stared with alarm at the Swede. "Though if that is why they're here, you do plan to disappoint them, I hope?"

"I haven't lost a relic yet."

The green track wavered slightly within the red safety

margin of the oscilloscope. Without taking his eyes from the now-steady strand, Einar rapped the pencil on the winch cables, satisfied that some external electromagnetic impulse had caused the fluttering.

As the dolly was pulled away and the crate swung from the truck to the museum steps, Chapman heard the unmistakable voice of curator Walston Tepper III, Wally to those who wished to annoy him. He watched as the dwarfish curator approached the truck from his private entrance, with a reporter and photographer sandwiched between himself and the gangly Claude.

His flattened face pointed upward, the curator waited until the crate was once again on the dolly and being wheeled into the museum before leaning on the truck's metal lip.

"Grant, I'd like your attention. This is Mr. Bouche from *Us* magazine and his photographer, Mr. Smith." The men exchanged greetings. Tepper impatiently waved a stubby finger past the crate that a pair of Chinese were beginning to fit to the hoist. "Back there, Grant, in the large crate. According to the manifest, that's the Madjan, correct?" Chapman indicated that it was. "Excellent," the curator declared. "I'd like the men to bring it out next, and then I want him uncrated."

"Before the others are unloaded? Einar wants to keep the flow going with the smaller figures. You'll throw him off."

"These gentlemen—" Tepper leaned closer, "—have to file their story by morning or we'll miss this week's edition. Please see that your man's efforts are redirected. Our fiscal year is in your hands."

"Excuse me," the reporter put in. "Are things really that bad?"

Uncomfortable at having been overheard, Tepper slapped on a broad smile. "Let's just say that in a good year, we inch into the black. This has been a bad year, and bidding against Barbalt at the Metropolitan for this exhibit did not help our solvency. If we fail to attract a minimum of three hundred thousand paying customers, we'll have to undergo serious staff cutbacks come the fall and the new school semester."

Chapman knew that Tepper was not overstating the institute's dire financial state. But the curator's ability to make personal ambition seem like benevolence rankled him, always left him feeling as though he had been hustled. Then he remembered something he'd read in Laojiu's report.

"Excuse me, Dr. Tepper." Chapman paused while the suspicious Tepper offered him his bulldoggish profile. "We can't do a thing with the Madjan until your preparations are finished."

"My preparations? Exactly what are you talking about?"

"The blood sacrifice. According to legend, no one was allowed to pay homage to the Madjan without at least a token offering of blood."

Tepper snorted while the *Us* reporter scribbled furiously. "Thank you, Grant. That was supposed to be an exclusive for the New York *Post*, a fine headline for tomorrow's edition."

"Sorry." Chapman realized that any angle he thought was outré, Tepper would already have covered.

Claude frowned. "Really, sir, do we want more of that kind of publicity? Today's front page was really quite sensational."

"As I've just said, we want press that will get people into the museum." To the journalist he remarked, "I've a skeletal pteranodon inside who is so dusty, he looks as if he has fur. That's fine for the winged dinosaurs because they were covered with a layer of fine, white hair. Not so the stegosaurs and tyrannosaurs or our Eskimo manikins and stuffed elephants. The problem is, gentlemen, that we haven't the money to hire the proper custodial help."

With a final snarl at Chapman, the curator excused himself to greet Cara Thomas, who walked over with her camera crew. After agreeing to interview Tepper after the Madjan had been uncrated, the network correspondent came over to the truck trailing her hot TV lights.

"Why is it that you men are doing all the hard work, and I'm the one who's sweating?" She tucked a finger behind her white scarf, at the same time shaking out her shoulder-length blond hair. A cloud of dust filled the air. "Look at that. I've still got sawdust in my hair from covering the circus this morning."

"Welcome to ring number four," Chapman declared.

"You've done these things before. I'm sure it'll be worse tomorrow night at the open—"

Einar pushed brusquely past the woman and her crew and surged into the truck. "So, I hear from dogface that we're to move the big guy next."

"Is that a problem?"

"Well, we had a nice rhythm going with the smaller figures. Hell," he moaned, "it's no problem. You know me. I just wish the runt had the courtesy to ask instead of playing dictator."

"It's part of his appeal."

"It'll be part of his epitaph if he tries it again," the Swede replied as he stood before the crate, examining it.

Because the crate was so tall that it had been barely squeezed erect inside the truck, Einar knew that they'd be unable to slide it onto a dolly. He ordered the men to a corner each, and with himself on the gauge, they walked the crate from side to side, moving it by slow measures toward the lip.

As they jockeyed the cumbersome weight forward, Cara Thomas decided to use their efforts as a backdrop for part of her report. She moved toward the lip and hadn't said more than a sentence when Einar's eyes went wide.

"Whoa," he cried, pulling the man nearest to him away from the crate, simultaneously swatting at one of the Chinamen and motioning the other men back.

"What's wrong?" Chapman gasped, his eyes dropping to the gauge.

"Jesus, look at it! It's writhin' like a snake. Nobody move. Don't even *breathe* until it's steady!"

The group stood around watching anxiously as Cara's camera operator turned his lens on the weaving oscilloscope. Although the crate was absolutely still, the green line continued to pulse.

"Bleedin' hell, we must have shaken one of the cables loose."

"How?" Chapman exclaimed. "I thought—"

"How should I know? I'll have to get inside. Christ, this bastard's more trouble than a roomful of Wally Teppers." The Swede retrieved a kit from the floor of the truck, grabbed a crowbar, and began prying away one of the slats. "This shouldn't have happened, no way it should have. I checked it over and over and then again. Hey, you," he called to the cameraman. "Be useful; bring your lights up here."

The bearded youth scampered onto the truck, leaving his camera running as he shined the white beacon to where the bar was pulling at the crate. When the slat had been torn away, Einar handed the crowbar to Renny, reached inside, and began ripping out fistfuls of padding.

The newswoman waved her hand in front of her face. "Smells as though they've got a dead cat in there."

Chapman smelled nothing, though he gave it no further thought as he huddled close beside Einar. "Can I do anything?"

"Yeah, watch the gauge for me." Einar reached inside, his arm vanishing to the shoulder. "I'm goin' to pull each of the cables a little. Tell me which one is causin' the meter to jump."

Einar wormed his hand around the statue and wiggled each of the taut bonds in turn. After each tug, he looked up at Chapman. Nothing caused any fluctuation in the steady up and down flowing of the needle.

Mystified, the Swede stepped back and scratched his head through his cap. He tapped the gauge. "I'll be damned. Either there's a short or some kind of activity in the air, like ultrahigh sound waves."

"You mean like a dog whistle?"

"No, it'd have to be something stronger, some kind of—" He spun and glowered at the cameraman. "Say, where's your bloody truck?"

"In the park. Tepper said it was all right to—"

"Tepper's a bunghole, mister. That's where the interference is comin' from. Hurry over and shut it down."

The cameraman looked at Cara, who stepped closer. "Just a minute, now. You've no authority to stop us from broadcasting."

"Never said I did. But if you don't close up, and I mean *fast*, I'm gonna walk over and rip out your fuckin' transmitter by its roots."

Cara frowned and then nodded at the young man. He handed his camera to the woman and ran toward the truck. She leered. "Let me know when the big boy is finished being Mr. Macho." Annoyed, she also stalked away.

Einar considered going after her and slapping her across the head but was too curious to see what would happen when the TV truck was shut down. He turned his attention back to the gauge, which in a moment fell dead still.

He beamed triumphantly. "See? Einar Björkman knows his frequencies."

"Better than he knows etiquette," Chapman teased, relieved.

Einar paid Chapman no attention. Replacing the padding as best he could, he ordered the men to get on with the unloading of the crate.

Chapmen went inside with the crew, feeling like the pied piper as the blank-faced reporters filed in behind.

The prying and snapping of the boards reverberated throughout the vast Hall of the Asian Peoples, echoing among the displayed armor and models of ancient villages, through the jade idols and painstakingly assembled mosaics that lined the walls and filled the glass showcases of the dark chamber. Adjustable track lighting had been installed from a temporary span, and it shone brightly on the center of the vast room where the statues were to be displayed.

As the uncrating proceeded, Chapman noticed Tally McGraw dwelling in the shadows to one side of the hall in her usual sit-in, turned antinuke protest, posture. It was a pigeon-toed poise that clung to a stubborn few fifteen years after its time had passed. The rest of her was no less antiquated as far as he was concerned. Her hair was stringy and long, and though washed, it didn't look it. Her round face was utterly without makeup but admittedly pretty. Her clothes were clogs, green stockings, a peasant dress, and a School of Visual Arts sweatshirt, moth-eaten from her days as a student, before she joined the faculty.

Tally dwelt, sketch pad in hand, studying the room with the intensity of a surgeon. She was watching to see how the light struck the statue, how the exhibit would relate to the existing displays, the way the statues should be arranged to provide maximum exposure within the roped-off sections that would be set up after the celebrity-studded opening night gala.

She moved after a long and pensive moment, her eyes never leaving the Madjan's crate. She walked over to Tepper, who was still involved with the reporter from *Us*.

"Must they be cordoned?"

The curator turned to her, his jowls trembling. "I beg your pardon?"

"I think it's a real downer to tell people that you don't trust them, besides detracting from the aesthetics."

Tepper smiled nervously. "Miss McGraw, I'm certain this can wait. Excuse me." He turned to the writer. "She's a bit eccentric. Has very good ideas, though, which—"

"I think that people should be given an opportunity to experience the figures close up. You know, there'll be a guard present, and that should be intimidating enough. I see no reason to—"

"Miss McGraw, if someone wants to carve their initials in the Madjan's girdle, there is no mortal reason why we should help them along."

"A rope won't stop them from doing that."

"Case *closed*." He waved his hand with excommunicating fervor.

The woman shook her head woefully and then wrote something in her sketch pad as she eased away toward the Madjan.

"Probably a poem about her experience," Claude said under his breath as Tepper resumed the interview.

Chapman, who had watched but not heard the exchange, crushed a soda can that sat upright in an ashtray, and then he strolled over to Einar. The Swede was on a ladder, working loose the last upper planks of the Madjan's crate. Chapman noticed with alarm that the oscilloscope was weaving again. He called it to Einar's attention.

"I *saw* it, damn your eyes, I saw it. But I don't know what the hell's causin' it!" The frustrated Swede wrenched a plank free and handed it down to Renny. "They must be broadcastin' again, those beggars. Left the truck on just to annoy me."

Chapman looked around. He smiled politely at Tally, who stood beside him, and then glanced into the crowd. He saw Cara Thomas and her cameraman commiserating with Reedy, looking like a trio of spies with their cold stares and hunched bearing. The NBC crew was the only TV unit present, and Chapman doubted that they'd bother to spite the Swede. He told Einar to go about the uncrating just a little slower to make doubly certain that the statue was secure.

After a few more minutes with the crowbar, Einar had ripped away all but the crate's metal frame. As the boards were being carried away by Renny and the Chinese, he began to unwind the padding. By this time, the crowd had gathered into a rough semicircle around the figure. Low chatter rose from among them as the statue was unveiled.

Still bound by the cables about its waist, the Madjan was a bridled Goliath, his ferocity undiminished by captivity. Indeed, lashed with metal cables to the beams, he seemed all the more formidable. Only when the bonds were removed and the crate dismantled entirely did a lifeless statue replace the vision of a bound god.

As conversation returned to its previous levels, Tepper moved to be in front of the figure as the first pictures were taken, although Tally was an unwelcome guest in the first of these, having ambled over as a student of art to study the remarkable statue.

As the flashes popped, the TV cameras hummed to life. Tepper smiled broadly as the swirl and beat of what he prayed would swell to an event had begun.

The Madjan's hard visage stared out, its mouth unutterably harsh.

For the first time in twenty centuries, the Madjan gazed on soil other than its own, peering through the pinhole of light at the core of the vortex.

It looked on people different from those it had known, subjects who hadn't the humility to bow.

It saw what was left of a once-powerful army, and it filled with rage and torment.

With a flash of will, it moved through the spiraling blackness toward the light . . .

Twenty-sixth Street on the East Side was a busy place, even at 1:30 A.M. The all-night magazine store on the southwest corner of Lexington Avenue played host to an impromptu debate among gays over a new activist newspaper; a coffee shop up the street was quieter, as hookers ducked inside to avoid police who had been cruising the neighborhood. For their part, the officers ignored School of Visual Arts students getting high on the stoop of their school; the kids were less abrasive when they were stoned.

Tally McGraw took the subway to Twenty-sixth Street and Broadway and then walked across town. She didn't feel endangered, never having encountered anything worse than apathy in the city streets. She felt as though she'd almost welcome a mugger or a derelict. One of the reasons she'd left the Vermont commune four years before was its isolation from the important battles, from the heart of the decision making. New York City was a compromise. It was not the rustic environment she'd come to love; the metropolis was a heterogeneous challenge that allowed her to be who she chose and think as she saw fit.

Tally paused at the entrance of the white-brick school to chat with two of her students, though she hadn't time to share a toke of hash with them. Nor would she have in any event. Her freelance assignments from the museum required mechanical precision; high, she couldn't pick up a pencil.

The pimply-faced young man looked up at her through bloodshot eyes. "How'd it go t'night?"

"Real good, Todd. The exhibit's going to be sensational, the statues—you'll have to see them to believe them. They're just incredible."

"Sounds neat," opined the young man's portly girl friend. "Got any Polaroids?"

"I own a Kodak," Tally corrected, hating the commonization of proper nouns, "which, would you believe, I left in my desk. I came back so I'd have it for tomorrow." She shuffled up the three front steps. "Can I catch you later? I'm due back in five hours with my finished designs."

"No problem." The boy sucked in a puff. "Glad to hear that profs pull all-nighters too."

Tally hurried inside. *Misguided generation*, she thought as she crossed the lobby. *We skipped our teens, went right into adulthood. These kids are eternal teens, interested in everything but curious about nothing. We were activists. All they've got are activities.*

Tally resolved that after the display had been completed, she'd find some way to get her kids involved politically. Perhaps she could use her art history course to find a social parable for the modern age.

The woman moved past walls and beams plastered with posters announcing concerts, art shows, lectures, and self-analysis groups. Occasionally, she saw little white mimeographed sheets dealing with school curricula. To the left, tucked into a corner by the door, was the registration desk. The post was dark, a nocturnal sight that never failed to distress her. Tally didn't like the thought of anything being closed or deserted; where there were no people, even dull ones like Todd, there was no life.

Her clogs tapped a deep clatter on the tiles, the half-century-old flooring scuffed with the past. She went to the stairs that climbed the far wall, stumbling as she spun around the banister, her desire faster at this late hour than her reflexes.

Good, Tal. Break your ankle and spend the night in a New York City emergency ward. You could do the sketches in blood and tears.

The art history room on the second floor had a lock on the door. Tally never used it, but the janitor did. She felt that no library should be shut off from the student body, regardless of the hour. After all, students studied at night as well as during the day. If a book disappeared on occasion, it was because someone had fallen in love with a subject. Tally could accept that more easily than she could the padlock, though old man Giddings would never be persuaded.

She reached through the collar of her sweatshirt and withdrew a leather thong. Its seven keys rattled one against the other. She thought for a fleeting moment that she heard another rattling down the dark corridor. She pushed the hair back from her ear and listened, deciding after a few seconds that it had been the echo of her own keys. She let herself inside, closing the door behind her.

Tally flicked on the fluorescent lights and sat down tiredly behind her desk. Between teaching three classes, attending her est seminar, and working at the museum, it had been a long day. She closed her eyes to ease their stinging, though she was aware that if she didn't open them soon, they'd stay shut until daylight.

A faint, tart smell wafted in, a distinctive odor that Tally could not place. She sniffed, presuming that the fumes came from what Todd was burning on the street. But it seemed too sharp for hash. Using it as an excuse to get up again, Tally ambled toward the drapes. She pulled them open and allowed her eyes to wander along the bank of windows. All the latches were tightly shut.

"That's odd," she murmured, and then resumed her sniffing as she turned back toward the room. Now the smell was more like incense than any weed; it was growing more potent by the second, without a source in sight.

As the aroma sweetened, she experienced an unusual gnawing in her belly, a sort of apprehension she hadn't felt since her campus days whenever she heard a police siren. Opening her desk drawer, Tally palmed the camera and slipped it into her shoulder bag. She started for the door, dropping the keys back inside her sweatshirt. They rattled for an instant; the corridor, like an acoustic barrier, once again seemed to pick up the jangling and send it back. Only the sound was louder now, even through the closed door.

"Giddings can't still be here," she told herself, "and I doubt ET's afoot." Tally's attempt at levity failed to relax her. With uncharacteristic urgency, she strode forward and reached for the knob.

A gust of heat rolled against her, forcing her back several steps. She stared into the emptiness before her as a fresh blast rocked her, accompanied by the sonorous rattling. Her mouth grew dry, and the smell that she knew for certain now was incense caused her to become light-headed. Tally straightened but couldn't move, weaving where she stood behind circles of amber haze.

"Dizzy . . . air . . ."

Tally thought to go back to the window, to push it open and dispel the sickly scent and the mounting heat. But as she started over, she was shoved roughly to the desk. She hit with such force that the air was pumped from her, leaving her gasping and barely clinging to consciousness.

She moaned for help in a voice so weak that she couldn't believe it was her own. She tried to rise but was driven down hard, gagging as the edge of the desk became a wedge against her belly. Tally slumped to one side, her bag falling to the floor, spilling its contents; the camera flipped open and began discharging pictures. But the woman didn't hear it, oblivious to all sound except her labored breathing and the jangling that was more distinct now, not so much the sound of a chain but the harsh din of metal striking metal.

Her breath died to a strained wheeze as something bore down on her. She felt as though each muscle in her chest were constricted, binding her ever more tightly. The sensation persisted even though she knew she was no longer lying belly down. The walls turned on end and fell to where the floor had been, her neck bending and twisting and the back of her head aching as it was forced against the hardwood of the desk.

Panting desperately, she became aware of a sharp pain in her back, as if there were hot metal beneath her, ribbed with spikes and rending her flesh. The room vanished, swallowed in a cloud of blackness, a reptilian tail forming, frozen in the void, streaked with rivulets of red. The smell of incense became overpowering now, and she knew she soon would lose consciousness. In her last moment on earth, Tally's tortured mind managed to focus on one clear thought: She wished that she had surrendered more quickly.

A flash of agony tore through her belly, and her eyes, wide at the instant of death, stared pitifully into a nightmare.

CHAPTER SIX

LINDA BERGENI AWOKE IN A FOUL MOOD. Still roiling over the eternal bickering that had spiced the evening she'd spent with her parents, she was unwilling to suffer in silence her mother's shrill voice. It tumbled from the telephone even before Linda was fully awake, filling her with defensive anger.

"I *know* he's dying," Linda interrupted Mrs. Bergeni's tirade. Getting her bearings, she reached over and shut off the alarm, which she wouldn't need now. "The fact that he is dying is why I said last night that he should be working hard to mend his broken fences, starting with his only offspring."

"It's not your place to tell him what to do."

"It is when it has to do with me or my career. I don't like hearing his ridiculous opinions, which as far as I'm concerned have messed up my career quite nicely."

"How dare you say such a thing! The man has never done anything to hurt you."

"Never intentionally, Mother. How many times do I have to say this before it sinks in? He stopped me from getting the education I wanted and needed. He wouldn't let me go to Kenya or to Paris or to Copenhagen not because it was too expensive to study there—which, by the way, I would have understood—but because of the niggers and the Frogs and the degenerates. I'm supposed to forgive him for prejudice which has stifled me like that?"

"He's dying," the woman repeated, upset more than angry with her daughter. "God will forgive him for what he did from love. But God will not forgive you if—"

"Yeah, yeah, I know." Linda slipped from bed, carrying the phone to the adjoining half bathroom. She fluffed her puffball of sandy brown hair and then began rubbing moisturizer into her dry skin. "Look, Mother, I'm sick of fighting. If it'll make you happy, I'll apologize, even though that won't change the way I feel."

"All right. When?"

"Give Father the phone, and I'll—"

"No, come by after work."

Linda balled her fist, refraining from punching something simply because there was nothing around that wouldn't shatter. "I can't come by tonight. Tonight is the opening; I have to be there. I know that doesn't mean a goddam thing to you—"

"I don't like that kind of language!"

"—that my whole career is a pile of *shit* in your eyes. I didn't go to the museum last night so I could be with you and Father, so I could be overhauled by the two of you. I can't miss tonight."

There was a long silence before Mrs. Bergeni said, "You act as though your father will be here forever."

"Believe me, Mother, he *will* be, still pulling on his end of the leash."

Mrs. Bergeni did not understand this ingratitude, and even Linda found it cumbersome. As hard as she felt inside, as resilient as she tried to be, she could not sustain her resentment. It shaded to exasperation and, as was its custom, collapsed beneath its own surplus.

Linda's brown eyes narrowed, and she swore quietly to herself. "All right," she conceded. "I'll stop by. I don't know when or for how long, but I'll stop by. Grant will probably be with me."

"He makes your father uncomfortable."

Linda lost control all over again. "That's just too goddam bad. Don't you know by now that anybody who gets into his precious baby's pants is no damn good?"

"If Grant loved you, he would marry you."

"Damn it, he wants to, Mother. It's me who doesn't to settle into something permanent."

"You don't care that people think you're a hussy?"

"Frankly, not in the least. What I care about is a career, making up for time and experiences and learning that my father cost me because of his stubbornness. I'm going to get my master's, and I'm going to travel. I can't be tied down to a marriage and do all of that. Look," Linda said, "I've got to get going." She rubbed off the creme with a washcloth and put a few drops in her eyes. "I'll call you some time during the—"

"I don't understand." Her mother was sniffling now. "I don't see how you can be so cold at a time like this. You meant so much to him."

"I am *not* cold, Mother, I'm resigned."

"You're so much like him." She was sobbing openly now. "He was resigned when you said you wanted to change your name, when you moved out of the house. You call him stubborn, and yet, maybe if you had been a little more considerate of his feelings, he wouldn't—"

"Wouldn't what, have cancer? Is that what you were going to say, that I took away his will to live?" The thought was so absurd that Linda couldn't even be upset by it. Instead, she said as sincerely as she could, "Mother, I've never done anything but love Father and you. But I'm me. Bergeni, Bergen— if it makes me feel less like an immigrant, you should be happy for me. But you're never happy, Father's never happy. You haul up a name change that's more than seven years old, and you make things that are natural seem criminal, whether it's leaving home or making love. I won't accept any of that, and if you're offended, I'm sorry, I truly am." She stole a backward glance at the digital clock. "Really, Mother, I'm late. We had a long and not very happy night together, and there's no reason to screw up today. Let's just cool it for now, both do a bit of soul searching and we'll talk later in the day."

"What time?"

Linda blurted, "When I *can*! My God, haven't you heard a thing I've said? Don't push me."

"You said we should search our souls and be a little compassionate. Is this how you do it, by yelling at me?"

There was no point in arguing; there never was. She surrendered just to get off the phone. "I'll try to call around two o'clock. It depends on how much Tally got done last night and this morning."

"I know you'll try your best."

"I always do," Linda confided. She bade her mother goodbye and hung up. She felt guilty in a visceral rather than in an intellectual sense for a change. She hoped things would change once her father was gone, though she doubted they would.

The slender woman hurriedly dressed in her autumn wool sweater and tight jeans, slipped into her brown high-heel boots, and grabbed a Ring Ding Jr. from an open box on the counter. Grant had turned her on to the cakes—they were pure trash, but what wasn't these days? She ate her breakfast when she got on the subway. It gave her something to do besides stare at the depressed humanity that crowded her.

As the train clattered on, Linda could not help thinking about her father, about the sacrifices he had made to feed and clothe her by driving a bread truck up to twenty hours a day. Perhaps she was being selfish, but even at this final judgment, his sacrifice did not warm her as much as his closed mind riled her.

Linda emerged from the train, and her personal life was mercifully, quickly, overtaken by her profession. She loved that feeling of leaving her private little honeycomb to become a citizen of the world, responsible for exhibits on loan to the museum, artifacts that added to the world's culture, that made the news. Although she would prefer Tepper's job and knew she could do it far better, that was a long way off. For now, work was a challenge, and that mattered a great deal.

Because she was late, Linda did not stop to buy a newspaper, barely noticing the headline as she hurried past the newsstand. The stop led right into the museum's cafeteria, and she took a moment to get a cup of coffee. As she poured it, Linda saw Susan Alomar motioning toward her. The cashier seemed more agitated than usual; she must have picked up something really juicy. Smiling, Linda capped her coffee and walked over.

"Let me guess." Linda held up her hand. "You're going on strike."

"*Madre de Dios*, didn't you hear?"

"Hear what? No more free coffee?"

The young Hispanic crossed herself, her eyes downcast.

"Good God, what is it?"

"It's Tally," she whispered. "I—I can't believe you didn't hear."

Linda felt uneasy as she urged the woman to tell her what had happened.

"She's *dead*. They found her at four o'clock this morning. And not only dead but torn to pieces."

Linda's mind shot back to the newspaper. "PROF SLAIN!" the headline had shouted. She shut her eyes and moaned her disbelief. "When?" she finally asked. "Do they know who did it?"

"All I can tell you is what I read in the paper and what I overheard one of the guards say when he came to work. They found her in her classroom, and whoever did it to her must have used an ax." The woman mimed several blows with a hatchet as though she were dicing beef.

Linda thanked Sue and, leaving her coffee, hurried out the glass door. She paused at the water fountain long enough to wash down the sudden taste of bile that welled in her throat. Then she ran up three flights of broad marble steps to the second floor.

Bolting into the Hall of the Asian Peoples, Linda expected to find people moving around as if in a daze; they weren't. The two security guards were seated on a bench, sipping their coffees and eating buttered rolls. Their usual chatter about sports and women echoed throughout the hall. A painter whistled as he touched up the stain on one of the easels that would display Linda's illustrations of the statues as they had looked in 20 B.C.; a pair of guides were familiarizing themselves with the dozen new arrivals, the statues all uncrated and arranged roughly where Tally had known she'd want them. Linda looked around for Tepper, who was sure to be lecturing someone about Tally's tawdry lifestyle, but he wasn't there. One of the guards told her that Tepper hadn't been seen since the night before. Hurrying to the elevator, she rode to his office on the fifth floor, a private level where the museum's exhibits were assembled and where she had her cluttered studio.

Moving briskly past rooms filled with cartons of fossils and partly assembled dinosaurs, of dioramas and displays being repaired or updated, she came to Tepper's brightly lighted office.

The chain-smoking Claude looked up at her from behind a

curling white tester. "Good morning, little Lin—"

"Is it true? About Tally? I just heard downstairs that she was murdered."

The young man nodded glumly, pushing the morning *USA Today* toward her. "WOMAN BUTCHERED!" it proclaimed, more boldly than the *Daily News*. She stared at the headline with renewed shock and felt her heart begin to gallop. "My God, Claude. Christ, give me an aspirin." He reached into his desk and handed her a large bottle of aspirin. She spilled a pair of tablets into her hand and crunched them down as she gave the bottle back to Claude. "Do they have any idea who did it and why?"

"The police haven't finished going over the classroom yet, but they called Dr. Tepper at four-thirty and kept him on the phone for over an hour. From the way he described the conversation, my guess is they think it was a bomb."

"Dear God, my poor Tally! We grew up together. I was responsible for her getting this job. Jesus, she was going to go to San Francisco until I saw an ad for Visual Arts. Oh, Jesus." She covered her face and began to sob.

Claude drew on his cigarette. "You know, I'm surprised they didn't call you. I hope you have an alibi."

Linda ignored Claude's remark, turning and walking humbly from the office. She stood in the hall, crying for several minutes until she was able to marshal a semblance of control. She went to her small studio to call Grant, and when there was no answer, she presumed that he already had left his home. Linda hung up before Gail came on, not wishing to talk to anyone but Grant.

She gazed out her window overlooking Central Park. The brightness hurt her tear-swelled eyes, and so she turned away, crying again. Chapman found her that way, standing with her back to the door, her shoulders heaving, when he walked in. She turned and breathed deeply when she saw him, relieved that the burden at last could be shared.

Throwing himself into her swivel chair, he held out his hand. Linda took it and squeezed. "What happened, Grant? Do you have any idea who could have done this?"

"All I know is that someone hit her with a vengeance. The police called me at four-fifteen, and I went over to the Chinese mission in case this was some kind of plot against the exhibit."

"Is that—" She choked and cleared her throat. "Is that what the police are saying?"

"The detective wouldn't tell me a thing except that the room was just about turned inside out and that a couple of kids smoking dope outside didn't hear a thing."

"Maybe they were too stoned."

"To hear someone crush a desk and a dozen chairs? I doubt it." He released her hand and stared absently at the floor. "There is one other thing, though. We're both suspects. I got that much from Detective Varley. It's a formality, actually. You, me, Tepper, those students, everyone in the address book Tally had in her purse, even that idiot Claude. I'm sure Laojiu is on their list, though he's out of reach because of diplomatic immunity."

Linda did not seem disturbed. "They've got to be thorough. God, I don't care how many people they suspect as long as they get whoever did it." Linda slid her hands into her back pockets and gnawed on her upper lip for a moment. "Christ, I could use a cigarette. I don't know why I let you talk me into giving them up."

"Because they're bad for you," Chapman said deliberately, as though talking to a child.

Linda snickered. "That's a real pearl, Grant. You honestly believe that kind of bullshit matters? Tally never put a thing into her body that wasn't one hundred and two percent natural, and not once did my fifty-two-year-old terminally ill father ever drink, smoke, gamble, swear, sit on a public toilet, or fuck around. It's all a joke, all that solemn goddam sanity of yours." There was a long silence as she paced and wiped tears from her eyes. "Claude'll have a smoke. I'm sorry, Grant, but I really have to have one."

Linda dashed from the room like a poodle in heat. Chapman rose and left more slowly, not looking into Claude's office as he passed on his way to the elevator.

Linda came down to the display hall a few minutes after Chapman. Noticing him lurking beside a table of press releases at the far side of the room, his eyes scanning the freshly printed pages, she shouted, "I only did half a cigarette, so stop your brooding."

"I'm not brooding."

"You are."

"I'm reading."

"You're not reading, you're full of shit." To the guards she yelled, "Anyone want to bet that he's read those things a dozen times in every draft?"

Linda was right. This particular packet of releases had been telexed to Beijing over the weekend. He folded the top sheet into his pocket and then noticed the guards and painter staring at him. "Oh, good, now we're *all* doing nothing. I thought we had an exhibit to prepare."

Chapman's humorless voice sent the painter back to work and turned the guards around; Linda braced her hands on her hips. "Well, you don't intimidate *me*, Grant Chapman. No one died and left you—" Linda's voice cracked and faded. Her shoulders slumped, and after a moment she walked across the hall. "I take that back. There's a spot on our staff for a lovable hippy, and I'm going to get hysterical if I think about it. Look," she strode over and hooked her arms around Chapman's neck, "I'm not going to dwell on Tally, I'm going to dwell on you because you're here and need me, and I need you. Life's too short for anyone to live it like Mr. Spock. Tally lived her way, and so did my father. But I care about you more than I care about anyone. All I want you to do is loosen up a bit, meet me halfway once in a while. That's not so much to ask, is it? The rest of the time I'm as easy as pie. You know that."

"I know it." Chapman smiled in spite of himself. Linda's ability to flush away anger and depression, to wash anything negative from her system, was remarkable. It wasn't selfish, it was a knack for survival and he was impressed by it. "All right, Linda. I'll stop pouting about the way you trashed me up there."

"It was a fit of pique, not a trashing."

"You've been spending too much time with diplomats," Chapman said, yawning.

They kissed lightly. "You must be exhausted," Linda said, stepping back. "Your eyes are all bloodshot. Can't you go home and get some sleep?"

Chapman looked at his watch. "The police will be coming at ten to search for explosives, and Laojiu is supposed to arrive after his breakfast with the Chinese foreign minister. I'll lie down in the lounge once everyone is settled. If I do it now, I may not get up."

Linda made Grant promise to take a break like a normal human being, then hugged him tightly. While Chapman strolled among the statues, she put in a call to the museum handyman to help her arrange the lights. Tally's notes had been confiscated by the police, and so they would have to improvise. Fortunately, because the room was windowless, one arrangement would suffice for both day and night.

The police rolled in like the Allies on D-Day, probing and dusting, a pair of specially trained German shepherds scurrying and sniffing. The job was finished in ten minutes, and they turned up no explosives. The officer in charge said they would return that night, well before guests began arriving for the gala debut. Chapman remarked that the secret service would be performing a similar chore since the Secretary of State would be in attendance, but a burly officer indicated that they'd be back just the same.

"There were secret service men all over the place when they got JFK," the husky Sergeant O'Toole pointed out. "It don't hurt to double-check things like this."

There was something naive about that line of reasoning, but because Chapman was a sucker for innocence, he let it pass.

Chapman was paged just then. Picking up the staff phone he learned that Laojiu and his daughter had just left the Consulate. He arrived at the curator's private entrance just moments ahead of the limousine. Chapman welcomed them warmly, and Laojiu wished him a pleasant good morning. Yu nodded politely.

As the threesome walked toward the hall, Laojiu asked, "There has been no news about the killing?"

Chapman had a flash, a brief, amorphous jolt that twisted the scientist's words from query to wish. The feeling quickly fled, seeming more absurd as the passing seconds left it behind.

"There's been no news," he said, "and we probably won't know anything more until the afternoon papers hit. Officials always read about crises on the front page before they hear about them through proper channels."

"You're joking, of course," said Yu.

"Not really. It's a racket that politicians and law enforcement agencies have going. They leak big news to the press in exchange for forbearance when they bungle an important job and want it played down. If there's been a break, it'll be headlined. If there's nothing new, you won't find it anywhere in the front of the paper."

Yu looked at Chapman, her wide brown eyes curiously hooded, as though she didn't know whether to believe him. He seemed to have a cynical view of things, one that she could not quite fathom yet.

Chapman introduced Laojiu and his daughter to Linda, the woman praising their discovery and thanking them for this chance to work with the statues. She showed them the rough sketches she had done. After regarding them dispassionately, the archaeologist asked to be shown to the office that the museum had put at his disposal. Though Linda was dumbstruck she smiled politely before turning away. After Chapman had taken the Chinese to the fifth floor, he found the woman still standing where they had left her in the middle of the hall, flipping glumly through her sketch pad.

"That's it?" she asked without looking up from her roughs. "No, 'Nice job' or 'Rotsa ruck,' just an 'Ah so' and off they go? Who the fuck do they think they are?"

"That's just the way they do things."

"Well screw them! And since when—" she looked up defiantly "—since when do you put up with that kind of arrogance much less *defend* it?"

"It's not malicious," he explained. "They've been uprooted and shafted, and I can't blame them for the way they feel."

"I hope you'll be as understanding if I take it personally. I'll bet they don't give Tepper that kind of cold shoulder."

"I wouldn't be so sure. Just calm down and do your job. I understand they've already sold twenty thousand tickets, half of them this morning. Word's getting around; excitement's building. Those are the people you have to impress, not Laojiu."

Having no alternative, the woman kicked and groused a moment longer and then concurred. Chapman's glib suggestion that they have Chinese food for dinner helped restore her coltish tenacity.

Chapman retired to the executive lounge to rest, while Linda threw herself against the task at hand. Both were interrupted by questions from a battery of detectives, but neither interview went beyond ascertaining their own whereabouts the night before and their knowledge of Tally's private life.

Despite the pall cast on the exhibit by Tally's murder and the ever present police, the lighting of the statues was completed by late afternoon. Tally had had the statues arranged in opposing parabolic rows rather than in a pair of phalanxes, as they'd been set out in Ch'en-shimm. Although Tally's antimilitaristic streak ran counter to Linda's passion for authenticity, the setup worked aesthetically, and she let it stand.

Dr. Tepper showed his face at intervals to rally the team of designers, carpenters, electricians, and custodians. He was as energetic, priggish, and single-minded as ever while he motivated everyone to put forth his finest efforts, even though very few of the staff members had been invited to attend the opening. Tepper seemed strangely unmoved by the tragedy of the night before. Watching him flit through twice an hour like a bee among the roses, she could not help but wonder if he'd have been as seemingly unaffected if it had been she who had been killed instead of poor Tally. Linda decided that she didn't want to know.

After the track lighting had been arranged, Linda concentrated on illuminating the color illustrations she had done of the statues. Tepper had at first balked at the $2,000 Linda wanted for the poster-sized renderings, but she had managed to persuade him that apart from their educational value, the two drawings were necessary to give the room some color; and they could, if popular, be mass-produced and marketed as art prints through the museum's gift shop. Linda had reluctantly agreed to sign away all rights to the works before Tepper would agree to the assignment.

Not having paused for lunch, by early evening Linda was ready for the dinner she and Chapman shared at Chan's on Second Avenue and Thirty-second Street. The smoke-filled restaurant was crowded, more so because waiters were busy wheeling carts laden with buffet-style *dim sum* dishes from table to table. The noise and the hazy atmosphere were part of Chan's environment and somehow made the fine food taste even better.

Pouring himself some tea between dishes, Chapman asked, "Are you going to see your father after the opening?"

"For a few minutes." She nibbled on a noddle. "After which I'm coming to your apartment."

"I should be flattered."

"You should not, because you *know* why I'm coming. As

much as I want to be with you, I don't want to be alone tonight. Remember, there were people right outside Tally's window and they scored zero on audio? I don't care how alert my doorman is, as soon as the sun went down I got scared shitless."

"You're welcome to stay, of course, though the police indicated there's no reason to suspect that there's a plot of any kind."

"I don't need a reason, I'm a natural paranoid. Don't try to tell me that you're not frightened."

"It's strange. I feel a lot of negative sensations," Chapman conceded. "Revulsion, pity, outrage—but there's no fear. It's not like when my Uncle Jack was killed in Korea. That terrified me. I was five years old, and I remember the tingling I felt in my guts when I overheard my parents discussing how it happened, how he stepped on a land mine and was blown in five different directions. I just don't have that same fear now."

"You're thirty years older," she reminded him.

"Age hasn't a thing to do with it. Fear is fear, like when Tarlo tried to chase me off with death threats. Scared the pants off me, and I saw people in a way I'd never seen them before—everyday people in the street, people you see without really seeing them. Believe me, I *saw* them. I imagined a knife in every purse, a gun in the pocket of every trench coat, every expression a leer as if the person wearing it were measuring me for a plot in Holy Cross. I was five years old again, watching the ground for land mines."

"Psychological warfare," Linda commented.

"Exactly. That's why I took up archery, right there on the roof of my building."

"Wait a minute. You took it up—to shoot people if they attacked you in the street?"

Chapman frowned. "No, Dumbo, it wasn't for protection. It was to show Tarlo that I could stay calm no matter what tricks they played, no matter what they threw at me. And it worked. I felt better, and the calls stopped."

"You really think they were spying on you?"

"I tested them, went to church—which I hadn't done in years. When I got back, someone called and told me that praying wouldn't help, I was a dead man."

Linda shuddered. After a beat she said, "And it's a hell of a topic for what's supposed to be a relaxing dinner. Tell me, when you were up on the roof playing Robin Hood, did you ever miss the target?"

"Occasionally," Chapman admitted, wondering why she wanted to know.

"Must've surprised the hell out of the people nine stories below." Linda arched her index finger to simulate an arrow dropping from roof to street.

"I shot against a brick wall, smartass." Chapman grinned and checked his watch. "Speaking of asses, unless we want Tepper to fit ours for a sling, we'd better eat up. His guests start arriving in an hour."

"Fuck him," Linda snorted. "I'm having a good time."

"You can afford to. If I lose this job, the only thing left for me will be managing a *Burger King*."

The couple grabbed a plate of sesame toast from a passing cart and garlic spareribs from another. While Linda alternated bites of each, savoring the clash of flavors, Chapman popped down a square of toast and called over the waiter for two sodas.

"You know," he said, "one reason I think I'm not worried is that subconsciously I've got this weird feeling that I know what killed Tally."

"What killed her? You mean like a bomb or—"

"No, I said 'who.' "

"You said 'what.' And you're scaring me."

Chapman sat back. "Never mind. What's important is that for some reason I don't feel threatened the way I did with Tarlo."

"Or with Uncle Jack."

"Exactly. I feel like an outsider, like someone watching the acrobats take all the chances. Either I'm blocking something out or I've matured or God knows what. I'm sad but dispassionate."

Linda's laugh was uneasy. "I'm glad to hear that, Grant, because as of nine-ten this morning, *my* already shaky composure rolled over on its dear little back, deader than a lump of clay. You'll have all of tonight to prep and prime me back into shape."

"Check your oil?"

"Maybe," she said as the waiter returned with their drinks.

Chapman asked for the check. When the empty plates had

been counted and the bill tallied, Linda reached for it. Chapman was faster, snapping it to his breast and holding it there face down. "This one's on me."

"The dishes will be on you if you don't tell me how much my half of the bill is. My money is just as green as yours."

"Maybe to Mr. Chan, but not to me."

"That's too bad." Linda lurched across the table, tore the check from his hands, and then counted $12 from her billfold. "That's all I've got. I owe you three more."

"You know, Ms. Liberated, it's not a crime to let your lover buy you dinner once in a while."

"That's the kind of BS my mother's always handing me. Wait a few days and you can take *her* out."

"You're morbid on top of being illogical and stubborn. Forget equality. I *make* more than you do."

"That's true, but that's also not *why* you want to treat me to dinner. It's your misogynic chivalry acting up again. When will science ever find a cure?"

"For who, me or you?"

Linda pounded the table, ignoring the disapproving glances from the neighboring diners. "Don't be a pain with that clever repartee of yours. Whose oil did you want to check tonight?"

"Here we go again."

"*Exactly!* And it's because *you're* too damn stubborn to give me any elbow room. You've forgotten to ask about a job for me at the Smithsonian. How long have I wanted to work there?"

"If you're such an ardent feminist, why do you keep threatening to punish me with sex?"

"Don't change the subject! I've been dying to work there ever since this job became a one exhibit per year bore. You haven't forgotten to ask; you just don't want me to go!"

"Since when is that a crime?" Chapman asked, annoyed. "I love you. Why should I want you hundreds of miles away?"

"You could hop on the train and be there in two hours. What about *my* wants? Don't they matter?"

"Let's turn that around, Linda. Don't I matter? You care more about a lousy job than you do about me."

Linda threw her head back and arched a brow. "Quid pro quo, as the people in your ex-profession like to say. If I moved to Washington, would you give up *your* job to be with me?"

"I'd consider asking for a transfer, yes."

"And if you couldn't get it? Would you go to work in a hamburger place just to be near me?"

Chapman regarded Linda in silence and then let his eyes fall to the check. "You're not being fair. It takes some getting used to, you know. I was brought up with certain values." He looked at her again. "I guess you're right. No, you *are* right. I've got a bagful of double standards—"

"Several bagfuls."

"—which are chained to me like Marley's cash boxes. I can't get rid of them overnight, and I won't lie and say that I didn't wish things were different, that you'd be happy with your job at a top-ranked museum and that whatever frustration you felt would go down easier because we're together. When I was in law, I found out the hard way that ambition isn't always a good thing or the most important thing."

"Nice words, Grant, but you wouldn't turn down Secretary of State or a full-fledged ambassadorship if someone offered. And if we were married, you'd expect me to go with you, even if I had a good career going right where I was. I can't think like that, not now. Maybe in a year I'll find out that I love you enough to chuck everything else. Maybe I'd go to the Smithsonian for a month and discover that I miss you too much to stay there. Can't we just take things as they come?"

"Is there an alternative?"

Linda shook her head.

Chapman put on a half smile, more resigned than persuaded. "Then we'll have to try, won't we?"

Linda looked up, just noticing the waiter who had apparently been standing there for some time. Slightly red-faced, she asked, "And what do *you* think we should do?"

"Pay check," he said in broken English. "We need table."

"There's a sage in every crowd." Linda sighed as Chapman reluctantly scooped up her money and handed the waiter his credit card. "He probably writes the fortune cookies to boot."

Chapman shook his head. "Like a jerk I'm probably going to wait for you."

"I'm not twisting your arm, am I?"

He slugged down the rest of his drink. "No, just breaking my balls." He rose and with a gallant flourish permitted Linda to go before him.

"Piss off," she grinned as they went arm in arm to the counter to sign the bill. Linda bought some breath mints to dull the potency of the garlic spareribs, and then the couple taxied back uptown. Chapman teased her about the fact that he had to pay, since he now had all the cash.

He peered into the point of light brought closer by the sacrifice and found the Woman of Peace who had been hovering about his statue. Yet he shied from this girl because she clung to her warrior. These strangely dressed soldiers and the armored chariots they propelled by thought itself were yet a puzzle to him. There would be no aggression, no offensive act until he understood their powers more fully . . . until his own strength had been renewed.

He searched the red-laced pit of the vortex for another Woman of Peace. Very soon he would need to drink, as the blood he'd recently spilled had run dry. He had never known a greater thirst or a more dangerous foe against whom to turn it . . .

CHAPTER SEVEN

THE FRONT STEPS of the museum were like day beneath the bank of spotlights. The huge statue of Teddy Roosevelt and his charger were utterly ignored, a strange object to be taken for granted, Chapman thought, since the crowd had come to see statues. Guests in formal attire were milling about the steps and inside the front lobby, though velvet ropes barred them from entering the museum proper. The few adventuresome reporters who tried to sneak upstairs were detained by guards or secret service agents.

As he stared from the fifth floor window of Linda's studio, Chapman found the monument rather forlorn. It helped coalesce something that had been eating at the back of his mind. He realized that it didn't matter what was on display tonight, whether it was the treasure of Tut, the art of Picasso, the Madjan, or some dung-covered statue hauled inside from the portico. The exhibition was exactly what Tepper had always wanted it to be: an event. People *had* to come. He recalled Linda complaining when they first met that a quiet display such as a showcase filled with moon rocks from *Apollo XVII* drew hardly a passing glance, and then mostly from schoolchildren.

The hype, he thought. *Laojiu realized back in China that the trapping of culture is all that saves this stinking game from appearing to be what it really* is. *It's nothing more than a buck-oriented publicity gimmick, damn Tepper. And while I'm at it, after all those high words I dished out at the embassy in Beijing I'm no better for having gone along with this.*

Linda swept into her studio, wearing a thigh-hugging beige gown. Chapman nodded approvingly; the woman did the same. "You know, I think this is the first time I've gone out with a guy who actually *owned* his tuxedo. You look pretty terrific, fellah."

"So do you."

She cuddled up to him. "Lots of conviction in that voice. What are you brooding about now, or still, as the case may be."

Chapman put his arms around her. "Nothing to worry about, just a fresh dose of self-reproach."

"For a change?"

"Laojiu was right. This whole thing is a farce, a circus with clowns and a whip-cracking ringmaster and—"

"Since you can't help what it's become, just enjoy it." she suggested. "That's what circuses are for. I'll tell you what I'm going to enjoy: what we're going to do after we visit dear Daddy. Arguing with you always makes me horny."

"Winning an argument is what you meant to say."

"That too. But it's going to be one big zilch after hours if you're miserable. I feel good in spite of everything, so you should, too."

"I thought I was supposed to be the chauvinist."

Linda told him to shut up and snuggled beneath his arm as they walked slowly to the elevator, each privately wishing that they could skip Tepper's event for one of their own.

As they stood in the hallway, Linda noticed that Chapman had forgotten to put on the flower she'd bought him. He hurried back to the lounge to get it. While he was gone, the woman felt suddenly very warm and unusually thirsty. She breathed deeply and turned toward the water fountain; she hadn't gone more than a few steps, when her ankle caved, pitching her against the wall.

"Are you not feeling well, Miss Bergen?"

Linda turned and through a brown haze saw the white-haired elevator operator scurrying toward her. The feeling of constriction passed, and she stood back up. "I—I think I'm okay. Wow." She inhaled again. "That came from out of left field."

"It's the glamor and excitement of the opening," the old man assured her as he took her arm and urged her forward. "Come and sit on my stool; you'll feel better in a jiffy."

Chapman came round the corner just then, fastening the white carnation to his lapel. Seeing Linda hobbling toward the elevator, he ran toward her.

"What is it? Are you all right?"

"Yes, no thanks to Chan and his goddam MSG. Made me dizzy for a few seconds."

"Are you sure you don't want to lie down?" he asked, helping her onto the stool. "We have time."

Linda repeated that she was fine and then rose to prove it. She was amazed that whatever had come over her had passed so swiftly; hooking her arm around Chapman's waist to reassure him—and herself, the spell having unnerved her slightly—Linda thanked the operator for his help as he took the cage down.

Chapman's eyes stayed on her until they reached the third floor. The elevator doors opened on a corridor crowded with security personnel and museum officials. In the hall beyond, Tepper was busy giving Cara Thomas a personal tour of the exhibit.

"Just smile and think nice thoughts," Linda reminded Chapman as they left the elevator and were passed by the secret service.

Because of the overwhelming size of her television audience, Cara Thomas was the first journalist permitted to view the exhibit. That hadn't sat well with other correspondents, but Tepper didn't care. Her video operator, an incongruous sight adorned in a tan tuxedo while he carried his camera on his shoulder, dogged the twosome's every move. Several feet in front of them, garbed in their work clothes, Laojiu and Yu were standing by the Madjan. Left in Tepper's care for the evening, they were waiting for the newscaster to complete her circuit of the statues. Then the archaeologist would give his first interview to a member of the press.

"I really do hate this more with each passing minute," Chapman exclaimed as he noticed Laojiu's humorless expression and his daughter's slightly more vituperative one.

"Knock it off," Linda rejoined. "It's not the end of the world for you or them. Let's all be adults about this, shall we?"

"The least I can do is stay near them, serve as a sort of buffer if necessary."

"Like a boxing referee?"

Chapman acknowledged the appropriateness of the metaphor by squeezing Linda's hand as the two of them made their way into the hall.

Tepper's deep voice crackled with enthusiasm as it filled the chamber. Hearing it, Chapman had to allow that though Tepper's single-mindedness often annoyed him, everything the curator did was for the good of the museum.

"When I first saw live television pictures from China," Tepper was saying in a merry basso that originated somewhere around his knees, "it was almost as thrilling as the broadcast from the moon. Now, less than a decade later, as a tribute to the farsighted leaders of the great nation, the American Museum of Natural History is proud to host a display of their most precious archaeological treasure, the warrior statues of Ch'en-shimm."

Cara Thomas asked, "Was there, Dr. Tepper, as is rumored, a good deal of political jockeying to get this exhibit for the museum? I understand upon good authority that several New York-area museums wanted it, in particular the Metropolitan Museum of Art."

"That's a myth, Cara." Tepper smiled. "There really was none of that, none whatsoever. This exhibit is clearly history first and art second."

Chapman swallowed a groan as he recalled the headaches everyone had had while the two museums slugged it out with quiet dignity, and when that failed, through their respective attorneys and finally the President. Tepper got the show only because the Met had gotten Tut.

The camera operator turned his lens on the Chinese as Cara and Tepper finally reached the foot of the Madjan.

"Dr. Laojiu," began the telejournalist, "the statue beside us was some sort of guardian angel to the warriors of ancient China, is that correct?"

"That is quaint but essentially accurate."

"It's a very male-oriented figure, muscular and heavily armed. How did women feel about this one-sidedness?"

"Why do you presume it mattered?"

"This was a god for *all* people, was it not?"

Tepper inserted diplomatically, "Cara, you must understand that women played a different role in ancient China than they do in our enlightened times."

"Enlightened?" asked Laojiu. "Your focus is much too short, Dr. Tepper. The mystique of the Madjan has endured for thousands of years and in one form or another has affected Chinese culture throughout the centuries. Current fads of liberation or equality are hardly the measuring stick by which to judge the Madjan."

"And how do you feel about all of this?" Cara asked, swinging her microphone to Yu.

The girl answered passionately, "I believe that it is pointless to consider such matters in terms of male and female."

"You put your faith in what, then?"

"Knowledge. Fear derives from no knowledge, ritual from partial knowledge. With full knowledge comes equality among all forms of consciousness. My father and I are currently deciphering ancient scrolls which—"

"Excuse me," Tepper interrupted, looking into the hallway where a secret service man was waving. "I'm told that the Secretary of State has just left his hotel. It might be best if we went downstairs now and continued this interview later."

Cara and her operator excused themselves and hurried downstairs; Tepper called Claude from where he'd been lurking behind the exhibit and asked him to escort Laojiu and Yu to the lobby. The curator himself remained behind, taking a moment to run a handkerchief across his perspiring forehead.

"You'd have made a fortune in PR."

"Huh?" Tepper spun and saw Chapman and Linda approaching from where they'd been loitering behind one of the woman's large illustrations.

"Grant, you almost gave me a heart attack! I thought one of the statues—never mind." He punched the handkerchief back into his lapel pocket. "So, did you hear the latest?"

"What's that? Have the police found out something?"

Tepper's brow creased and then cleared. "Oh, no, not about that. We're up to forty thousand. If I didn't know any better, I'd swear that Claude murdered Tally McGraw."

"What on earth are you talking about?" Linda snapped.

"Forty thousand! Tickets *sold*, cash in the drawer. Ticketron said they unloaded five thousand during lunch hour alone. And the museum switchboard has been unbroachable all day, the calls coming in since the story broke at seven o'clock on *Good Morning America*. About Tally, that is."

"I'm sure she'd be happy as a clam to know that," Chapman threw off, hoping to cut off the maledictory comments he knew Linda was preparing.

Tepper shrugged. "Yes, I suppose it is a rather lurid way of looking at things. But frankly, Grant, I need a crowd right now more than I need self-respect." Tepper checked his pocket watch, replaced it, and nervously tugged at the frilled sleeves of his shirt, which poked from beneath the black tuxedo. "I'd best be going, and I suggest you go down as well to greet your boss."

"He always leaves the hotel five minutes after he says he is. He likes to be eagerly anticipated."

"Oh, I see. All the same, I'd better get down and look to my guests. They're the impression makers, and we want to make a good impression on them. Linda," he said, as if noticing her for the first time, "since Claude is gone, would you take a second to check on the caterer in the arctic hall? I want to make sure everything is perfect, and an artist might have a few good last-minute suggestions to make on the arrangement of the cold cuts." Tepper excused himself again and then waddled quickly across the hall, casting sideward glances at the statues as though he were a general reviewing his troops.

"That miserable, rotten, foul, stinking son of a bitch," Linda snarled. "From the Madjan to pastrami. How dare he!"

"He's an idiot; forget about it."

"*Forget*? Grant, he just set feminism back to where it was under Emperor Ch'en. And what he said about Tally. The man's really debased; he's a fucking ghoul!"

"Trust me, it comes from too many years in public service. You tend not to see people anymore, only demographics and bottom lines. Come on." He kissed her on the head. "If we start brooding over everything there is to get depressed about—"

"We'll make a bad impression on the impression makers, right? Grant, are you selling out on me?"

"Not a bit. I just don't want to be any more miserable than I have to be. And if you're miserable, so am I."

"Bullshit. You're selling out. I know that sweet, loving, conciliatory voice of yours."

"Look." Chapman frowned. "Let's just do what we have to do to get through tonight. We can hash out the right and wrong of it later."

"A voice loaded with compromise," she continued, "just like Tepper."

There was a strained moment which Chapman broke by saying gently, "You're not being fair. If we went back through the years we've known each other, I'm sure we could find instances where you've made professional and personal concessions."

Linda laughed bitterly. "For God's sake, Grant, please don't start lecturing me. I've had enough of that crap the past few days to last the rest of my life."

Chapman debated the matter privately and then let the subject drop, having detected more embarrassment than resentment in Linda's words. As contradictory as she sometimes became, he knew that she was neither insensitive nor a hypocrite. Linda always needed time to calm down, and raking her over hot coals would only produce the opposite effect.

"I've got to get downstairs," Chapman said. "We're both overworked and under-rested and generally worn pretty thin. Why don't we do what you said a few minutes ago and act like adults, help each other instead of doing a last tag number?"

"I'm game."

"Then let's go." He took her by the elbow and began walking toward the corridor. "After all, we don't want people to think we've been doing what I hope you're still looking forward to doing later."

"No, not the impression makers."

Chapman grinned as they walked slowly from the hall. Linda felt a chill and shuddered. Chapman put his arm around her. Behind them, at the center of the far arc of statues, the Madjan looked out with dead clay eyes.

The thirst was great, but he would have to be patient.

He felt their shadows upon the vortex, the shadows of the Women of Peace who had come to the statue. But they were with men now, and he would not attack any warrior until he was stronger, until he had an army of his own.

Patiently, his spirit swept beyond the void, searching for one who had broken away from her protector. Finally there was one, and he reached forth to make her his own . . .

The offices of NBC-TV News at Rockefeller Center's stately network headquarters were in keeping with that division's lofty on-screen image. The landmark tower was a grim Art Deco monument that rose above a monolithic statue of Atlas shouldering the world.

Cara had left the Ch'en-shimm opening early in order to be first on the air with footage of the statues inside the museum and the Secretary of State's late arrival. She and her cameraman had gone straight to the twenty-ninth floor of the skyscraper in order to select scenes for the eleven o'clock news.

While "Duke" Snyder was making a comment about the quality of a segment they were watching, Cara suddenly stepped back from the video machine and swore. The camera operator stared at her for several seconds and then asked what was wrong.

"Nothing is wrong, except that we're a pair of asses. At least I am, since they pay me to think on my feet."

"What'd you not do now? Forget to interview the Madjan?"

"I've been working too damn hard, I told them that just the other day." She pushed her long, brown hair away from her face and looked very intense. "That footage I shot last night after that boor Einar left. We took pictures of the McGraw girl, didn't we?"

"I'm sure I covered her."

"And," Cara went on more excitedly, "there's no telling who else might have been recorded."

Duke caught on. "You mean, like someone watching her."

"Exactly."

"Gee, I'm surprised the cops didn't ask us to turn this stuff over so they could have a look-see."

"Because no one knows we took it, remember? That was all done with room lighting, to be as unobtrusive as possible."

The operator switched off the video machine, since neither of them was paying much attention to that day's footage. "Why'd it take you twenty-four hours to think of this?" He grinned.

"Because between arranging to beat out Barbara Walters tonight and agreeing to subhost the *Tonight* show next Monday, my mind's been in twenty different places." She seemed very pleased. "My God, Duke, I hope there's something in it. I've been itching for a nice, juicy legal battle, and refusing to turn over important evidence to the police will fit the bill perfectly."

"Meaning you go to jail and our ratings go up."

"Precisely."

Duke thought, *And the salary you've got to renegotiate in two months goes up, up, up.*

Cara ordered Duke to get the tape from the nearby vault while she hurried to her purse to pop a pair of tranquilizers. After washing them down with fruit juice from the cooler, she turned her attention to the footage. It began with a shot of Tepper, Tally, and the press gathered around the just uncrated Madjan. "Duke, why didn't we use this shot on last night's news? The way the shadows bleed under room lighting is really creepy."

"You didn't like the up angle on Tepper, said it made him look too impressive."

"That's right, it does. Why'd you bother with such a low angle shot of a ten-foot-tall statue, anyway?"

"Because he wouldn't have fit if we'd shot him straight on."

"What's wrong with a pan?"

"Like I tell the rookies, a pan is great if you're frying eggs. Why distract the viewer with a moving camera? I thought it made more sense to let them concentrate on what those Chinese dudes were saying to Tepper." The operator looked over to the wall clock. "Listen, Cara, I'm going to run tonight's footage over to evening news or we'll never get it cut in time."

"All right, you know pretty much what I want."

Duke did, in fact, since he usually changed her selections in the cutting, and she never knew the difference. "I'll be down in room 909 if you need me."

"Fine. See you there in fifteen minutes."

Duke instinctively shut off the light, but Cara paid the dark no attention. She stared attentively at the flickering nine-inch color monitor on which the tape was playing. After a minute of fruitless squinting, she decided to roll over the nineteen-inch television set for a better look at the faces of the guards, employees, and reporters in the background.

While the woman was crouched behind the sets switching the wires, she heard a muffled clanging in the hallway. She finished hooking the video player to the new TV, ignoring what she presumed was the cleaning woman's cart, and then stepped around and began replaying the tape.

"Much better," she admitted as she knelt before the television. The clanging returned then, distractingly loud.

"This is Ms. Thomas," she yelled, "and I'd like some quiet out there!"

The volume of the din increased, sounding more distinctly like the clattering of dozens of metal objects. Cara tried to force her attention to the screen but was distracted less now by the noise than by the boldness of someone ignoring her order.

"Shit!"

The newswoman pulled herself from the TV and strode to the door. En route, she paused to hold her hand up to the air vent, since she suddenly felt very warm. The cool air was churning in as usual, and with a huff of overall annoyance, she pulled open the door.

The sharpness of the odor that assaulted Cara caused her to stagger back a step. The picture that came to mind was of a burning candy cane, something not unpleasant but pungent. She heard the raucous clanging more clearly now, yet as she looked along the brightly lighted corridor, she saw nothing.

"Who's there?" she shouted. "Whatever you're doing, you're delaying the news and stinking up the place."

There was no answer, only a tingling low in Cara's belly. A moment later, her breath broke unexpectedly into whimpering gasps.

"Anxiety attack!" She shut her eyes and leaned against the jamb. But she found herself growing more and more tense with each passing instant, and she knew that what she felt was not self-generated.

"Wh-what's ... *happening* ... to ... m-me?"

As her chest knotted, with the siege simultaneously spreading through her thighs and legs, she turned and staggered toward the telephone. Halfway there, Cara felt someone enter the room. "Duke?" She turned and with a tremor of relief looked for her cameraman. Her eyes strained against the blackness, but she saw only a blurred, luminous glow forming within the doorway and spreading inward as a gray, omnipresent cloud. She watched as the shape became clearer and more distinct.

"Oh no," she managed as her eyes went wide with recognition. "Oh, God, *no!*"

Marshaling her strength and wits, she managed to look away. With a will still barely her own, she made her way to the vault. Stumbling inside, she shut the door of the metal-walled chamber and reached for the intercom.

She fumbled with the mouthpiece, dropped it, stooped slowly, and retrieved it. Punching out 909, she hissed into the mouthpiece since nothing else would come; the louder she tried to speak, the more breathy her voice became.

The clanging had blossomed into the strident hammering of metal. It was muffled for a short time by the steel walls; then the vault itself began to vibrate with the ringing thunder.

Cara looked around, watching with fresh terror as the walls shook, rattling the shelves stocked with tapes and cans of film. She forced her lips to the intercom, but before she could utter any sound, a cold, rough force yanked her violently from the mouthpiece, pushed her against the racks, and bent her over a stack of tapes. The cartridges spilled, though Cara was not aware of them. She lost all perception of sound and sight as something both filled and crushed her, driving everything from her mind except the soul-searing pain. Her legs twitched and rose as her back slid slowly to the floor. Perspiring as though she'd been thrust before a furnace, Cara quickly felt her back moisten more thickly and warmly with blood. A heartbeat later, her every pore bubbled red and she screamed, though her cry was lost as the film cans and tapes began spinning around the room as though trapped in a vortex, the walls and ceiling denting outward as though battered by countless explosions.

Duke and the nightly news producer heard the scream over the intercom and rushed to the elevators. Duke ran far ahead of the heavyset man, caught a waiting carriage, and hurried up alone. Arriving on the twenty-ninth floor, he rushed into the room. The large chamber was illuminated only by the television, whose tape was still running as he flicked on the light. At once, Duke saw the vault bulging with rents.

The producer skidded to the cameraman's side. "Holy hell, what happened here? And where's Cara?"

"I don't know, Ollie." Duke ran to the vault and unlocked the door. Cara's broken corpse slid from among the ruins, thudding on the carpet before a flood of film cans and twisted shelves. Her blue eyes stared wide and lifeless from her badly lacerated face. Her expression was fixed, as though on film, in a moment of torment.

"Jesus wept," Duke exclaimed as he knelt beside the woman. He gently fished into the wreckage for her wrist in order to take a pulse. His fingers grazed a ragged sleeve of flesh just below her elbow where the forearm had been severed. He noticed then that her other arm and both legs were gone, as though ripped away at the roots. Averting his eyes, eyes not unused to witnessing horror, he felt her neck for a sign of life. There was none.

"I'll call the police," said the producer, who crossed himself as he turned away. As he punched out the number on the telephone, he heard Cara's voice, and his eyes were drawn to the still unreeling tape. Incongruously alive, the reporter was describing in tones of kidding, mock horror the fierce visage that filled the screen, the hard face of the awesome Madjan.

The Ch'en-shimm party was all Dr. Tepper could have asked for and then some. By ten o'clock, no one had left except Cara Thomas and her crew; even Secretary of State Leumas was still there. He'd arrived late, it was true, but it was unlike him to remain anywhere that wasn't a negotiating table for more than an hour.

Tepper was a ball of glee, spinning and aglow like a disco globe. "Grant," he spouted, cornering the only guest who was standing by himself. "Grant." He poked him in the ribs as Scotch sloshed over the lips of his glass. "Smile, you party-pooping grouch. We're a hit!"

"I'm not sure whether it's the exhibit or the museum's wine cellar." Chapman's voice seemed to come from afar as he held up his glass of chablis. His eyes drifted from the curator back to Linda. The slender woman was standing not far from the Secretary of State, not having moved from his orbit since Chapman had introduced them an hour before. He suspected that she was planning to inquire about a job at the Smithsonian, even though Chapman had told her that it was the vice president who was ex officio head of the board of regents. To

Linda, everyone over subcabinet level was Washington royalty. There hadn't been enough of a break in the glad-handing for her to speak with Leumas, though his wife had turned to Linda at one point to ask her if she knew what was in a particular dish. Linda had made a polite guess, though a passing waiter corrected her.

"I've got my event," Tepper continued at a gush. "People will be lined up for tickets hours before we open tomorrow. We'll have to extend the show a week or two, maybe a month or two."

"Now, wait a minute," Chapman protested. "We promised Laojiu—"

"What does that matter? Beijing will love the good press." He did not notice the Scotch dripping from his overfilled glass onto his shoe. "And you arranged it, Grant, *you* pulled it all together."

"Don't remind me."

"You tiptoed through the minefield and brought the museum a miracle. You're a heck of a diplomat and a hell of a professional!"

Chapman snickered. "I try to do my job and keep my promises. When they conflict," he said portentously, "I keep my promises."

"Good motto, very good." Tepper had missed the hidden threat. His thick thumb floated over his shoulder toward Laojiu, who was standing with Yu and members of the Chinese diplomatic community. "Uh, tell me, does he seem to be having a good time? Does he like the food?"

"He's been pleasant to all of the guests if that's what you mean."

"Will—"

"—he be averse to spending more time in the U.S. than we'd originally planned?"

"You read me loud and clear." Tepper fell stone-silent as he looked across the crowded hall. Detective Varley, who was in charge of the Tally McGraw investigation, was scuttling toward him like a sand crab. A walkie-talkie was pressed to his lips, and if his face was any indication, what he had to say was not good. "Uh-oh," Tepper warned. "Methinks that trouble is on the way."

Chapman turned and felt his stomach drop.

"We've had another bloodbath," said the tall, needle-thin

detective when he was near enough not to be overheard. Tepper chased down an oath with the rest of his Scotch, while Chapman's gaze sped protectively to Linda. "This time our killer picked a biggie, plastered Cara Thomas all over the NBC film library."

"My God," Tepper blurted out.

"How do you know it's the same person?" Chapman asked.

"Because everything's just like it was last night, only more so. Body torn to pieces, room turned upside down."

"Why do you say more so?"

"Ms. Thomas had locked herself inside the steel vault they've got up there." Varley cocked his elbows like a rooster and jabbed outward. "It's like someone did this in clay. Blew off the half-ton door, ripped the woman and the vault apart, and punched dozens of dents in the high-gauge steel. I've got my boys up there right now, sifting through the wreckage for hints of explosives."

"Do you think," Tepper inquired weakly, "that someone has targeted my exhibit?"

The detective ran a hand through his close-cropped gray hair. "Off the record, yeah. So what I want to do right now is get Secretary Leumas out of here as quickly and quietly as possible. His secret service people have been advised, and they're waiting for us to get our act together so that there won't be a mad rush for the door. What I want you to do—" he regarded Chapman "—is to hustle the Chinese out of here hard on the Secretary's heels, and then we'll tell everyone else the party's over."

"What do I tell them," Tepper asked, "that won't be thought of as rude or cause a panic?"

"Just tell 'em there's no more booze and they'll leave. If that doesn't work, tell them you've got to tidy up for the opening. No big announcements. Just circulate and leave word that the party's over."

"A bloodbath," Tepper wheezed incredulously as he shuffled off. Chapman followed close behind, delaying until he saw that Varley had left. He hurried to where Linda was standing. Chapman took her hand and tugged her to one side just as the Secretary was finally free.

"Grant! What in God's name are you doing?"

"Don't talk," he snarled, "just listen. I want you out of

here. Don't ask any questions; just go down the stairs and out the door."

"What is it? You're scaring me."

"Trust me and go. I'll meet you at the apartment in a half hour."

"But why?"

Chapman didn't answer; he walked over to where Secretary Leumas was conferring with one of his secret service men. From the corner of his eye, Chapman saw Linda storm away; angry or not, he didn't care, just as long as she was safely away from the museum.

The Secretary allowed his guard and Chapman to usher him and Mrs. Leumas off, though he lingered for a moment here and there to press a bit more influential flesh. "You know," he told his wife as they finally emerged from the museum into the crisp night air, "I never even got to look at the statues."

"You'll see them in Washington," the woman assured him.

Chapman asked as they slid into the waiting limousine, "Washington, sir? Are there plans to bring the exhibit there?"

"Oh, just a lot of talk on the deputy ambassador level. This one looks like it's going to be such a hit that a tour is all but certain. And by the way—" he patted Chapman on the shoulder as he took a seat beside his wife "—I want to tell you how proud I am of the job you did here. Absolutely fantastic, a really first-rate bit of diplomacy. Frankly," he said to Mrs. Leumas, "I'm afraid we're going to lose this guy. The vice president was talking to me this morning about kicking him upstairs onto his staff." To Chapman again: "I'd hate to hold you back, but I'm going to fight to keep you, Chapman. You're too valuable to me."

Chapman mumbled out his thanks as he settled back into the seat. Laojiu probably sensed all of this, but if there was a tour, Chapman knew who'd be tagged to break the news. He was beginning to hate himself for having done his job so well, and he took no consolation in the Secretary's praise.

As the long black car pulled from the museum and rolled downtown along Central Park West and then Broadway, Chapman found his mind drawn like a grisly spectator away from the problem of Laojiu to the scene described by Detective Varley. It finally hit him. That had been no fantasy spun by the detective—Cara Piri Thomas was dead. He looked out at the unsuspecting city, which soon would be rocked by the news. Chapman felt somehow personally responsible for the fear that would settle on everyone in New York. It was the job of government to see that things like this didn't happen, to see that people were safe and educated and striving toward a society that was above senseless, savage acts. Not personally, but as part of the machine, he had failed.

Anything else you can blame on yourself? he asked in a flourish of calm introspection. *The temperature, the state of the economy, maybe a bad harvest or two. When does Tarlo let your conscience go?*

The Secretary of State looked at the museum program rolled in his hands. "Does Toby save this garbage?"

His wife nodded patiently and turned to Chapman. "In two years, our daughter has filled seven huge scrapbooks with mementos. Too bad she had to be at school this week for exams. She'd have so loved to be here."

The dashboard telephone rang, and the secret service man seated beside the driver scooped it up. When the brief conversation had ended, he buzzed the Secretary's extension on the other side of the partition.

"Excuse me, sir," the young man announced, "but we're going to have to ride around the city for a while."

"Why is that?"

"They don't want us going right back to the hotel room."

"Oh? Is someone using my room for something?" The official smiled at his own slightly risqué joke.

"Yes, Mr. Secretary," the agent answered straight-faced. "The police are checking your suite for a bomb."

"A bomb?" Leumas complained. "We get a dozen threats like that every day. Don't the police realize that?"

"You let them check," Mrs. Leumas said sternly. "Ask them to drive down to the Bowery so I can see these bums everyone's always talking about."

The Secretary relayed her request and then folded his arms impatiently. "It's such a bother." He pouted. "They listen for ticking and look for hidden wires, they feel for lumps in your mattress and under the toilet seat and in the shower drain. Don't they realize that if someone wanted to kill me, kill anyone, they'd succeed?"

"Stanford, you know how I hate it when you talk like that. These men are experts at what they do."

"So are most paid assassins." Leumas shook his white-maned head. "Always a new problem. By the way, Chapman, Ambassador Scott couldn't make it tonight, but she tells me that you know Wayne Teres."

"We went to college together. As a matter of fact, I just saw him at the embassy in Beijing."

"He's not there anymore; he's back in the States."

"So the ambassador told me."

"What she didn't tell you because she didn't know is that he killed a prostitute while he was on marijuana. We got him out before the Chinese could try him; I'm all for sacrificial cows when they're necessary, but not when they're madmen like Teres."

"Mad? Sir, do you mean clinically psychotic or just a little—"

"I mean mad, Grant, mad as a hatter. Too many drugs, too much pressure, who can say what drove him over the edge? The guard at the embassy found him giggling like a fruitcake. He's still giggling over at Bellevue. The Chinese won't tell us what exactly happened over there until their own detectives have finished an investigation."

"Dear God," Chapman sighed. He listened with detachment as the Secretary talked informally about a thought he had had after hearing the news, of recommending to the President that Chapman take Teres's place. Chapman neither embraced nor rejected the feeler; he merely thanked the cabinet officer and told him that it was indeed something to consider. In the meantime, he waited impatiently as the suddenly inspired official ordered the car to turn uptown and raise some political capital by driving unannounced through Harlem, in order, as he would later explain to the press, "to witness conditions as they are, and not as they are prettified for visitors from Washington," even though he barely glanced from the tinted windows as they negotiated the desolate streets of the neighborhood.

Four minutes into their tour came the phoned all-clear, and fifteen minutes later the car finally rolled up to the Waldorf. There, the Secretary greeted newspeople waiting to ask him about his evening and about international matters. Chapman gritted his teeth and checked his watch repeatedly, waiting for the opportunity to excuse himself and head for his apartment. It was ten more long, frustrating minutes before he finally could leave.

114   Jeff Rovin

• • •

Linda took a cab to Chapman's place and admitted herself, immediately switching on the air conditioner to take some of the uncustomary stuffiness from the place. Fuming still at the high-handed way Grant had treated her, she flopped down on the bed and considered how she was going to handle him when he appeared. Her reverie only fueled her anger, and Linda didn't want it to peak too early; switching on the TV, she absently watched the eleven o'clock news. She knew that she should phone her parents and tell them she wouldn't be coming, but she did not. In her current state, one snide word from her mother would be enough to send her into a tirade.

A few minutes into the newscast, there was a bulletin announcing the death of Cara Thomas. Linda stared at the TV with disbelief and then shot from the bed to call Grant at the museum. "The poor dear," she rehearsed her apology as she dialed, realizing that he must have known what happened and didn't want to frighten me. But before she finished, Linda heard the rattling of keys in the hallway and, slamming down the phone, bolted from the bedroom.

"Thank God you're here," she sighed as she pulled open the door.

There was no one there. Poking her head into the hallway that led into four apartments, she saw that it was empty. Linda peeked at the elevator next to the apartment and noticed that it was descending. "Must've been the cables rattling," she decided. She watched the carriage pass her floor and stop in the lobby; the sound did not stop, however, nor did it seem now even to be coming from the elevator shaft. The staccato jangling was more clearly now a metallic pulse that ebbed and rose, like electric rock percussion, Linda thought. Without ever quite vanishing, it actually grew louder with each recurrence. The clattering came from nowhere in particular, yet she was in the midst of it, as though it were being squeezed from the very air itself.

Linda walked cautiously down the hallway, in turn putting an ear to each of the apartment doors. Every time she did so, the sound seemed to come from behind her; when she would turn, it was once more everywhere.

"Come on, kid, don't scare the piss out of yourself like this. It's probably only your sinuses ringing."

As she walked slowly back to the open door, still listening

carefully for the elusive source, Linda found her breath becoming strangely labored. It was as if the air had thickened to a soup. She drew on it hard but at the same time was aware of an almost imperceptible fog swirling toward her from Chapman's apartment, warming her and causing her flesh to crackle and sweat. She stopped and wavered and then leaned against the elevator door.

It's like . . . at the mu-museum, she thought as the cloud seemed to gather rather than disperse. Then, with the clanging painfully loud in her ears, hands grabbed her and spun her around, and she fell backward.

"Linda," Chapman snapped as he shook her. "What are you doing out here? Is something the matter?"

The noise, the unbreathable air, the heat, and the mist all swirled into one and seemed to be sucked through a funnel. Everything was clear again, and Linda threw herself at Chapman. She murmured incoherently as she clutched at him, placing her head on his chest. Chapman stroked her back and her hair, allowing her to recover in her own time. After a few minutes, she looked up at him.

"I don't know what happened to me. I heard a noise and figured it was you. But when I came out to let you in, no one was here, just this hideous ringing and banging, like cymbals smashing glass or something."

Chapman went over and examined the firewell and the smoke detector on the wall.

"It must have short-circuited," Chapman said, indicating the alarm. "That sometimes happens when there's static electricity in the air."

"The alarm?" She looked at it dubiously. "No, it was more than just sound. There was also this . . . this incredible humidity which—Grant, I could actually see it rolling along the floor. And there was a smell, something sickly sweet like charred honey or molasses or something."

"What it probably was," Chapman said calmly, "was a neighbor overcooking a pie or pudding and setting off the alarm." He looked into his apartment through the open door. "You thought the smoke was coming from in here because the air conditioner kept churning it back into the hallway."

"Maybe." Linda sobbed. "Jesus, Grant, what's happening?"

"Relax," he cooed, "you're letting yourself get worked up

over nothing." He put his arm around Linda, led her into the apartment, and kicked the door shut.

"You call what happened to Cara Thomas nothing?"

"How did you find out?"

"I saw it on the news. It said they found her just like Tally. They gave one of those special numbers to call if you have information."

"Finding her in the same condition as Tally doesn't mean a thing. Cara probably made a lot of enemies in her line of work; the two deaths may not even be related."

"The police don't think that, do they?"

"No," Chapman admitted.

"Which is why we had to wrap up the party as fast as we did, right? I should have known." Linda managed a weak grin. "Otherwise, Tepper would have kept it going all night, maybe even all week." She smiled and hugged Chapman. "Thanks for not telling me. I would have just locked myself in my office and stayed there."

Chapman pulled off his tie. "Not to bring up a sore subject, but what did your mother say when you called to tell her you weren't coming?"

"I didn't call. And it's too late now. Besides, I'll get the same ration of guilt whether I phone now or in the morning. Just hold me." She crushed herself closer.

"Okay if I shut off the air conditioner first? I'm freezing."

Linda promised to warm him, and after switching off the unit they retired to the bedroom. There, Chapman put Cara Thomas and Wayne Teres from his mind. Tonight there was only Linda, and as they fell on the bed—Chapman breaking from her long enough to flick off the news—he rediscovered the passion, affection, and mutual emotional need that allowed their relationship to bridge its frequent chasms.

CHAPTER EIGHT

THE CHINESE CONSULATE, a quiet place during the day, at night took on the air of a monastery. The outside was pale ivory in the reflected glow of streetlamps and occasional headlights from passing automobiles, and the inside usually was not lighted at all. The interior was Spartan. Though enlivened here and there by a framed watercolor or paper cutting, by a plant or tiny jade statue tucked into a corner, its sparse decor added further to the impression of seclusion, which ironically was what China was struggling to shed.

Laojiu and his daughter had been given the third-floor guest suite. Except for the downstairs guard they were alone, having being chauffeured from the party. In the adjoining study—little more than an alcove with a desk, a standing lamp, and a shelf of history books, atlases, and current mainland fiction—the archaeologist carefully unrolled an ancient scroll from its aluminum cylinder, leaving four others still inside. Next to him sat Yu, pen in hand, a notebook bent open before her.

His fragile glasses perched on his wide bridge, Laojiu began reading from the top of the right-hand column of the scroll. His voice was slow and clipped like that of one just learning to read as he struggled with a forgotten language in writing that was barely legible after more than two thousand years.

" 'The . . . stars . . . paint . . . two . . . kinds . . . of pictures, one that . . . is . . . physical and . . . the other which . . . is . . .' I can't quite make this out, but it is a form of the word 'spirit.' No doubt, Yu, Kuo is referring to astronomical constellations and astrological designs." Laojiu read on, the twentieth century and his own problems forgotten as he was all but swept through time by Kuo's vivid, heartfelt account of the ancient world in which he moved.

As Laojiu began a fresh passage describing the nearing completion of the temple of the Madjan, Yu laid down her pen.

"Your petulance is distracting me," Laojiu said after a moment, his eyes not leaving the scroll. "And you are missing key passages."

"Father, let us go home."

"Please write," he insisted, and continued reading slowly.

Yu obliged, though after a few minutes she once more put aside her pen. "They're taking care of the statues, we've seen that. Chapman is a meticulous and honorable man, and sometimes, as now, I want so badly to be at the dig that I can feel the dirt beneath my feet, smell the ancient earth as we explore its secrets."

"We have made a commitment here, one which I will honor."

"None will thank you for it."

"That is not why I am here."

"But I ache." Yu made a fist. "And wouldn't it be nobler after all to betray an ignorant multitude than to betray the quest of knowledge?"

Laojiu looked up, peering over the top of his wire-rimmed glasses. "I ache no less than you, child, of that you can be very certain. But as much as we dislike this work and resent it, I wonder if, as Chapman says, it is part of our mission to explain antiquity to people whose focus goes no further than a day or two, whose primary fascination is with murder and bloodshed. Is knowledge better served by those who hoard it or those who distribute it? Where would we be today if Kuo had not taken the time to preserve his thoughts and observations?"

"If Kuo were as magnanimous as you imply, he'd not have survived in Ch'en's court as long he did; no society treats its benevolent members with respect. Whatever Kuo did for posterity had to have been complemented by ambition, greed, or some other selfish motive which honed his instinct for survival. Emperor Ch'en was not benign, nor was General Jiang. Our own rulers use those of us whom they see fit, and their conscience is not stirred as yours appears to be."

"I will serve what is right rather than justify what is wrong."

Yu's eyes narrowed. "And what will you do if another government asks to display our finds? Do we become showmen, carting our props from village to village like minstrels? Would you be satisfied, Father, if this were to become our work?"

"We can speculate endlessly about the future, yet until it is here—"

"I do not *trust* those who organized this program. Mao is a god one morning, a mortal before the sun has set. Our future is clearly defined: today's promise becomes tomorrow's lie. Despite the claims of the minister of culture, this exhibit will not begin and end with New York. It will spread to London and Paris and wherever else the government wishes to curry favor." Yu gave her head a challenging tilt. "I expect acknowledgment of such from the man who hammered into my head the primary value of the past, which is to allow us to anticipate the future."

Laojiu smiled. "You are an incomplete philosopher, my dear. Consider this saw of mine as well: Do not dwell upon the contemporary; it is neither long-lived nor paramount, only a passing thing. More importantly—" he nodded toward the scroll "—do not let it distract you from the time we do have for research. Come, let us continue."

The archaeologist returned to his reading and Yu to her transcription. However, in spite of his own admonition, Laojiu's mind was not entirely on the manuscript. He asked Yu if she would mind getting him a glass of cold water; when she had left, he sat back in his seat.

Being away from his work troubled him, yet he was consumed by more than just that. His little speech to Yu brought back memories of a similar talk he'd had with a young Chinese woman who caught cold on a remote night dig and who, before either realized how ill she'd really become, was soon too weak to travel. She had died in that field, in a tent that swayed gently before the night wind.

The girl returned with two glasses of water, complaining of the heat in the mission and draining her cup in a single long swallow. They resumed their work, but only briefly. So demurely that Laojiu could not become impatient with her, Yu announced, "I feel like that cartoon figure Yun-fan in the newspaper."

"I fail to see how this pertains to the wisdom of Kuo."

"Don't you, Father? He always tries his best, yet rarely is that enough to satisfy those in his modest sphere." She skillfully sketched a short, frowning face in her notebook. "Kuo . . . Yun-fan . . . Laojiu. Call him what you will, he has a cruel taskmaster."

"His own conscience."

"No, his own modesty. None of you realizes his own power. One point tells you nothing, two a line, three a plane. You form a plane, the three of you. Below it, the masses roil. Upon it, the strong tread with impunity." She drew a trio of dots and then erased one. "Remove but one and you leave the leaders on a tightrope." Yu looked at her father. "Remove two and they are immobile. Remove the third and they fall. Remove *yourself*, Father," she implored. "Be what you have always been, not what empty threats and assumed obligations will make of you."

The archaeologist grinned in spite of himself. "As fond as I am of geometry, Yu, this is a political matter. When necessary, you will find in fact that our leaders have learned the divine art of walking on air."

"If they can work such miracles," she said stubbornly, "then why do they need our statues?"

"Because the people they rule, unlike politicians and scientists, require symbols around which to flock. Leaders identify themselves with artifacts of which the public approves. They are no different from Emperor Ch'en." He tapped his bony finger on the desk, beside the scroll. "They need their Madjan."

"You don't," she protested. "Nor do I."

"We neither lead nor truckle through a life of symbols because we have minds."

"But we are servile for all of our fine qualities."

Laojiu handed his daughter the pen. "Kuo also served. Yet consider how valuable his legacy is compared with the inconsequential bequest of some who held even greater sway in his time, men such as General Jiang." Laojiu feigned surprise. "And how cyclical life is. Kuo's comments about the officer lie before us in the scroll, to which we had best apply ourselves before it is too late for me to see or think clearly."

The jangling was remote, dragging her toward it from a deep sleep.

"Oh, shut up!"

Despite Linda's admonition, Chapman reached over to the nightstand and grabbed at the telephone for what had to be a wrong number, a crank call, or an international crisis.

"Yes, hello."

The voice on the other end was garbled, and it was a long moment before Chapman recognized it.

"Mrs. Bergeni?"

Linda was up in a shot. "Oh, Jesus Christ. Oh Jesus, oh God, don't tell me he's dead, don't do it!"

Chapman motioned her quiet while he pressed the receiver to his ear. "Yes, yes, I understand. All right." He squinted at the digital clock. "It's four-twenty-five. We'll be there within the half hour." He depressed the cradle and dialed the number of the State Department's car service. "Your dad's in a coma," he said as he waited to be connected. "Who's Dr. Griffin?"

"Our neighbor, a fucking podiatrist."

"Well, he's there, and they've called Jelkowitz's service."

"Shit." Linda tried to orient herself as she flicked on the light and searched the floor for her clothes. Chapman ordered the car, and fifteen minutes later they were at the Bergeni apartment on East Twenty-fifth Street on the river.

Dr. Griffin answered the door. "I'm sorry this has—"

"How is he?" Linda barked.

Griffin's great shoulders heaved as they stepped inside. "Not well, I'm afraid. I did—"

"You're here!"

The charge wailed from the bedroom as if announcing a banshee. Moments later, Linda's mother appeared. She was a large woman, though she hardly seemed so now, hunched in the doorway of the bedroom. Even across the living room, they could see that her eyes were red and puffy, her cheeks glistening with fresh tears.

"You're here. The wayward daughter has returned. If you had come last night, even if you had called, you would have been able to talk to him one last time." The woman came forward slowly and did not look at Chapman. "There were other things more important to you than your father, than your promise to—"

"Mother, shut *up*," Linda snapped as she pushed past her.

"Yes, go now that it's too late! Too late, Linda. He won't be waking from this."

Chapman did not go with her; he slid into the small kitchen. He felt detached from all of this and wondered if he'd feel anything if the old man had been his father-in-law.

Mrs. Bergeni sat down and stared into space. Dr. Griffin huddled over her and offered comfort as best he could. Chapman admired the man for trying; it was more than he could bring himself to do.

Linda returned a few minutes later and put on some coffee. "I'm going to stay, Grant, at least until we see whether this is stable or what."

"I understand. Do you want me to stick around for a while?"

She shook her head. "The less of an audience Mother has, the more manageable she'll be."

"Okay. I'll be at the apartment until seven-thirty if you want me. After that, I'm picking up Laojiu and heading for the opening."

Linda stood on her toes and kissed him, wishing them well. "Call me here," she said, "if you learn anything about Tally or Cara. That's still got me on edge."

Chapman said that he would. Then he went over and offered Mrs. Bergeni a few compulsory words of consolation. The woman muttered her appreciation with equal sincerity.

Although it was still dark outside, Chapman decided to walk the three miles home. The buildings of lower Madison Avenue were imposing in the darkness. He made for them as he left the Waterside Towers complex on the East River. To Chapman, this area of Manhattan was the real heart of the city, of the world. It represented all that was right and wrong with society: the opportunity for achievement and material things, the temptation toward compromise and shame. Behind him, to the right, was 41 Madison. The law firm where he'd once worked was there, along with some of the larger toy companies. Tarlo was at 200 Fifth, just across the small park.

For at least a year after the debacle, Chapman had avoided this area as though it were radioactive. He didn't know what he'd have done had he bumped into one of his former colleagues. Although none of them had been blamed by Tarlo Toys for Chapman's acts, and Chapman himself had been disbarred for having exposed a client confidence, the firm lost the Tarlo account. Its stockholders were enraged by the $1 million out-of-court settlement the company had agreed to after they had won their case.

But that was years ago, and now he came here often. This place had taught Chapman a great deal about himself, and he was nostalgic about any event or place that had helped him mature. What made this particular moment even more flavorful was that it had been at about this same hour that he'd left the office and gone to the New York *Post*, tortured by the Tarlo memo. He could still feel the punch in the gut it had given him and the twelve hours he'd spent behind his desk tossing it angrily through his mind and reinforcing the decision he'd made. Tarlo had manufactured a toy spaceship whose electron torpedoes were just large enough to lodge in a child's throat. It could have been an innocent mistake, other toy companies having been similarly irresponsible. But Tarlo had done it intentionally to promote their flagging safety-oriented subsidiary Child-Pruf line. He couldn't believe it when he'd read the memo from Inventioneering, their design contractor, but it was true. He'd seen through the $10 million damage suit brought by the parents of a child who had choked to death on the projectile and won it for Tarlo. Later, he found the memo while rounding up their depositions and decided to take it to the press. The *Post* did a horrendous story but a proper headline as he knew they would: "TOY COMPANY KILLERS!" Now he worked for the State Department, their token do-gooder.

As Chapman waited for a garbage truck to rumble east on Thirty-fourth Street, he noticed the first sunlight glinting obliquely along the East River. He began to imagine a time when he might see that same sight from some other place, someplace quiet like Utah or Sri Lanka or even China as Secretary Leumas had proposed. Maybe he would do some writing as Reedy had suggested, and maybe Linda would come with him, giving up the rat race to sculpt or paint or do whatever the hell she pleased.

There were a lot of maybes, he knew. But pursuing them was beginning to make a lot more sense than sitting around and letting his ego be stroked by professional con men like the Secretary of State.

It was six-fifteen before he reached the apartment, and the first thing Chapman did was check with his answering service. Linda hadn't called. He confirmed with the TLC limousine company that the car would meet him at the regular place in two hours. After showering and shaving, Chapman walked over to the Moon, a kitchenlike cafe on Eighty-first Street and Second Avenue. There he had his health food breakfast of tofu salad and soy crackers, a meal that made him feel better about guzzling two quarts of saccharin-sweetened soft drinks every day. The limousine met him there and then went to the Chinese mission for Laojiu and Yu.

Whether it was the sensational, late-breaking publicity or a flourishing of interest as a result of media coverage, the line for tickets to the treasures of Ch'en-shimm went almost completely around the long museum block. Chapman could not help but question deep inside whether, like Tarlo, the museum had in some unthinkable way manufactured the publicity to draw a crowd.

The doors opened at ten o'clock, and the line began slowly to file through. The Chinese couple was seated at a table near the exit, where visitors could ask them questions about the dig and look at Linda's illustrations of the statues in their original habitat. Chapman stood behind and off to one side, his job being to help the Chinese with anyone who might dawdle too long at the desk or become unruly. Because of the two murders he was more alert than he might otherwise have been; he watched those who approached the Chinese with the same criteria used by airline personnel to evaluate potential hijackers.

The first visitor was an overweight, silver-haired woman who carried a large pocketbook in the crook of her elbow. "Excuse me," she said, clearing her throat, "but I would like to ask a question. Do you think there was ever a Chinaman who visited Poland or maybe might have seen pictures from there?"

Chapman wondered how Laojiu would react to the woman and to the large, eclectic batch lining up behind her.

The archaeologist answered soberly, "The Chinese traveled widely, madame, according to the archaeological record and those few written documents which survive. It is quite possible that they went as far from the mainland as Eastern Europe seeking a market for their advanced sciences and inventions."

The woman looked from the man to his daughter to Chapman, amused by the fact that the scientist had spoken to her as an intellectual equal and had treated her query with respect. "I'll just tell you quickly why I ask," she continued, throwing a warning glance at Chapman lest he try to cut her off. "When I was a little girl, my grandfather Sol told me stories about a statue called the Golem. A giant statue, with powerful arms and an unhappy face. Your Madjan reminds me of the Golem, who is said to have come to life to protect the Jews. That's why I was wondering if maybe a Chinaman saw a Golem and created this statue when he got home, the same way that we took Chinese food from China."

The scientist answered patiently, "The creation of a symbolic protector in stone is not limited to one era or one culture or people."

"Oh, no," the woman insisted. "The Golem wasn't just a symbol. My grandfather said he actually saw a Golem come to life in Prague. He said its eyes glowed after a rabbi said some magic word, the name of a demon. Later, they found the tsar's constable crushed to death after he tried to get familiar with a local girl. Jewish girl."

Laojiu nodded, enjoying this unique cultural exchange. "I have heard of such legends. However, the Madjan is not a benevolent demigod like the Golem of your people. He lived to be served, and in return he protected those who worshiped him—or so it is said. What is more likely is that the ancient Chinese sought through the Madjan to honor the principles of strength and conquest for which he stood."

The woman did not fully understand, but she smiled and nodded politely.

"Please exit to your left." Chapman pointed, urging the woman aside to make way for a pair of Hawaiian men who were brandishing cameras and healthy tans.

The woman took a moment more to thank Laojiu, muttering to herself as she turned away, "He still looks to me like a Golem."

Yu bristled. "He predated your Golem by a millennium." The woman ambled on, and Yu calmed down as her father gripped her hand beneath the table.

It was nearly an hour before the crowd waiting to talk to

Laojiu broke for a moment, at which point Chapman asked if they would like some coffee.

"We do not drink it," the archaeologist responded, sipping a glass of water.

"Tea, then?"

"Thank you, but the water is fine."

Chapman changed the subject. "Tell me, do you know anything about astrology or psychic phenomena?"

"My work requires me to study certain aspects of these fields."

"Something that first woman said interested me. Before I was made a partner at my law firm, I handled a toy company and an astrologer in a bizarre case. A man claimed that his wife had been killed by a ouija board which some mentalist had used as a focal point for a blast of psychic energy. My movement for summary judgment—dismissal of the case— was granted by the court, but I amassed an interesting bulk of information on the way. Do you think it's possible to use inanimate objects like that, or like a Golem or the Madjan, as a channel for subconscious emotion?"

"It's one very provocative school of thought," Laojiu admitted. "Certainly my ancestors believed in it." A young man who introduced himself as an archaeology student had his girl friend snap his photograph with Laojiu, after which the scientist continued. "Writings which I have uncovered indicate that the gods were considerably more able than humans in this matter of manifesting their presence through icons, though many occultists sought to accomplish this as well."

"Fascinating," said Chapman. "I'll tell you, I find mythology as a rule more credible than contemporary religions. Whether or not there really were gods, at least the ancients respected things that were important to them: the rivers, trees, the sun, even heroism in combat. It wasn't just weak-kneed faith."

Yu turned to Chapman. "It is unusual to hear a Western man speak this way. Do you not believe in a supreme being?"

"While I was studying law," he recalled, "a friend and I— Wayne Teres at the embassy—Wayne and I came across this case where a woman had killed someone and then claimed that God had ordered the murder. She was found guilty, of course, but Wayne and I took it one step further. We found her innocent and put God on trial instead. Wayne defended, I prosecuted, and we played with the script of this trial for months. In the end, we had to let God go because I couldn't produce enough evidence to satisfy the court that he even existed."

"Then you don't believe in him?" Yu asked.

Chapman answered reflectively, "Tally McGraw believed in God. She was convinced her blameless hippy soul would go straight to his heavenly little commune when she died. Must have been packed inside her pretty tight for him to have to rip her apart like that." His voice grew bitter. "Any god who does that to his faithful is a joke as far as I'm concerned."

"There is that paradox," Laojiu allowed. "The Madjan at least granted protection in this life as well as everlasting glory in return for fealty."

"I'd have signed up for that policy." Chapman grinned and let out a sigh. "Pretty heady stuff. I'm going up for a soda. Are you sure I can't get you anything?"

"Nothing. Thank you again."

Motioning to one of the guards to take his place, Chapman hurried to the fifth-floor lounge. Plugging coins into the soda machine, he held back a dime to call Linda.

Linda answered the phone on the first ring with a glum, throaty greeting. Without any chitchat, she informed Chapman that nothing had changed since the morning. "Mother's asleep in the chair where you left her, and I'm happy about that. I've never heard her so bitter. As soon as Dr. Griffin left, she was off and complaining a blue streak about me, about my career, about you—everything."

"Let her roar; they're swell pictures."

There was a moment of silence, and then Linda said, "Please, no bits from *King Kong* right now. I'm in no mood."

"Thought you could use some humor. Sorry."

"What I'd appreciate is a punching bag with her face on it. She wore me out mostly because I won't beat Mother down, not when she's going through this shit. As much as I really don't like the woman, it's not in me to hurt her. Christ." Her voice trembled. "I'm so high-strung! I popped two tranquilizers; didn't do a goddam thing."

"Did you try to get some sleep?"

"With someone dying in the next room? I can't just tune out like that."

Chapman hated to end the conversation, but he didn't like the thought of Laojiu and Yu alone with a killer on the prowl.

"Listen, Linda, I've got to get back to work. I'm going to try to go up and see Wayne Teres during lunch, but I'll call you in the afternoon. You'll leave a message with Gail if there's any problem?"

"Why can't I call the museum?"

"Because the switchboards are still jammed with people who want tickets."

Linda hung up with a perfunctory "I love you," and Chapman hurried downstairs. The conversation had left him feeling strangely distant. He realized it was because he'd found the talk with Laojiù so uncharacteristically rewarding. All he wanted at that moment was to rejoin the archaeologist and pick his brains in this matter of gods, humankind, and morality. It was a refreshing change from arguing about Mrs. Bergeni, the Smithsonian, and whether or not Linda should smoke....

CHAPTER NINE

THE DIALOGUE CHAPMAN hoped for never materialized. He returned to the hall and found it more like a mob scene from a Cecil B. DeMille production than a cultural display. People were crushed into every niche, and the guards had their hands full just keeping spectators off the loose velvet ropes that surrounded the statues.

The queue beside Laojiu's table had thickened to a disorderly mob. The guard Chapman had tagged to replace him had given up trying to keep people in line and was preoccupied simply with keeping everyone from jamming against the desk at once. Chapman threw himself into the fray, resorting to the elementary school standby, "We're closing this position if a line is not formed!" in order to restore order. Grumbling about everything from the confusion to Chapman's Gestapo tactics, the mound of humanity reluctantly complied.

By lunchtime, having been forced to prune all manner of chaos before it could flourish, Chapman was ready for a nap, not a hasty trip to Bellevue. But he'd obtained permission from the State Department to pay a brief visit, and he felt he owed as much to Wayne Teres.

After turning the Chinese over to a beaming Tepper for lunch with the U.N. Secretary General, Chapman caught a cab and forced himself to rest on the traffic-delayed ride uptown.

He had never been to the mental institution, and it was with a feeling of awful vulnerability that he hurried up the cement walk to the imposing edifice. His eyes played across the bars that fronted each window, the frosted glass that prevented reality from interfering with the treatment of the patients.

Chapman entered the off-white lobby and a white-cloaked attendant came for him at the front desk and showed him to Teres's room. The burly young man drew back a pair of deadbolts and then fished for a key on the ring hanging from his belt.

"Is all of this security due to regulations?" Chapman inquired. "Or is five-foot five-inch Wayne really dangerous?"

"I been knocked down by a little old lady," the youth said with the reverence of a quarterback discussing an opposing lineman. "She thought she was a weredog, a mixture of herself and her dead pooch. Yeah." He put his eye against a peephole to make certain that Teres would not run out when the door was opened. "It's regulations."

"Does he get any fresh air or sunlight in there? I noticed that all the windows are translucent."

The attendant seemed bored with Chapman's naivete. "Your friend thinks he's on a Club Med cruise in the Caribbean. He takes me for a porter who won't let him out of his cabin because there's been a coup in Colombia. His doctor doesn't want to destroy that illusion because, odd as it may sound to a layman, it's Teres's only hold on reality."

Chapman felt sick as the young man pulled open the door. He hoped he was emotionally prepared for this encounter, even though part of him still didn't believe it was all happening.

"Holler if ya need me," said the attendant. "I'll be right outside here."

Chapman barely heard him or the heavy locking of the door as he stepped inside. His eyes were on Wayne, who lay sprawled on his back in bed. He looked much the same as he had in Beijing, except that the moustache had been shaved away, and his hair, clipped shorter, was oily looking. Chapman didn't imagine that they washed and blow-dried it every day as Wayne used to. Stripped to his undershirt and jockey shorts, he didn't hear Chapman walk in; he continued to stare at the ceiling, his arms bent behind his head.

"Afternoon, Wayne."

Teres looked over, his detached gaze focusing gradually. After a moment he brightened. "Holy moly—Grant!" He bounded from bed. "Grant, I didn't know you were on the boat." Chapman had to fight back tears as Teres embraced him and then pumped his hand over and over. "I mean, since when have you gone in for this swinging singles trip?"

"Had nothing else to do," Chapman said softly.

"Wow, great to see you, really great. Say," he ejaculated, "how'd you get in here, anyway? I heard they're keeping all us American types indoors until they've flushed out the Cubans. They're the ones who're behind the coup; did you know that?" Chapman shook his head and then turned away. Teres continued. "Yeah, it pisses me off too. But hey, the world learned its lesson in Grenada. Nobody fucks with Americans anymore. This'll all be over soon enough, and then we'll go find us some chicks." He put his hands on his hips and stared at the floor. "You know, I promised myself I'd swear off poon after what happened in China. But after a few days I'm rarin' to go again. Hey, Grant, did you hear what happened at the embassy?"

"I caught snippets here and there. You want to talk about it?"

Teres swung around Chapman and squatted to look up into his face. "First you tell me what you heard. I love listening to how twisted stories get in their fourth-hand versions."

"Well," Chapman said, trying to sound nonchalant, "Secretary Leumas said that they found you in your office with a dead woman."

"Mei, the woman you met."

"Yes, I assumed as much. He told me that the guard answered your phone call and hurried over, found you saying things he couldn't quite make out. Basically, though, that you were calm but distraught." Chapman turned away and picked up a copy of *Hi-Fi* magazine so that he wouldn't have to look at Teres. *Giggling and babbling like a baby is what Leumas really said. God help me, but this hurts.*

Teres laughed out loud. "Calm but distraught, eh? Come on, fellah, I'd recognize your diplomatic horseshit anywhere. What I was doing, Grant—and dig this, because it's *real*, not some turkey show we used to watch, like *Night Gallery*—I was holding her arm, which had been cut off. I was holding it fingers down and doodling on the floor with her blood. That's why they sent me on this vacation. They thought I'd cracked up. Truth of it is, Grant," he walked over and said in a whisper, glancing furtively at the door, "I did it because it seemed to make a lot of sense at the time."

"How so?"

Teres threw out his arms. "That lady was blown to pieces. I mean *kaboom* all over the room." Chapman was suddenly very alert. "Yeah, it was a fuckin' mess. I picked up her arm because I never really thought it was her sexiest part." He shrugged. "If you've gotta face the fact that someone you care about is dead, the best thing to do is think bad thoughts about them till the shock has passed."

"Wayne," Chapman said urgently, "who else knows about the condition in which they found the girl?"

Teres whispered, "Just the Chinks and the embassy guard—" he took another suspicious look at the door "—plus you and me. They refused to tell the State Department; not even the President was given the lowdown."

"Why?"

"Because the bigwigs in Beijing don't want to scare off the diplomatic hookers! That's how they get a lot of their secret information. Hey, I can understand that. They didn't even have to threaten to kill me and Jerry the guard if we told anyone. I'm telling you, old buddy, because I know you can keep a secret. If you don't—" he peered ominously at the door, "—the Chinks'll hotline Castro, who'll divert some of his Colombian team to this boat and cut the nuts off you know who."

Chapman didn't doubt Teres for a moment. Except for his tragic cover story, forged in the trauma's aftermath, Teres was as lucid as ever. What concerned Chapman now were the implications of what the former diplomat had revealed. There was no question but that Varley would have to be told about Mei, if only to prevent him from pursuing leads that would not accommodate the Beijing death as well as those in New York. Chapman did not understand the connection, nor was he pleased to have to betray Teres's confidence. But three women directly associated with the exhibit had perished in the space of as many days. If it was in his power to affect events, he would do so rather than risk the chance of seeing yet another woman die before this day had ended.

Chapman rolled up the *Hi-Fi* magazine and tapped Teres in the soft part of his arm. "Wayne, this sounds like a pretty grisly business. Were you able to give the Chinese any idea who might have killed the girl?"

"When they came to the embassy, I told them I thought that Godzilla did it. Then I remembered that he's from Japan."

"Seriously," Chapman said firmly, "what do you think? Was it a bomb?"

"*Godzilla*? No, I loved it. Raymond Burr could've been better, but it wasn't a bomb." Teres donned a cheek-splitting grin. "I'm pulling your leg, Grant, you sober-faced old fart. I don't know what happened." He sighed. "I wasn't stoned, didn't hear a sound, and was gone less than a minute. I didn't do it, there was no one else in the building, Jerry couldn't have made it to my office and back while I was away, and I always keep my windows locked. You figure it out." He walked over and flopped back on the bed. "Maybe I'll think of something when we reach port. A few days on the beach, some cards, a little sex. Who knows, it may come to me in a flash of godly inspiration."

Chapman stared compassionately at his friend. He had a hunch that the doctor was right, that only the thin thread of Teres's delusion prevented him from unraveling completely. Privately, Chapman wished his friend a long and peaceful voyage. Aloud, he said, "Say, I've got some business to take care of elsewhere. Okay if I catch you later?"

"No problem. How about dinner one night in Caracas?"

"I look forward to it. I really do."

"All that sun and surf; it'll be a blast. I can't wait."

It was difficult for Chapman to leave the room, in part because he knew that it would be difficult to return. Wayne was in no pain physically or emotionally and seemed in good spirits. But he was an honest and cheerful fellow and a good friend; he deserved better than a cage, even a clean one like this.

Chapman phoned Varley from the front desk and said he'd like to meet him at the precinct house as soon as possible. The detective told him he'd be there for another hour or so. Chapman wouldn't reveal the reason for his visit, however, feeling that Wayne should have at least some secrets from the hospital staff.

As he was leaving, Chapman walked over to Wayne's attendant and slipped him a twenty-dollar bill. The young man asked what it was for; all Chapman could think to say was, "Throw him under a sunlamp every now and then. He likes that."

"Hey, you crazy too?"

"Could be." Chapman shrugged. He left Bellevue feeling as low as he'd been in recent memory.

The iris opened to admit the river of blood and continued to widen as the red poured through.

Throbbing with the heat of resurgent power, of strength which had been dormant for too many centuries, the god found his thirst for it as heightened as his need. Even before the taste of one slaughter had faded, he had sought and found a new victim, and then another, and now scoured the mortal world for a fresh Woman of Peace.

Soon, very soon, he would be mighty enough to move among them, and his army, his brave flock of warriors, also would stir anew. Those who had defiled his temple would perish, their kingdom razed. And then, feasting upon their blood, he would turn with supreme vengeance against his ancient foe—the earth dragon . . .

The silver-haired woman looked around the vault of the bank. A curious sensation filled her, causing her to tingle and her brow to flush. She gazed through the lobby, toward Fifth Avenue, and saw nothing unusual. She turned to the well-dressed young woman who was flipping through documents in her safety deposit box.

"That's very strange."

"What, Mrs. Feingold?"

"Did you just feel a hot breeze go by?"

"I thought it was rather chilly in here actually." The woman looked up. "Are you quite all right?"

"I think so," she said without conviction as the warmth passed. "It was probably just indigestion from that egg salad I ate at the museum."

"Have you been to see the Ch'en-shimm exhibit?" the customer asked, genuinely interested.

Mrs. Feingold nodded. "I had a ticket through the sisterhood. It was very nice. You should see it."

"I plan to. Mikhail said he'll arrange for passes."

Mrs. Feingold forgot her discomfort, reminded of the conversation she'd had that morning with the archaeologist. She made a mental note to herself to run down to a bookstore after work to see if she could find a book about the Golem and about Chinese explorers.

Yu splashed cold water on her face and then looked at herself in the mirror. Unless she had contracted food poisoning during lunch, there was no earthly reason for her to feel as she did all of a sudden, nauseous and warm. She'd felt fine moments before when she'd entered the museum lounge, had felt nothing more than filthy when she'd come to the ladies' room to wash the city dirt from her face. Then the ringing came, like little bells echoing inside her head. Now, as she patted her cheeks dry, what she saw was not her face but a red mask that threatened to burst into flame at any moment.

The water had barely cooled her flesh; breathing slowly, she concentrated on walking toward the door, toward her father, toward help. Taking each step in turn, she negotiated the few paces between the bank of sinks and the door. Pushing against it, she found the rush of fresh air rehabilitating; the instant her father came into view, the jangling and queasiness faded as though drawn into a silent whirlpool of oblivion. Yu nodded as Bonnie, a VIP guide for the Ch'en-shimm exhibit, went past her into the rest room. Walking slowly to the center of the lounge, she sat heavily beside her father on an old leather sofa.

"You look pale, Yu. Do you feel ill?"

"A bit dizzy, that is all."

"Shall I summon a physician?" Laojiu's voice and face were calm, though behind them lurked great concern. He had been careless once, and he would never be so again.

"No, I'm well now. There was a stifling heat in the room and a strange odor which I presume to be a disinfectant. Americans may be used to the trappings of hygiene, but I seem to react badly to them." Reading doubt in his features, she said, "I am fine, I assure you. Whatever it is has passed, though you seem to have a glaze about you. The lunch wines perhaps?"

He smiled. "No, Yu, nothing as easily brought on or gotten

rid of. I was far from here, lost in the tall grasses of Tahnsien."

Judging from the unusual delicacy of phrase and his wistful expression, she asked, "Tahnsien in which century?"

"That of Kuo, as you've no doubt guessed."

"Your spiritual ancestor," she remarked in jest. "I'm finding it increasingly difficult to distinguish between the two of you. When I think about things you say, I honestly can't recall whether I heard them during our reading of the scroll or in conversations with people at the museum."

"At least you seem to know what year this is. Did I tell you that after you retired last evening, I turned to the final scroll? Do you know that Kuo's wife and child left Ch'en-shimm shortly before the earthquake, to settle in the woman's native village, which is now Kuldja."

"Your birthplace?"

"That is right, and the home of my ancestors for as long as our line is known. I wonder if it might be that Kuo and I are bound by more than just our innate curiosity, joined by blood as well as intellect."

"It certainly is a satisfying thought. Intellectual thoroughbreds. Society may not be persuaded about the genetics, but it is something to look into."

"It is indeed," Laojiu admitted. "Yet it is both fitting and compelling for another reason. There is more than just the pride I would feel being Kuo's distant progeny. This Chapman is a bright young man. What we were discussing before about gods and the supernatural pointed to a fundamental breach in the thinking of myself and Kuo. You and I and Chapman, and many other thoughtful people, put no credence in religion. Our religion is science, the miracle of nature, if you will. But Kuo was a scientist, a fine one, and he believed. He believed in an earth dragon, in the supernatural power of the Madjan, in astrology, in demons, in an afterlife. His perceptions in many areas were remarkably astute. Can he have been wrong in others?"

"It is not without precedent."

"But Kuo himself is without precedent. He understood the fundamentals of psychology centuries before they were recognized by others; he was a superior scientist, using his skills to support many of his astrological predictions, and he knew in the second century B.C. what European astronomers were first discovering a thousand years later. He did not let knowledge or his quest of it obscure truth, and that is a quality much to be admired and emulated."

"You feel we have certain biases," Yu began, "which he—"

"Exactly. His mind was uncluttered by predisposition. His only prejudice was his fondness for truth."

"You will write Kuo's biography, I trust."

"Absolutely, once I have lived for some time inside the mind of this man, unearthed more of his work if any."

Yu started as though she'd been touched suddenly from behind. Her vision swung to the lavatory as a dull thud sounded from behind the door. Laojiu followed her gaze, and together they watched as blood began to seep from behind it. The thick ooze crept from the bottom, over the marble lip, and onto the tile floor.

Laojiu pushed off from the sofa and ran to the door. Something prevented it from swinging in, and so he hooked his narrow fingers behind it and gently pulled the door toward him.

The black girl's body didn't so much fall out as pour out, sloshing from the ladies' room onto the scuffed green floor and lightly rocking there in a crawling sea of blood.

Laojiu's black shoes became islands in the rapidly expanding flood. Unperturbed by the gore, he knelt and delicately grasped her one red-soaked wrist, the other having been severed brutally at the elbow. He found no pulse. After looking curiously up and down the torn and twisted corpse, Laojiu laid down her arm and walked slowly to the courtesy phone.

"Varley's Suite: This Way" was what the shirt cardboard sign said, ornately rendered in a spectrum of markers and signed "Jeanette Varley." The detective's daughter had contributed the only spot of color along the corridor on the second floor of the precinct house. The faded olive walls must have looked worse, Chapman thought, when they were fresh and without character.

The door was open, and Varley motioned Chapman inside, waving him in through a cloud of cigar smoke. Chapman gagged involuntarily, and the detective obliged him by opening a window.

"I hope you've got something for me," the man stated as he

returned to his desk, hoisting two large feet onto several layers of splayed files and dossiers. "I'll tell you what I wouldn't dare tell the commissioner: This one's got me hamstrung."

"Are you free to tell me what you've got so far?" Chapman inquired innocently.

"Sure, because what I've got is nothing. No fingerprints, that goes without saying. But also no shoe scuffings, no threads of fabric, no strands of hair, no trace of spittle or any other bodily fluid. In short, not a goddam thing. All we know is that both victims were in the neighborhood of thirty years old, female, Caucasian, had been at the museum, and were left in almost the same identical condition, as though they'd been crushed."

Crushed. The description that woman gave of the Golem came rushing back into Chapman's mind. "Detective Varley," Chapman began slowly.

"Warren," the investigator interrupted. "I hate formality."

"Warren," he went on, "I've had some information in confidence which may put the two killings in a fresh light." He hesitated, reluctant to betray Teres.

"I'm all ears."

"I have to stress that this was told to me because I'm not the sort of person who takes someone's trust lightly."

"It will go no further than necessary," Varley said ambiguously.

"You see, there will be complex international ramifications if—"

"Chapman, cut the crap!" the detective blurted out. "We're not negotiating a SALT treaty, we're trying to find out who killed two innocent women."

"Three."

The word hung in the air like a midnight chime. Varley stared for a long instant and then snapped from his stupor and sat up, fishing a pad and pencil from among the clutter before him. "Did you do it?"

"No, sir."

"All right." He noted the time and date. "Let's have it, concisely and from the beginning."

Chapman recited the story of the Chinese hooker as briefly as possible, wishing to get his Judas role over and done with. Behind a facade of professional detachment, Varley took down the pertinent facts, all the while chewing his dead cigar and tossing these revelations through his mind, hoping the new facts would mix with what was already known to form some sort of discernible picture.

When Chapman had finished, Varley sat back in his seat and studied what he had written. The ensuing silence was broken by the buzz of the phone intercom. Varley absently picked up the receiver.

"Yeah, Sergeant. Who? For me?" His eyes went to Chapman. "Okay, I'll take it." To his guest: "The museum's calling. Do they know you're here?"

"No one does."

Varley waited while the switchboard connected him. The message from the museum's security chief was terse and drew an oath from the detective. "I'll be right there," he promised.

"Trouble?"

Varley slammed down the phone and rose, snatching his jacket from the back of his chair. He looked at Chapman for a moment and then said simply: "Four."

Chief of security Webster Hall had collared the special-events photographer from the museum's *Natural History* magazine, and as they burst into the lounge, the young shutterbug from Kentucky stopped, swallowed hard, and then declared, "Jiminy, she's worse'n the gutted deer I covered last month."

Hall told him to shut up and cover the victim from every angle and also to shoot the lavatory and a complete mosaic of the lounge. When Varley arrived, he complimented Hall for thinking on his feet and then called for help from homicide.

Even before the coroner arrived and performed a preliminary postmortem, conducted on the premises at the detective's insistence, Varley knew what they'd find. It would be the same as with the other victims, the body not only mangled but crushed, not just dead but neurologically wasted from a flash of feral energy. He turned from the chalky black corpse to the Chinese, and with a sigh more frustrated than angry, he flipped out his notebook.

"From the top, please," he said, addressing the couple as one.

Yu looked from her father to Bonnie. Not quite certain about what she was supposed to say, the girl answered succinctly, "As you can see, this woman died in the toilet."

"Did you see her go in?"

"Yes, she entered as I was leaving."

"You were in there first?" Varley asked. Yu nodded once. "And there was no one else in there?" Yu shook her head. "I see. How did you know that something had happened? Did you hear anything, see anything, smell—"

"I sensed something," Yu interrupted. She searched for the proper words. "I felt a dome of humid air rush up behind me, flowing toward there." She indicated the lavatory. "I turned with it."

"This blast of air went *toward* the bathroom?"

"It wasn't a blast; it was heavy but controlled. It actually rolled around me."

"It didn't rush away from the bathroom, like an explosion."

"No, nor was there the sound of an explosion."

"Sir, did you hear anything at all?"

Laojiu said, "There was a muffled bump, just once."

"That could have been a well-packed explosive hidden somewhere in a stall or trash can. Tell me, did either of you smell anything before or after, like leaking gas or—"

"Yes," Yu interjected, "before. There was an odor, a sweet smell but penetrating. I was quite overcome by it. And while I was in there, I heard a distant clanging."

"Water in the pipes," Chapman guessed, though he was troubled suddenly by Yu's recollections. What she had just described was not unlike what Linda had experienced the night before at his apartment.

Varley took a second to scan his writing. "Grant, would you mind turning away for a second?"

"I don't follow."

"Diplomatic immunity is going to go down the drain for a minute or two. I have to ask," he said, looking at the couple, "exactly what the both of you were doing when the girl was busy being murdered."

"We were sitting here," Yu explained, "discussing Kuo."

"Who?"

"He is long dead," Laojiu informed him, "not a realistic suspect."

Varley erased the name from his pad. "Go on."

"We heard the thud," said Yu, "and then silence. My

father tried to open the door, and when it wouldn't push in, he pulled it out. The girl fell with it."

"Did you scream? Forgive me, but you don't seem terribly upset by any of this."

Laojiu said, "My daughter has seen atrocities as vile on the North Korean frontier. And for your convenience, we freely waive the immunity granted by our station. I have felt too deeply the bitter pain of death, and resent your implication that we might be involved with this tragedy."

"I'm a cop," Varley explained, "not a Welcome Wagon lady."

"I will, however, tell you where to find your killer."

Varley stared distrustfully at the Chinese. "Okay, Mr. Laojiu. I'm all ears."

"Look in the shadow of your next victim. I have yet to see death turn willingly from a fresh conquest."

Varley folded away his note pad. "Thank you, that's very illuminating. I'm trying to find a lunatic, and you're spouting off like Confucius."

"You flatter me."

Chapman coughed and stepped between them. "Detective Varley, this kind of interview won't bring us any closer to a solution."

"That's true, pal. But if he keeps pushing me, it'll let out a lot of anger that's building inside of me. You better learn this right now, 'cause it looks like we've got a long haul ahead of us. I've got no patience for prima donnas, smartasses, or game players. There's always room in the city jail for one more joker who wants to play bait the cop." Turning to Laojiu, Varley said, "Stick around, Pops, I'll have more questions for you and yours later. Don't take it personally, but the only thing I give a good goddam about right now is wrapping this case up. I hope that's a goal we have in common."

"I'm sure it is," Chapman offered as Varley turned away.

While Chapman apologized to the bemused Chinese for the detective's blunt manner, Varley padded around the room. He played with the few common denominators he had cited to Chapman and then considered one more: that Tally had died in a room where the windows were closed, Cara in a sealed vault, this girl, Bonnie, in a lounge without windows. From what Chapman had revealed about the girl in Beijing, she too had died in an enclosure.

The detective walked pensively into the ladies' room and checked it more carefully then he had on first surveying the scene. There was clearly no way but the door to get in or out. He bent down and ran his hands over the tiles, finding them to be securely in place. The sinks and toilets were torn up or shattered. Looking at them, there was no question in his mind but that there had been an explosion in here, a powerful one.

"Either the Chinese are lying," he murmured, "or this place was hit by a kind of silent explosive I've never heard about." Stepping around the corpse as he left the lavatory, Varley went to the phone and called the precinct to ask that they send a demolition expert.

As Varley completed his call, Dr. Tepper rolled in. The sight of the corpse stopped him cold, as though he'd walked blindly into a brick wall. He had to look away to keep from vomiting. Varley walked over.

"Your little show seems to be cursed, Dr. Tepper. I thought only Egyptian relics had problems like that."

Gasping down what he had just eaten, Tepper said, "Yes, it's ghastly stuff, all of this. I came right over from '21' when I heard."

"Any reason you can think of that someone would want to kill this girl?"

"None, but I didn't really know her. I—oh, hang it, Varley." He flushed. "Isn't it obvious to you what's happening?"

"Another sage," the detective quipped.

"We're faced with some kind of conspiracy, something political in nature or possibly even a religious cult."

"Are you privy to some factual tidbit of which I'm not aware?"

"Of course not. I'm only using common sense."

Varley pursed his lips. "Good for you. The rest of us have to make do with only years of experience. Speaking of which, we novices at the station considered those explanations the night the McGraw girl was killed. But it doesn't wash. No one has come forth to take credit for the killings, and that's always the M. O. in cases of terrorism."

"Maybe this is a new kind of terrorism."

"Sure," Varley replied. He pulled out his pad and pencil. "I want to do a bit of research into the Chinese, since these killings coincided with their arrival. Do you have any kind of file on—"

"Excuse me," Tepper blurted, "but Chapman knows them better than I, and besides, I'm not feeling in an especially investigative mood just now."

"Dr. Tepper," Varley began darkly, "almost twenty-four hours passed between the deaths of each of the first victims. Now, twelve hours after Cara Thomas was torn to bits, we've got another shredded corpse."

"Please, must you be so vivid?"

"And by dinnertime we may have yet another. Maybe it'll be you. Or our killer may start going for two or three victims at a throw to save himself carfare."

"You talk as if I'm enjoying this. Lord, my nerves are shattered!"

Varley jerked his pen toward Bonnie. "So are hers. If you've got anything on Laojiu and his charming daughter, I want to see them. Clippings, bios, press releases, all of it."

Tepper sighed, "If word gets out that you suspect them of murder, this show becomes a white elephant."

"My heart bleeds. Shall we go to your office?"

Tepper nodded and told Varley to follow him. The detective asked Webster Hall to have the explosives people sent directly to him. Then he hurried after the browbeaten curator. Laojiu, Yu, and Chapman left moments later, feeling little better than the detective.

Waterside Towers was Linda's favorite place on earth. Her parents moved there in 1973, a year after Linda had moved out, or run away, as her mother had described it, to live with Jon, the art director of a top glamour magazine. The live-in situation lasted fourteen fiery months and was responsible for turning Linda against any relationship that encroached so thoroughly on her privacy. She knew it wasn't fair that Grant should suffer for wrongs committed by an insensitive jerk like Jon, but the concrete had set and was eroding very slowly.

Unfortunately, Linda could not afford to live by herself after the breakup and moved into the one-bedroom apartment her parents had taken at this new three-building complex. Linda knew that by returning, she would be forced to endure several months of "I told you so" from her father and being dragged to Sunday mass by her mother. After a time, though, no one spoke directly of her sins, and they were once more a loving, quarreling, but sharing family. Then came the museum post in 1976 and the final break with her home, along with the downward slide in her relationship with her parents.

But Waterside Towers apartment 20D was still a precious place to her, the house that had offered her sanctuary after the debacle with Jon. As night suffused the clear spring skies over Manhattan, with skyscrapers winking on their thousand lights, she lay on the couch and stared out the bank of windows. From beneath the panes the air circulator filled the room with its comforting, almost narcotic drone, a humming that used to put her to sleep more effectively than any chemical transquilizer.

She loved this sleek but cozy refuge above the world's confusion; she hoped her mother would never give it up.

Mrs. Bergeni was asleep in her armchair, where she'd been sitting all day. Linda looked from her to the butcher-block clock on the kitchen wall.

It was almost six-thirty and Linda rose stiffly. She'd been on the sofa reading and watching game shows for most of the day, ever since Dr. Jelkowitz had come and gone over twelve hours before. She'd found it almost comical how helpful he'd tried to be, telling Linda and her mother with the sobriety of a priest that their beloved Ernesto would probably not be waking from this sleep. She'd felt like remarking, "That's why they call it a deathbed," but decided that the quip would have exceeded good taste. Linda dealt with the impending tragedy by amusing herself; her mother had escaped into sleep.

Both of us folding into ourselves, she thought, *rather than helping the other. Even now, it's too late to change the pattern of twenty-eight years.*

Linda paused to look in on her father. The bedroom was dark and utterly quiet save for the long, labored breaths that were the fifty-two-year-old's frail tether to life. His rapidly failing strength troubled her more than his inevitable collapse. He had always been such a robust man; cancer had punched the stuffing out of him.

It's bad enough life has to end, but for it to leak away like this, without dignity—a quick death is better. She thought of Tally then, and of Cara Thomas. *Better*, though *no more pleasant in the area of self-esteem. The only way to beat that humiliation is to kick and scream all the way to the grave, which is what I plan to do. And if there's any way to keep on kicking after that, Linda Marie Bergen is going to do that, too.*

Linda reinforced her conviction by standing beside her father's collapsing shell a moment longer; then she stepped into the bathroom. While she was spreading on lipstick and fluffing her hair, she heard her mother sniff. Linda finished the application and then returned to ease her mother back into reality. She refused to apologize for the fact that her efforts, even in this, were on her own behalf: The more comfortable her mother was, the less foul her temper was likely to be. The investment of effort seemed reasonable though not obligatory to Linda.

Mrs. Bergeni insisted that she remain in her chair but at the same time wanted a bowl of vegetable soup. Reading between the lines, Linda discerned and resented the order that she go make it.

"You're too good to say please?" Linda sneered under her breath as she headed toward the kitchen. She spilled a can of soup into a pot. While she was stirring it and trying to think tranquil thoughts, the doorman called to announce Grant.

Chapman was a welcome but hardly cheering sight. After kissing Linda at the door, he told her about what had happened to Bonnie Franklin. Linda's fears, made remote by the security of Waterside, bubbled swiftly to the surface.

"There is a plot," she charged, her words amplified as they bounced around the bare corridor. Hearing them spoken seemed to feed Linda's sense of urgency. "So what do we do now? Pretend that it'll go away like the sniffles or just get the hell out of New York for a while?"

"I can't go, but I won't try to talk you out of leaving."

"That's caring of you," Linda interrupted. "And if something happens to you, do I console myself with memories of your nobility? Does the exhibition really mean that much to you?"

Chapman didn't feel like defending his priorities and said, "There's a nut running loose, maybe a couple of them. Whether that nut is part of a conspiracy or not, I want to be here in case I can be of some use."

"Sure, just climb on a line and dangle like bait! For once why don't you think of yourself?"

"Look, we're pretty sure this thing started in Beijing with

the death of a Chinese girl at the American embassy. It's fair to speculate that running away won't help anyone worth a damn. Leave if it makes you feel better, but I think the smart thing for us to do is to stay together as much as possible. The four women were alone at the time of their deaths, and that may have some bearing on who is or is not a victim. Something's got to turn up soon, and Varley thinks that when it does, the killer will either vanish or come out in the open. Either way, I want to be here when something breaks."

"Even if it's my neck," Linda complained.

"What's new here?" Chapman asked, changing the subject.

"Grant, I want to go out for dinner. I want to go somewhere to sit and relax and put everything from my mind. Please, I really need it."

Chapman's jaw tightened and Linda backed away behind hands held up as though holding him off.

"I know that expression, Grant, and I'm not up for one of those you can't run away from life lectures. If I am running away, it's because I need it. I don't need any other justification than that."

Chapman turned away. "I'm not here to lecture anyone," he said, drawing a deep breath to remain calm. Still wearing his trench coat, he walked into the apartment and bid good evening to Mrs. Bergeni. Linda swore and hurried off toward the kitchen when she heard the soup sputter, and Chapman entered hard upon her heels.

"Linda, it isn't that I don't sympathize with you—"

"Spare me," Linda said. "I know you don't agree with the way I handle things, but it works for me. I can't be a martyr the way you can."

"Doing what's right doesn't make me a martyr."

"Nowadays," she snorted, "just doing what isn't wrong makes a person a martyr." Linda stared into the soup. "Anyway," she said as she stirred it, "I'll be ready when I'm finished with this. I've got to get away from her, from the murders, from all the craziness."

"Why don't you move in next to Wayne? He's beyond pain."

Linda thrust the spoon into the pot. "It's going to be one of those evenings, I can tell. You're going to be snide because you think I'm copping out, and I'm going to get more and more pissed off while you stay calm and easy, which is going to piss me off even more, and—shit, Grant, I don't need any of this, I really don't."

"Fine," he said softly, looking directly at her. "When you find that you do need something, like me, you know the telephone number."

"You're leaving?"

"You're driving me away."

"Well, you poor, persecuted son of a bitch! What happened to all that crap about us staying within earshot until this museum cutup is caught?"

"Your parents are here." He tried to sound authoritative. "You'll be safe enough."

Linda's eyes narrowed, and she hurled herself around to tend the soup. Quietly, Chapman showed himself from the apartment.

He felt no guilt about leaving, only disappointment. After crossing the pedestrian walk that spanned the FDR Drive to Twenty-fifth Street, he hailed a cab on Third Avenue and rode home. Twice he considered turning it around and trying to make up for the argument; twice he grew angry just thinking about it. Settling back into the seat, he couldn't help but wonder if midnight tonight would bring the number of killings to five. He believed that Linda would be safe at the apartment; all the same, he resolved to phone her when he got home just to make sure.

The churning darkness was receding, lay almost behind him as he drank down the last tendrils of blood. His glowing eyes scanned the strange world that spread before him. Soon he and his army would enter that world, and their long-dormant arms would thrill with fresh battle; the glory that had been his would return.

His strength and appetite aroused, the Madjan cast out his spirit for another Woman of Peace who was worthy of receiving it . . .

CHAPTER TEN

LAOJIU PACED THE SHADOWED ALCOVE, his white-slippered feet hardly making a sound as they bore him on his small mental treadmill. Yu was sleeping in their quarters down the hallway; as usual, Kuo had kept the professor awake and reflective into the waning hours of the evening.

His hands were tucked into his long black robe, his face drawn and sallow. He had read all but the astrologer's last scroll now, and he was profoundly disturbed. Tonight's revelation came from Kuo's recounting of a ritual to honor the Madjan. The service, he said, was conducted using human blood, a fact that Laojiu had known. Kuo himself had remarked that even the scholars in his previous retreat honored their gods with blood. What alarmed him was the regularity. The astrologer had made these notations at the beginning of the five-year war. During these times of trial and sacrifice, the Madjan was offered a goblet of blood each day. The frequency was increased only when the tide of combat went against Emperor Ch'en.

Laojiu lingered by the desk to reread his notes. " 'There is so much blood about, spilled on the battlefield. Yet Ch'en adds to it willingly by hacking at these young Women of Peace. The priest, wisest of the fools, says their blood forges the red chariot which the Madjan rides from the void. By now this must be a mighty carriage indeed, for they slaughter a battery of girls daily. One day I hope to ask the god, *Why*?' "

The archaeologist stared with red-stained eyes at the ceiling. "You leave me more riddles than solutions," he admonished Kuo. "You attempted to demythologize the earth dragon when you wrote, 'Whether the earth trembles and wakes the dragon, or the dragon shakes the earth when he stirs, the results for we who crawl upon the surface are dire.' You recognized that earthquakes may have occurred naturally, dared to doubt the long-held belief in this creature. Yet you persisted in your faith that the Madjan was *real*. Why? Why were you as blinded as those you ridiculed when it came to the Madjan?" Laojiu eyed the scroll. "Or were you persuaded by evidence? These Women of Peace. Help me to understand, Kuo. Are we today seeing their like again? Is that possible? Can it be that your science is right and mine is wrong, that there is a world of which you are aware that I dismiss as the fantasy of a child or a religious zealot?" Laojiu sat down heavily and began to unwind Kuo's thin final scroll. "My last clue, and how I grieve that it is such. Work barely begun before Ch'en-shimm fell into the earth, writings which offer me one last chance to discover—"

Laojiu shook his head. "I mourn what I do not possess, yet have I the capacity to believe what I may find within the text before me? Have I an open enough mind to draw the logical if not the rational conclusion, accept the oneness of the ritual of the Women of Peace and the tragedy we have seen this week?" He adjusted his spectacles and turned to the writing. "Let us hope so," he said as he began reading the account of the last days of Ch'en-shimm.

Yu was in a deep sleep, dragged there by exhaustion and kept there by thick, comforting dreams that protected her from the lingering horror of what she had witnessed that day, the girl sprawled like a slaughtered animal amid her pumping blood.

She was with a young soldier on a blue lake, in a lush green setting that had never existed for her but that she had always desired. The waters were calm, unstirred by wind or current, and Yu had just snuggled closer to her olive-garbed lover, when she became suddenly very much aware of the sun. It was on her cheek, warm and then hot and then burning hot. She turned to avert her cheek and opened her eyes briefly; the soldier was gone.

The sun beat more fiercely with each passing instant, and Yu decided to cool off in the water, which was where she presumed her companion must have gone. But before she could jump, a queer haze of yellow sunlight had settled on the lake. It was followed by a gurgling sound from the water at the back of the boat. The woman bent over the side to see what was the matter, but the face she saw in the red bubbles was not her own. It was Bonnie Franklin, wide-eyed and covered with oozing blood.

Yu recoiled with shock. After a few seconds had passed, confusion gave way to disbelief, and she ventured another look overboard. Bonnie's face was gone, and Yu's own clear features reflected back at her from the greenish lake. She smiled, relieved that it had been only her imagination. Just then the water revealed the soldier rising behind her, an ax raised high above his head. She spun, expecting to find nothing, just as he brought the blade down at her. Yu threw herself against the soldier's feet, and they both fell to the bottom of the boat.

Without quite knowing how it had happened, Yu found her lover on top of her. His hands thrilled her as they ran up and down her side and more urgently across her thigh. She forgave what no doubt had been a joke on his part or a hallucination. Yet the young man making love to her now was not quite as she had remembered him. She tried to wriggle from beneath him, but as her small hands pushed out, it was not flesh they touched. She opened her eyes and saw a leaden mass that was at once alien and familiar.

The yellow air exploded into crackling sheets of flame as the soldier looked down at her, a grim, evil caricature of himself carved in stone. Burning and unable to breathe, Yu clawed from the bottom of the boat and from her nightmare.

She awoke, but the horror refused to dissipate. Her eyes flickered open and found the room at the Consulate alive, crawling with hot gray smoke. Her first thought was that the building was on fire, though she noticed that the smoke didn't billow upward so much as surge from all about the room, gathering at the foot of the bed and carving itself into a solid, dreary figure. At that same instant, two blood-red orbs began to glow from within the solidifying terror. It loomed closer, was upon her as the soldier had been in her dream, crushing and passionless and palpably cruel.

"Ma-mad—" she screamed, but the word clung in her throat. With the pain of the entity's assault, Yu's arms flailed out, her hand striking the nightstand and hurling the telephone to the floor.

The din floated down the quiet hall to Laojiu's study. He looked up and listened; there was a second crash, and he spun from the desk, shuffling quickly along the corridor.

The bedroom was black, and Laojiu flicked on the wall switch. Light shot away from the floor like a judgment, from the broken glass lamp that lay at the foot of the nightstand between their twin beds. The stark glow beneath the dented shade cast Yu in a sharp, devilish light whose suggestion of hell was heightened by Yu's writhing on the blood-spotted sheets.

The girl felt weightless when the light flashed, and her tremors stopped at that moment. The pressure and the heat, the pain and the tart odor of incense rolled back into the dissipating fog and in the span of a lone heartbeat shrank to a pinpoint. Freed from the awful presence, Yu screamed.

The professor scurried to his frantic daughter, ignoring the few cuts she had somehow sustained on her face, arms, and midriff. Scooping her up, he cuddled her to him, her arms encircling him as she began to cry. It was a more violent outpouring than the archaeologist had ever seen from Yu, and his mind raced to its own explanation. He had expected a volcanic release such as this for quite some time. She had not let down her stern front in the many months this exhibition had been talked about and planned; whatever small thought or dream or event had triggered this, it was past due, and as he held her, he felt more joy than concern.

After Yu had sobbed away the crest of her agony, Laojiu set her against the brass headboard and then sat back from her. He looked more carefully now at her wounds, and he used the hem of the bedsheet to dab at the cuts. The worst of these was on her thigh, where her pajamas had been torn; examining it in the poor light, Laojiu thought it seemed less a gash than a rupture. He ministered to it in either case, at the same time trying gently to draw Yu from her trauma.

"The body looks after itself," he said soothingly. "This has happened for a reason."

Yu shook her head violently, though she said nothing, more concerned about coming to grips with what had happened than with reporting it. More than a minute passed before she felt rational enough to speak.

"He was here, in the room with me."

"Who was here?" her father soothed.

"The Madjan. It was he who did this to me." She indicated the cuts on her arms and legs. "He would have slain me had you not come when you did."

Laojiu stared at her and continued mechanically to dab at the blood. "I saw no one," he said at last.

"You are not in the thick of combat. I begin to understand," she said not so much to him as for her own enlightenment. "The Women of Peace—their blood is his strength."

"So we read this evening in Kuo's document. I suspect that the astrologer's vivid writings are at the root of your nightmares."

"No! I tell you the Madjan walks the earth, his spirit feeding on blood, renewing himself for a fresh encounter with the earth dragon."

"You believe this?" he asked, struggling to reinforce his own failing disbelief.

"Father, had you arrived any later than you did, I would be dead now. Crushed, just like the other women. The Madjan drew blood, acted in complete accord with the ritual of Ch'enshimm. It's fantastic, of course, but there is no other explanation. I know what I saw. And he brought with him the heat of the basin, the smell of incense, the same sensations I felt in the museum shortly before Bonnie was slain." She looked hurriedly toward the clock, which lay face up on the floor. "It is ten minutes past midnight. In the morning, we shall hear of a woman having died a few minutes later. She is being murdered even as we speak."

"This is madness."

"I am not mad! I swear on my mother's grave that the Madjan was in this room."

Laojiu reached down and raised the shattered lamp. "This is your attacker." He held up a fragment of the broken base; there was blood on its ragged edge. "Events and exhaustion both have colored our judgment. A few minutes ago I found myself thinking similar thoughts to those you have mentioned. But even the most open mind must recognize what is possible and what is not. The universe is run by natural law, which this violates."

"You presume to know all of nature's laws."

"I assume no such knowledge. I simply have yet to find one law contradict another, and what you suggest contradicts many." He lay the bedsheet aside and took her hands in his. "There is a part of me which wants desperately to believe this, Yu. Upon my very breath it does. In the midst of the bloodshed, the agony—to prove such a thing would actually fill me with joy. It says that this world is not the end to life, that there is another sphere in which your mother may dwell, even alongside my friend Kuo. You know how quickly I would embrace this notion if there were the remotest chance of it being so. It is not so, Yu. It is the hopeful, frightened conclusion of tired and frustrated minds."

Yu's eyes continued to bore into those of her father and then fell. With the passage of each minute, the immediacy of her vision ebbed and with it her conviction that any of it had ever happened. "Surely," she said at last, "midnight is not the time to try to postulate any new idea."

"We are in agreement there." Laojiu smiled. He retired to the bathroom to dampen a towel and cleanse Yu's wounds properly. After putting her to bed the professor retired as well, his mind too cluttered with fact and fancy to tell them apart. He hoped that the morning light would dispel the evening's long shadows.

Still, as the archaeologist lay on his back in bed, staring into the blackness, he found himself possessed by a frightening thought: How well would logic serve him if the day brought word of a new death clocked at a quarter past midnight?

He put the idea from his mind by playfully allowing that there was an afterlife and drawing up a list of questions he would like to ask Kuo. His concentration crumbling beneath the burden, Laojiu slid into sleep.

Linda sat in a chair in the living room, alternately dozing and listening to the tenuous, shallow breathing that came from her father's bedroom. The phone rang; she ignored it, as she'd done for hours. Linda had no desire to talk to Grant, to hear either his self-righteous brandishments or his mewling apologies. She began, as she had often in recent weeks, to reconsider their relationship. Linda was glad that she hadn't married the man. As a husband, Grant never would have walked out on her the way he had, and she really didn't want to be around him tonight. She had been too tired to debate any issue at all, unlike the constantly inquisitive Grant. Linda knew she'd probably feel differently in the morning; she always did. For now, though, all she wanted to do—

Linda sat erect. She felt a flushing heat roll from her chest to her head, causing perspiration to leak from her upper lip and forehead. Fearful that she might be about to suffer a recurrence of whatever had hit her the last two nights, Linda rushed to the bathroom and swallowed two aspirins. Realizing on her return that she had been seated near the radiator, which had just kicked on, she decided to sit in her father's room. There at least she could feel that the death watch was more nobly a vigil.

Walking over to her mother's chair and pulling her blanket up under her chin, Linda yanked a bridge chair from the hall closet and perched herself at the foot of her father's bed.

The radio came on, pumping Chopin into the morning. Chapman sat up and rubbed his eyes with the warm heels of his hands. He squinted into the slate of light that streamed through the window and let his gaze drop to the black phone on the night table.

"Screw you, too," he snarled, and instantly regretted giving in to his temper. Linda hadn't answered his calls because she didn't want to argue, not because she didn't want to talk to him. He had to learn not to take people's actions so personally.

As Chapman stared at the phone, it jangled, startling him. He answered at once. "Good morning, Katherina. How are you?"

"Chapman, it's Warren Varley," the detective's voice rasped. "Sorry to mess up your love life, but I want to see you and Laojiu for breakfast this morning." The detective continued before Chapman could assemble his thoughts. "I've just got a call from the state police. Another girl, also alone, was murdered around midnight. She lived in Rockville Center and had been to your damn exhibit yesterday."

"My God." Chapman shuddered. "This is more than just coincidence; it has to be!"

"You said it, not me. In a nutshell, I can't afford to play

any more games. I want to meet with you two on neutral ground because I've got some hard questions to put to your friend. Can you get him over to Hickory House on Park and Thirty-second by eight o'clock?"

"That's over an hour from now. Sure," Chapman said. "I can try, anyway."

"Good."

"Tell me, though, is he a suspect or are you asking general questions?"

"Both," Varley admitted just before the click.

Gathering himself up for the task of winning Laojiu's cooperation, Chapman dialed the number of the Chinese Consulate. While punching the buttons, he paused and started from the top; this time he tapped out the Bergeni number. After two rings, Linda answered.

"Wake you?" he asked in a monotone.

Linda waited a beat and then said that he had.

"Where'd you sleep, on the couch?"

"In a chair near my father's bed."

"I called last night."

"And I didn't answer, or I'd've told you that you're rude and selfish and probably would have hung up."

"There are two sides to every story," he said evenly.

"Yeah, but mine is the one I've got to live with twenty-four hours a day. Grant," she said with an edge of disgust, "I don't want to start the day like this. I'll have my fill of arguing when my mother gets up. Can we talk about this later, like over lunch or something?"

"Linda, I want you to stay put until I come for you." Linda asked why, and Chapman explained about the latest killing. He went on, "I don't mean to worry you."

"Too late!"

"If the pattern holds, someone else will die within the next few hours. Promise me you won't go out until I can get over there."

"You'll have to eat whatever there is in the house."

"Fine. See you soon." Chapman held on for a moment longer, trying to decide whether he should apologize for what had happened the night before. Even though he didn't consider himself to be at fault, he hated leaving the air murky like this. However, before he could say anything, Linda had hung up.

Feeling fitful pangs of anxiety, he resumed calling Laojiu and prayed that among the three of them, they could make some sense of this blind carnage.

As he listened to the grim tidings, both logic and reason drained from Laojiu's mind, leaving it numb. The arguments were all against him, and as much as he could not believe them, he could no longer deny them. It was morning. Things looked clearer by far than they had the previous night, but not in the direction he had anticipated.

Yu listened to the terse conversation and said nothing. Dressing, she said that she would like to go to the Chinese bookstore down the street. Laojiu refused, insisting that she remain with him.

Chapman arrived by cab ten minutes later, after which he, Laojiu, and Yu walked to their appointment downtown. It was a warm spring morning, the sort of day that made one treasure life and feel profoundly secure in the temperate embrace of nature. Chapman and the Chinese felt none of that joy. Streams of New Yorkers flowed by, many clutching newspapers that announced the latest killing. With the trust that had grown between them over the past few days, the three discussed openly their fears and sifted through and then discarded a multitude of theories.

"There's only one thing of which we can be certain," Chapman was saying as they crossed Forty-second Street at Park Avenue. "Our culprit seems to be proficient enough at killing. That should point us in some direction, toward a soldier, a member of some secret service group, someone with experience."

"Deductively, your thinking seems sound," Laojiu said cautiously.

"It's got to be something like that. Who but a government agent would have entry to the places where our people have been killed? The embassy, and a day later the museum in order to tail Tally McGraw, then the NBC library and the lounge where Bonnie was killed, and now a college dorm where everyone has to be announced before they can go upstairs."

"Have you ruled out a ghost or a poltergeist, or even a Golem?" Laojiu asked.

Chapman eyed him curiously, thrown by the seriousness of the archaeologist's query. "They fall somewhere in the category of that woman I told you about, the one who claimed that God told her to kill someone." Chapman could see that his answer was not what Laojiu had been seeking. Turning the question around, he said, "More to the point, I haven't ruled it out because I haven't considered it as a possibility. Should I?"

Laojiu weighed his response with unusual care. "If you will permit me a metaphor, I am held fast on one pole of a magnet, unable to approach the other pole regardless of how I struggle."

"Meaning you want to believe but can't."

"Meaning," the archaeologist explained, "that scientists must not only draw upon their own experiences but those of others. You are a bright man, Chapman. I would like to tap your more wistful side."

"Are you asking if I believe in the boogey man?"

"Imagine that this case does not exist. Answer rhetorically. Clinically."

"I've never given it much thought," Chapman said carefully, "but I can accept the possibility of a preternatural consciousness. On a scale of one to ten, I'd put these specters and demons in the middle, between UFOs, which I believe in, and God, which I do not."

"Why UFOs?" Laojiu asked.

"Because they make sense to me."

"Explain, please. I have reasons for asking."

Chapman felt just a little foolish as he said, "Well, though it wouldn't surprise me to find out that UFOs are the works of alien beings of some sort, I really think they're the ships of chrononauts, time travelers from our own future looking into the past. I don't lose sleep over it, but I wonder about it now and then on those long transatlantic trips."

Laojiu reflected for a moment and then said, more to himself than aloud, "It's interesting. Your imagination is healthier than my own, yet even you are not convinced."

"Convinced of what? That a ghost is behind these killings?"

"Correct."

Chapman dragged a hand through his hair. "I'm dubious, I'll say that much. Although," he said, throwing up his hands, "in fairness to the spirit world, I can think of a number of other things which logic dictates shouldn't exist. Emotion is one. It's independent of and immune to just about every physical force I can think of. Dreams are another. They suggest a consciousness living inside of you, one that functions without your cooperation or consent. And, sometimes, I still can't believe there's such a thing as sex. Before I was twelve, nothing could have convinced me that such a thing as an orgasm existed. I lived one third of my life convinced that in being bruised, tickled, or just plain tired I'd felt about every physical sensation there was. Twenty-three years later, I have to keep my mind open a crack to the possibility of being surprised again." Chapman fell silent for a moment, then said with a capricious turn of his mouth, "When I was a boy, you couldn't convince me that there was no such things as goblins. They were as real as the closet in which I knew they were hiding or the bed under whose mattress I was convinced they were lurking. I believed in them, sometimes even spoke with them, until an older cousin of mine heard me mumbling in the dark and told me I was crazy. I'd always looked up to her, and what she said was like a pan of cold water in the face. Chased away the ghost-believer in me nice and proper."

"What if you had resisted her?" Laojiu asked. "Consider, academically, what you might believe in nearly a quarter-century later."

"That ghosts and demons are real?" Chapman grinned. "I doubt it. I've never been fond of people calling me crazy. I take it too much to heart."

"So did I at one time." Chapman grabbed the preoccupied scientist by the elbow to prevent him from crossing Thirty-sixth Street against the light. Laojiu went on, "Twenty-two years ago, the head of the archaeology department at the university where I taught told me I'd never find Ch'en-shimm. I did not concur and made a private commitment that when I discovered the lost city, thereafter I would support my own convictions above all. It was a reactionary attitude I had then; it goes without saying that no one can be right all the time. But I believe, still, that nothing should ever be dismissed out of hand. Not the power of human will and certainly not the extent and form of nature's will."

The threesome walked in thoughtful silence to the restaurant. Chapman held the door for the Chinese, watching Laojiu as he followed Yu inside. Chapman had to admit that of all the people he had met during his years in the diplomatic service, this man was at once the most brilliant, the most prepossessing, and the most refreshingly honest.

As the trio made their way through the crowded eatery to a table behind the adjoining horseshoe counters, Detective Varley arrived. He scooted after them, and they all sat down together.

"Sorry I'm late, but I got a call as I was leaving. News about Tally McGraw."

"A lead?" Chapman asked hopefully.

"Not exactly." Varley signaled for the waitress and ordered coffee all around. "But it's fitting that word came as I was leaving for here. It'll save me a lot of needless questioning. First things first. The call I got was from the coroner. The forensic team studied the tissue and bone samples where her limbs had been severed." The waitress arrived with their coffees. "Turns out her arms and legs weren't exactly torn off. It was as though something that weighed a ton or more was placed on her—didn't fall but was *placed*—" he lowered his palm slowly to reinforce the difference "—causing our girl to burst outward."

"Why the distinction between some heavy object falling and being placed?" Chapman asked.

"Because Tally, and I presume the others, were not mashed. It's more like they were *popped*."

While Chapman tried to digest what he had heard, recognizing that that was all he might digest this morning, the waitress asked impassively for their breakfast order. Chapman passed, Laojiu requested a grapefruit, Yu selected cornflakes, and Varley asked for the breakfast special. When the waitress had shuffled off, Varley shifted his gaze back to Chapman.

"So," he said as he sipped his coffee, "while the information is interesting, it doesn't help much. It leaves us with Goliath and Dumbo the elephant for suspects."

"I still can't believe that's right." Chapman shook his head.

Laojiu offered, "Seldom does fact cater to our desires."

Varley agreed as he withdrew his note pad. "Dr. Laojiu," he went on, "I had a number of questions for you, most of which are now irrelevant."

"Pertaining to my own guilt, no doubt?"

Varley answered noncommittally, "Pertaining to what now appear to be dead ends. So I'll keep it simple. First, do you have any colleagues whom you would categorize as jealous of your success? Second, more for your daughter than for you, has anyone called up or come over and made what might be described as unseemly or antagonistic remarks?"

Laojiu slid his coffee to one side untouched. He folded his hands on the table. "I have many envious colleagues, I am sure, though none who is a murderer."

"Would you mind giving me their names? I'd like to look into their whereabouts."

"I would mind very much. I have already said that they are not murderers."

"Yes, but that doesn't rule out sabotage, rape, and vandalism," Varley returned, undaunted. "I can't worry about hurt feelings when women are being torn to shreds right and left." The detective continued while their breakfast was served. "You all saw Bonnie—mashed like a squirrel under a car. I'll settle for a few insulted archaeologists over a Bonnie any day."

When the waitress had set the food down and gone, Chapman turned to the professor. "I can check these people out very sub rosa through the State Department. Even your own government needn't know why we're asking. I can tell them we're interested in some sort of archaeological symposium."

"Now we're cookin'!" Varley chimed. "Good thinking, Grant. I'll withdraw the question if you two will agree to take care of it."

"Better us than him," Chapman whispered to the scientist.

Laojiu breathed deeply and then sat quietly staring at his hands. After several seconds he nodded.

Varley added, "You might also see if any of them knows a sumo wrestler. Those guys are pretty hefty as I recall."

"Sumo is a Japanese sport," Yu offered.

Varley shot back, "Grant knows what I mean. You must have something like that in China." He pushed his pad aside and dug into his breakfast. "Now then." He looked at Yu. "As to threatening remarks and the like?"

"Last night I was assaulted," she said calmly.

The detective's face froze. After a long pause, his jaw began to move again, chewing down a piece of egg. "Who and when, and—damn it, why didn't you say something before? Grant, did you know about this?"

"Not exactly." He should have surmised something in the archaeologist's questions. Grant was annoyed that he'd not been astute enough to pick up on it.

Yu said, "Knowing about it does not matter, because you cannot stop him. Our quarry is the Madjan, and he will not be turned aside by mortal skills."

"The Madjan," Varley snickered. "The stone monster from the museum, that's who we're fighting." He sat back and noticed Chapman shift uneasily in his seat. "Grant, this young lady or some other unfortunate woman may be a hunk of hamburger in the city morgue come afternoon. Will you please tell her that this is not a joke!"

"I don't think she's joking," Chapman ventured somewhat sheepishly.

"Of course not. And I'm working for Darth Vader." He ran a hand across his face and then regarded Yu. "Be serious, lady. I'm too busy for—"

"My daughter had a nightmare about the Madjan," Laojiu interrupted, "and she is convinced that the dream was real. Without debating that particular matter, please note that these girls, each of them, were killed in the same fashion as the sacrificial victims of the Madjan. Kuo wrote that none ever laid a hand on these girls, yet they were at death 'as a bladder which, filled too fully, had burst.'"

"That Kuo guy again," said a suddenly pensive Varley. "Maybe our killer read Kuo and is reenacting the ritual. Who'd he write for?"

While the detective scribbled his observations in the note pad, Laojiu said, "I and my daughter are the only ones who have read Kuo."

"Nonsense," Varley barked. "You just don't remember having told someone about the ritual or publishing an excerpt of it in a paper."

"I remember quite well every moment I have spent since devoting my life and career to Ch'en-shimm."

"Grant," Varley looked away from the stubborn archaeologist, "I'll need the names of those other scientists as soon as possible. When can you have them?"

"By the afternoon, I suppose."

"Good enough. In the meantime," he said cocking a thumb at the Chinese, "don't let the two of them out of your sight. I'm going to send a few men over to the Consulate to keep an eye on it round the clock." He finished his eggs and pitched his napkin onto the plate. "A jealous rival, that's the key!"

"You *think* it's the key," Chapman qualified.

Varley looked suspiciously at the State Department official. "Come on, you don't believe this nonsense, do you?"

"He doesn't disbelieve," Laojiu interjected, "which is much the way I feel."

Varley nodded and finished his coffee. He looked at his watch. "Grant, didn't you say that you had to check in with Tepper at eight-forty-five?" Chapman looked questioningly at the detective. "Phone's in the back. I'll walk you over, since coffee goes right through me."

Picking up the detective's sledgehammer hint, Chapman excused himself. Yu watched as the two men walked together down the narrow flight of stairs at the rear of the cafeteria. When they stopped outside the lavatory, Chapman turned to his companion.

"I know what you're going to say—"

"No, you don't, Grant. Listen, as nutty as this case has made you, that man's sick! He's gone off the deep end from sitting alone in that ivory tower of his for so many years. I want him out of the country."

"What?"

"You heard me. I want him out as soon as possible."

"Those extra police?"

"You guessed it, to keep him in at night, not to keep the Madjan out. The Madjan!" he laughed. "Nuts, if I recorded that conversation, I could have the crackpot committed. I pretended not to suspect him, but I'm convinced he's covering for himself or for someone else, and at the moment I'm betting it's him. The girl died at the embassy shortly after he left; girls start dying all over New York shortly after he arrives. He didn't want us to take his goddam statues in the first place, and now he's paying us back."

"But how? You said yourself the girls are—"

"Popping. So maybe Laojiu found out some kind of secret that the ancient priests of China used to convince their followers that some clunky statue was raping women. Anyway, that's the hunch I'm going on. I want you to go back there and stick by him like glue. He seems to trust you. Find a way to eat with him, maybe do research with him, shit with him if you have to. Just don't leave him or his stuck-up daughter alone." Varley shook his head. "I hate being jerked off, and he's a pro. The sooner you realize that, the sooner we'll have this mess wrapped up. And I promise, Grant, that's going to be soon. The commissioner's on my ass because the mayor's on his ass because the newspapers are on his ass. You get my drift?"

Chapman nodded. "And then there are the victims."

Varley ignored the crack and reached into his pocket. He folded three dollar bills into Chapman's hand. "For my breakfast. I'm going out through the kitchen. If I see that phony bastard again, I may not be able to control the urge to arrest him."

"You know, Detective, I can't help but be reminded about the Bill of Rights, that part about being innocent until proven guilty."

Varley snorted. "Seems to me that kind of trusting attitude got you into hot water once before."

Chapman's jaw clenched and his eyes narrowed. "You're a bastard, Varley. Has anyone ever *not* told you that?"

"Sorry, but you've got to understand we're dealing with some heavy-duty crime here. We can afford to handle muggers and punks with that kind of kid gloves attitude, but homicide is shoot first, ask questions later. All that stuff you learned in Criminal Law 101 is bullshit." He yanked out his handkerchief and blew energetically. "Anyway, make my apologies to one and all. I'll talk to you later in the day."

"Wait a minute. I told Linda I'd stop by this morning."

"Where is she?"

"Waterside, apartment 20D."

"I'll have someone stop by and check the place out, make sure it's secure. My guess is she'll be all right, as long as she's with someone."

Chapman thanked the detective and walked slowly upstairs, folding the dollar bills over and over in his hand, considering this latest weight on his conscience. It just wasn't in him to spy, not on Laojiu, his Asiatic colleagues, or anyone else. He realized he was going to have to fight Varley on this.

Slipping the money into his pocket, Chapman rejoined Laojiu, who was staring at the unfamiliar bustle behind the counter. *Is he staring at the waitress?* Chapman couldn't help wondering. *Did he eye the dead girls as carefully? And while I'm at it, who's to say that Laojiu isn't innocent and Varley is the killer?*

Although he thought about it briefly, Chapman didn't

believe that about Varley. He didn't think Laojiu was a murderer either. But the option?

A rampaging god! Open mind, my foot. Wanting to believe in the occult and actually believing in it are two different things. Those statues have got you spooked, and if they've done that to you after only a few days, imagine their impact on Laojiu after a couple of years. No wonder he's jumping at shadows!

But the grim face of the Madjan stayed in his mind as though it had been branded there. And as they finished their breakfast, talking pleasantly if superficially about the museum and exhibit matters, Chapman actually found himself frightened. The Madjan's eyes seemed to blaze to life in Chapman's mind, and he shuddered as a gust of warm air blew past him.

The hooves drummed to his rear, clapping nearer and nearer as he filled with the lifeblood of his victim. Behind them rose the shrieks of those who had honored him through the millennia and who would serve him again once the barrier had been breached.

The darkness had been all but conquered, and soon, very soon, he should turn his might upon the world that had so violently wronged him. His eyes like flaming beacons searched the hell of his new temple for yet another Woman of Peace . . .

CHAPTER ELEVEN

GAIL FISHER WAVED across the hall at Chapman. She presumed it was he, standing behind Laojiu's table at the museum, looking less movie-star handsome than his voice intimated but not the sort of man she would ever turn away. Playfully, he saluted the woman. She could read his lips mouthing, "Who's answering my phone?"

"Lunch hour!" the short, thin redhead yelled, though he hadn't heard her, distracted by a question from Yu. She continued to file through the exhibit.

Gail was glad she had come here. Chapman had sent her a pass, and she had wanted to see the statues and also see him at least once in her life. Besides, she told herself as she admired Chapman once more between admiring the figures, she never really did anything constructive with her lunch break. An hour a day, five days a week, over two hundred fifty hours a year. Time like that should be used for more than just a deli sandwich and chitchat around the switchboard. Her only regret as she exited from the hall was that she had been in line between an old man and a gay couple. What she'd wanted above all was to show some tall, rugged man what a connoisseur of art she was.

Gail paused at the museum map in the corridor. The dinosaurs were on the floor just above. She'd probably find only young kids and decaying professors up there. The planetarium? Drug freaks and eggheads. The African dioramas? The thought of all those poor, stuffed, furry creatures put her off.

Maybe I'll meet someone on the subway, she decided as she left the museum, pausing to buy a pretzel from a vendor on the corner of Seventy-ninth Street.

The train let her off at Forty-third Street, and she headed for her small office in a Ninth Avenue loft. Gail cursed the vendor as she entered the elevator—his pretzel had given her acute indigestion and made her dizzy. She managed to press the button for the seventh floor where the doors didn't open so much as burst into the office, spraying metal and the remains of Gail Fisher about the reception area.

Chapman took lunch with Yu. Her father had agreed to sit for a series of photo portraits with Tepper. Chapman had let him go, deciding that Varley's suspicions were way off base. In addition, without further prodding, Laojiu had agreed to have the list of names for Chapman before they returned to their post.

Chapman looked at Yu across their cafeteria-style table in the museum's crowded downstairs area. She ate her shepherd's pie with regular strokes, while he only picked at his scoop of tuna salad.

He jabbed his fork toward her tin. "Don't you feel the little microwaves crackling through your body? Do you realize that that thing was frozen solid ten minutes ago?"

"You make it sound unappetizing, yet it is perfectly tasty."

He downed a mouthful of soda, swirled it around his tongue like mouthwash. "Do you think you could ever live in another country?" he asked suddenly.

Yu never knew quite how to respond to Chapman, wondering whether the small talk was part of his State Department persona or whether he was genuinely interested. "I would do whatever my work, my father's work, demanded. Is that what you expected to hear?"

"I hoped to hear something that might help me know you a little better."

"Is that something you say to everyone you meet in your work?"

"Yeah, it's what I tell all the girls." Chapman winked. She

did not recognize the cliché and he went on. "You do yourself and me a disservice."

"No." She weighed her words with care. "I merely sense that your position entails a certain measure of insincerity. I don't want our intercourse to be, as they say, 'part of a day's work.'"

Chapman smiled at her innocence, her vulnerability. "I'd hoped you would know me better than that. I can't be nice to someone I don't like."

"Can you be cruel to someone you do like?"

The question took Chapman by surprise and he said so. He pushed his plate aside and folded his arms, asking Yu to elaborate.

"Didn't Detective Varley take you aside before leaving and instruct you to report to him on our comings and goings?"

"Good God, no," Chapman lied, but he didn't want to sustain the facade. After a long moment of silence, he admitted that Varley had done exactly that. "But I couldn't go through with it, so—" He paused, shrugged. "When Varley calls, I'll tell him to find a new accomplice."

Yu smiled slightly. Chapman realized it was the first time he'd seen that expression on her delicate features.

"I have grown comfortable in our relationship, more so than I thought I would. You have charm and sensitivity. It is a shame that no one we have met comes close to being your equal."

Chapman blushed and, not knowing what to say, said nothing.

"To answer your question, a country means nothing to me. Integrity and curiosity should be the only human boundaries. Artificial borders and visas prevent people from exploring the cultural riches that other societies have to offer." Her large eyes widened slightly—sensuously, Grant thought. "What about you? Would you accept a post overseas?"

"That depends," said Chapman.

"On what?"

"On who I had to leave behind. Or," he leaned forward slightly, "who I was going to be with."

It was Yu's turn to blush and, excusing herself, she went to buy a cool drink.

• • •

All the silly old expressions fluttered through Linda's mind like banners drawn by distant airplanes. "He died in peace," "He's better this way than suffering," "Now he's asleep in the loving hands of his maker." Mrs. Griffin had uttered them each during the past few minutes. But the thought that dominated even her grief, the phrase that in a perverse way kept her from succumbing to tears was, "Where the fuck is Grant?"

Linda sat with her arm around her mother, who was sobbing heavily as Jelkowitz held court in the bedroom with a pair of dark-suited men from the funeral home. Mrs. Bergeni's occasional choked phrase railed against the injustice of the world and the loss of her beloved Ernesto; Linda railed more quietly against Grant for not calling.

When Mrs. Griffin returned from the kitchen with a glass of water requested by Mrs. Bergeni, Linda broke away to try once more to penetrate the museum's busy switchboard. She understood how he couldn't come over that morning; the policeman who stopped by had explained it all. But for Grant to be too busy to phone was unthinkable. Linda promised herself that if by some miracle she did get him on the phone, she would promptly hang up.

Claude took the call when there was no answer at Laojiu's table. He tendered his condolences to Linda and promised that he would go and find Grant at once and have him phone her. He located him in the cafeteria and gave him the news about Linda's father. Driving his palm to his forehead for having lost track of time, Chapman asked Claude to show Yu back to her table in the gallery and went to the nearest pay phone.

Mrs. Griffin answered and called Linda over.

"Claude just told me," Chapman said when she'd gotten on. "Are you all right?"

"If you really cared, why'd you wait until now to get in touch?"

"Didn't Varley's man explain?"

"It was a woman, and yes, she told me that you couldn't be here. But that didn't mean you couldn't call." She began to sniffle. "I could have used a hand around here when I had to call Jelkowitz and the funeral home and keep my mother from tearing her hair out at the same time."

"I'm sorry, but between Varley and the damn show—"

"What about fucking courtesy?" She ignored his remarks. "A call, just to see how I was, how my shitty morning was going, when you planned to get your so-much-in-demand ass over here!"

There was nothing Chapman could do except apologize again and promise to be right over. Linda told him not to bother, but when she didn't hang up on him, he said that he was coming just the same.

Putting his faith in Laojiu's innocence, Chapman decided—hoped—that it would be all right to leave them alone for a few hours. After explaining the situation to Laojiu, who gave him the list of names, Chapman headed for Waterside Towers. As he neared the buildings, the warm thoughts he'd briefly had for Yu vanished, the familiar, less romantic world once more in control.

The Bergeni apartment was a void, with all feeling and color and sense of home gone. Linda and her mother were alone now, the body having been taken away, the doctor and Mrs. Griffin gone. Chapman felt that it was cold there, like a stage whose actors had given up on the play.

Chapman kissed the indifferent Linda on the cheek and walked over to her mother. She was seated in her husband's wing chair, staring through red eyes at the city. He bent over her. "I'm very sorry, Mrs. Bergeni. Your husband was a fine, fine man, someone I respected very much."

"He liked you," the woman managed to croak as she gazed into the past and into her own frightening future. "He always hoped that you two would marry."

"I wished that too."

"And he wondered many, many times how such a decent man could ever have become a lawyer."

"It's something I often wondered about myself." Chapman patted her hand. "If there's anything I can do, please let me know."

Mrs. Bergeni thanked Chapman, her face pale but her expression peaceful, as though she were consorting with an angel only she could see. Leaving her, he walked over to Linda, who was still standing by the door. Taking her around the shoulders, he ushered her into the kitchen and then ran a comforting hand along her back, and up and down her arm.

"Can I ever make it up to you?"

"No."

"I really don't blame you this time. I should have called, and I won't even try to mount a defense."

"Did I ask you to?"

"Not this time."

"I think I'd like it better if you just shut your mouth and hold me," she whispered. Chapman obligingly pressed her to him, and as the burden of sorrow was finally shared, Linda fell to sniffling. "I guess I overreacted a bit on the telephone. You always end up catching my shit."

"In a better world with a better me, that's what I'd be here for."

"No, it's not. I ask for space, then curse you out when you give it to me. I'm a selfish child who ought to be kicked in the ass once in a while."

Chapman pulled her head to his chest and stroked her hair. "I think under the circumstances I deserved that and more. You're just punishing yourself because you feel guilty about your father."

"Guilty? After two years of waiting and watching him waste away, I'm glad it's over."

"What about before those two years? No regrets?"

"What are you trying to do, make me feel bad? I need that right now like I need an ulcer."

"You've got a wall up inside you, and if it doesn't work itself free—"

He hadn't quite gotten the words out before Linda wriggled herself closer to him and began to cry hysterically, tears that spilled from the depths of her. Chapman looked past the sobbing woman and saw her mother sitting calm and undisturbed, staring out the window. He thought back to when his own father had died, relived the teenage shock of his mother's gentle austerity being pushed aside by sorrow, her elegance corroded by weeks of crying, her cheeks becoming gaunt, the flesh under her eyes wrinkling and bulging with black. She was never again the strong woman she had been, and when she died years later, there was an eerie gladness about her that helped Chapman through her brief illness. He thought of that whenever things looked blackest for him. In the end, he would remind himself, even sorrow is fleeting.

Linda rubbed her eyes across Chapman's chest, and he heard Laojiu's list crumple in his shirt pocket. He said nothing until she had backed away. "Fell a little like a rag doll left in the rain?" Linda nodded and quickly began gnawing her lower lip to keep it from trembling. "What you need is a bit of diversion." He eased toward the telephone behind him. "And what I need is some help with my ever-pitiful Chinese enunciation." He fished out the list and passed it to her. "I've got to give Varley these names. When I get him, if you'll be so kind as to read them out, a name and address at a time—"

"Pretty simple-minded diversion, Grant."

"I'm a pretty simple-minded guy."

"I mean, most people would come up with some really clever and spectacular distraction like 'Let's go shopping in Barbados' or 'Why don't we go buy you a car.' "

"Problem is—" he consulted Varley's card and punched out his number "—I'm just an underpaid diplomat and not a game show host."

Linda looked toward her mother as Chapman asked for Varley. Told that his extension was busy, Chapman left Linda's number with the desk sergeant. "I don't look forward to having to deal with Mother over the next few weeks," Linda confessed. "I'm sure she's going to walk around with my father's ghost on her shoulder. Now everything is going to be, 'If Ernesto were here.' "

Chapman pushed his hands into his pants pockets and leaned against the wall beside the phone. "She may surprise you. The lady's pretty sturdy, considering what she's had to put up with over the past two years. I saw it with my mother. Facing the fact that after forty-odd years you're going to be alone is not an easy thing to do."

"You forget, she had a whipping girl." Linda pointed to herself. "It's easy to be tough when you've got a daughter who recognizes guilt as the fourth dimension and moves through it as freely as if it were height or—"

The phone jangled, and after excusing himself, Chapman scooped it up. He started to explain that he had the list but wasn't going to be Varley's eyes and ears when the detective cut him short. Linda watched as Chapman's high spirits drained away. She felt her belly tighten as he looked at her with an expression that was as close to defeat as she'd ever seen in him.

After promising Varley that he'd get right over to the museum, he hung up and said numbly, "There's been another killing. Same method, same everything."

"Who?" Linda asked, adding hopefully, "I mean, it's no one we know, is it?"

Chapman said, "It is. Gail Fisher."

Linda gasped involuntarily. "Why? Who can she have offended?"

"I think we're beyond finding a sane motive for these crimes. The bastards! The goddam bastards." He pounded the wall. "Someone must have seen her wave to me. But who and why?"

"Varley still has no clues?"

"Varley." Chapman snickered. "Varley wants me to be at a meeting with him and Tepper in a half-hour. I'm supposed to find a way to get Laojiu and his statues shipped back to China."

"But that's ridiculous. Why punish the museum just because the police can't do their job?"

"You're asking the wrong person. This whole damn thing is senseless. Jesus." He crossed the room and leaned against the counter top, "Can you believe I finally saw Gail for the first time on the day she died. Attractive little woman with a big cheek-splitting smile. How the hell her death serves any mortal cause I just don't understand."

Linda felt a rush of compassion. She went over and hugged Chapman from behind, half leaning on him. As she held him in silence, she felt a tug at her waist and fell backward a few steps, her hands sliding from around Chapman. He turned and saw her standing in dumb silence in the center of the kitchen.

"What happened?"

"I'm not sure. It's like the other—"

Linda folded at the waist and seemed at once to scoot and jerk away from him. This time she hit the wall two paces behind her.

"Grant, I'm not *doing* this—something pulling—"

Chapman hurled himself toward her, catching Linda under the arms as she suddenly passed out. Her brow was hot. Scooping her up, he carried her from the kitchen. Before he could call Linda's mother for help, Mrs. Griffin walked in and saw them.

"Fainted," Chapman explained as the woman hurried over. "Shock, from the way she was shuddering."

"There's a doctor downstairs, in the lobby of the second building."

"That's where I was taking her. Will you call ahead and tell them what the problem is."

Mrs. Griffin ran to the telephone while Chapman hurried out the open door toward the elevator. Her words stuck in his brain. *She was being pulled.*

She's been building up to something, he told himself as he ran blindly through the small lobby and outside to the neighboring tower. *Two dizzy spells and now this. Poor girl's been through a lot between Tally and her dad and this whole bloody killing spree.* Chapman decided that Varley and his meeting would just have to wait, that Linda's needs came first. What he feared and regretted, as logic speared his idealistic bubble, was that whoever the killer was, he or she would not wait before striking again.

The Madjan retreated from his tenuous assault, satisfied that he would soon be renewed. He drank down the blood claimed earlier and turned from this warrior and his woman to find a woman alone, a Woman of Peace.

The vortex was a buzzing memory, and his spirit reveled in the sights of this strange, new civilization that soon would fall and worship him. And if the earth dragon in jealous fury dared raise its thorny head, it would at last be smitten.

The snorting mounts and watchful soldiers stood with no less anticipation by his side, waiting until the might of the Madjan was sufficient for all to rise and conquer . . .

Chapman's call to the museum put Varley in as foul a mood as he'd ever known, not only because the detective felt as though the weight of the city's well-being was solely on his shoulders but because the one intelligent, rational man he'd met since this case began had just deserted him.

After jamming the phone down, he resumed pacing before Tepper's desk. "All right, we'll coordinate what we can for now."

"We haven't agreed on a thing, you know." Tepper poked an eel-shaped letter opener up and down on his blotter. He didn't much care for the detective and cared even less for the scheme he'd proposed. "In my opinion you're being rash and impractical. Apart from the logistics of refunding all that ticket money, how can you in all conscience surrender to a faceless killer? Moreover, how do you even know that closing the exhibit is what he wants? No." Tepper stared at the backs of his extended fingers. "This is not something I can agree to."

"Then what's your better idea? What would you do next? What stone have we left unturned? If you had a daughter and she were a potential target for this lunatic, what would you do? Wouldn't you try something to assuage him, buy yourself a little time to figure out what the hell's going on? Announce that this circus is leaving town, and if there's no killing tonight at midnight, rest just a little easier knowing that this is some sort of vendetta?"

Tepper ran the pointed tail of the eel beneath his fingernails. "I am not an officer of the law, Warren, I am the curator of an institution which cannot answer for the actions of a psychopath and will not accommodate him with any shifts in policy."

"You're an asshole," Varley corrected, "and you're going to do exactly what I tell you to."

"I beg your pardon."

"You heard me. Either you close the show willingly tonight, or I swear to Christ I'll find a reason to lock you up and close the show down anyway." Poised on his knuckles, Varley leaned over the desk. "What you and I are going to do right now is go downstairs, tell our Chink friends that the party's over as of five o'clock so that they can get word to their cohorts, if they're in fact behind this whole plot, and reassess the whole thing tomorrow morning. We're going to do that together, Tepper, or I'm going to do it alone. Which is it?"

"You have no authority for this!"

"How about if I punch your fuckin' heart out and blame it on the killer? Is that authority enough?"

The curator sat back in his chair, appearing to consider the proposal but, in fact, putting himself beyond Varley's immediate reach. "What you're proposing is really a feint," he clarified. "It may not be necessary to close the show down permanently."

"Maybe. Anyway," Varley said as he stood up, "I'll bet attendance starts falling off real soon even if you stay open. All those women came to the museum—and all those women died.

The publicity is going to start working against you, wouldn't you say?"

Tepper weighed Varley's interpretation carefully, with an uncharacteristic depth of concentration. At last he said, "Fine," shoving the eel into his pencil holder. "We'll try it your way for now. But I want to take this plan under consideration with my board before a final decision is reached tomorrow."

"Sure." Varley played along, having neither the time nor the inclination to argue further. He cursed Chapman again for leaving him alone and then trudged from the office behind the waddling Tepper.

The two men entered the hall melodramatically, as though returning to the stage to take their bows. Tepper's flourish was the more contrived, intended to match Varley and show who was in charge. Calling over a pair of guards, Tepper quietly ordered the desk cordoned off. When that was done, and the grumbling crowd told to come back later, the curator positioned himself next to the Chinese while Varley bent over the table.

"We've had another killing, a young woman who was here this morning."

"Yes, we've had this information from one of the guards," Laojiu replied.

"Then it won't come as a total surprise when I tell you we've decided to shut down the display and send you two home."

Laojiu folded his hands on the desk top. "You fear for us to remain in New York?"

"We are concerned for your welfare," Tepper put in.

"Impatiently so," Laojiu said, scrutinizing the detective's posture. "You seem braced for a footrace."

"We've had enough bloodshed," Varley said. "I intend to do whatever seems necessary to stop this disaster."

"Including deporting us."

"No," Tepper chimed, though he was made a liar by the unyielding stare Varley leveled at the archaeologist.

Yu, who had been listening with mounting outrage, snarled, "Yes. Yes, he's deporting us because he thinks that we're responsible for these savage attacks." Her eyes narrowed. "As though we were mad dogs, without feeling, uncivilized things with as low a regard for his people as he has for us. Where is Chapman?" She rose, looking toward Tepper. "I won't have my father suffer this indignity any longer!"

"He's with Linda." Tepper found himself apologizing. "Her father passed away, and she is not feeling all that well, as you might imagine." Yu's expression dulled visibly as the curator, his manner more assured, turned to the detective. "Surely we can leave this for now. Yu is right; Grant should be present. This is, after all, a matter for the State Department and not for the police department."

"You'll be surprised at the commissioner's powers in matters of this nature. I can't make it any plainer than—"

There was a scream from the crowd around the Madjan as a girl tripped and bowled over an old man. One of the guards hurried over to keep them from being trampled in the twining crunch of people filing before the statues. Tepper felt the sweat creep from under his collar as visions of another death at the museum flooded his mind.

Varley checked his watch. "Have Chapman here in three hours if you can. As a matter of fact, I'd appreciate it. He's had experience translating some of life's tougher realities to dimwits. But come five o'clock, the Madjan goes out of business, or so help me the name of this museum goes through the sewer with a shitload of arrests and investigations."

It was more the detective's disrespect than his edict that bothered Yu. As he stalked away, she was restrained from lashing out only by her father's hand which rested calmingly on her own. The archaeologist looked up at Tepper, whose eyes followed Varley and then fell with a sigh.

"I was once asked, Dr. Tepper, why for twenty years I refused the help of my government in locating Ch'en-shimm. I think you can see the danger in serving a master other than yourself."

"You're a fortunate man," Tepper said in agreement. Excusing himself, he decided to contact the mayor's office and Chapman's superiors at the State Department to see if Varley could in fact shut down the display as he had boasted.

Tepper ordered the archaeologist's position reopened as he stormed from the hall. The guard resumed his post behind the Chinese as the queue of visitors was reborn, and the day crept slowly onward.

CHAPTER TWELVE

"YOU DON'T NOTICE all the lumpy-bumps when you're walking. God, this whole city must be a disaster area for cripples."

Chapman nodded as he pushed Linda's wheelchair across the concrete plaza that separated two of the three Waterside Towers. "Makes you appreciate what the handicapped are fighting for, doesn't it?"

"No question." Linda let her head roll over the leather back of the wheelchair. "Never mind being jiggled from head to foot, can you imagine lugging this thing onto buses and down subway stairs? I'm going to write my congressperson when I get home."

The chair clattered along the cobbled cement, carrying Linda through the amber light and chill air of late afternoon.

"You're not going to write to anyone," Chapman said after a moment. "You're getting into bed and trying to get some sleep."

"Balls to thee and thine! Dr. Norvig pronounced me perfectly fit."

"Except for that part about being emotionally exhausted. In my book as well as hers, that means I tuck your little bod between the covers when we get back and see that it stays tucked."

"I really don't need any of this, you know." She clapped

her hands on the black-varnished armrests. "I feel perfectly fine. Maybe I had some kind of muscle spasm, that's all."

"What about the two times you felt dizzy this week and your general crabbiness over the past few weeks?"

"I haven't been crabby, just oppressed."

Chapman backed the chair up a pair of steps and into the lobby.

"Crabby," he said as they waited for the elevator.

"People have been riding me," she returned. "My parents, Tepper, Claude, Tally when she kept hesitating about helping me out because of commitments."

"What about me?"

The doors opened, and Chapman rolled Linda into the carriage. "You were away," she answered.

When they reached the apartment, the wheelchair was left outside so as not to cause Mrs. Bergeni undue concern. As it was, she was sleeping; Mrs. Griffin welcomed them with a handwritten message for Chapman to ring Tepper while she grilled Linda about her medical examination. Chapman left them to place the call. He had to tap out the number several times in succession before hooking into the switchboard, all the while hoping that he'd not be greeted with word of yet another killing.

When Tepper came on, his voice was aflutter with desperation. "Grant, they're going to do it, they're actually going to let him shut down my exhibit. It was supposed to be a sham but it's not! No proof, no clues, just a hunch and—Grant, if you're worth anything as a diplomat, you've got to stop them, got to! We'll be a laughing stock for years, and I won't be a party to that. If we lose our credibility over this, I'll be forced to resign."

Chapman told him to calm down. "Who's going to shut down the show and why?" He knew that Varley must be behind this, but he wanted to know who else had gone over to his side.

Tepper rattled off the names: Varley, Secretary of State Leumas, the mayor, and the board of trustees. "They can't do it, not after the investment we've made, the time and loan of our good name to this event. What kind of arm twisting can you perform?"

"From the sound of it, things have gone too far for me to do anything."

"Can the display mean so little to you that you'll step aside just because some flatfoot has panicked?"

"It's more than that, and you know it. Don't forget, this show was my idea. I end up with just as much egg on my face as you do, maybe even more. But Christ, Wally, if there's even a remote chance that this will stop the killings, how can I argue with what they're doing?"

"Yu is! Laojiu is! They're as angry about it as I am."

"They are?" Chapman was genuinely surprised. "I can't believe that they wouldn't jump at this opportunity to get back home."

"That's just it, Grant. They're not *going* home."

"What do you mean?"

Behind an edge of impatience Tepper explained, "Varley wanted them deported, but instead the exhibit is simply being moved, that's all. Moved from here to the Los Angeles County Museum of all places."

Chapman was silent for a moment as he tried to make sense of what he'd been told. The logic escaped him. "Whose idea was this?"

"Your employer, Secretary Leumas. It's a compromise, he said, a face-saving device to keep Beijing from being insulted because we're throwing their statues back at them. Also, the Commissioner says it's a good experiment—if you can believe it—a little test to see if the killings follow the statues west."

"Jesus," Chapman complained, "I don't blame Laojiu for being teed off. They're treating him like a shuttlecock."

"Fear not, he isn't alone. They're flying Einar up from the Pentagon even as we speak. He was about to go over to Tibet on some government project, but they wanted him to start crating tonight."

"This is insanity." Chapman looked at the oven clock. "Look, I'll be up there in a few minutes." He saw Linda's ears perk, and she glowered at him. He jabbed a rigid finger repeatedly at the mouthpiece, as if each gesture were an exclamation point identifying this as a critical matter. Linda continued to scowl as she wound up her conversation with Mrs. Griffin and walked over.

Chapman was asking Tepper to keep the archaeologist calm above all, when Linda edged beside him, arms crossed.

"I'll be there as soon as I can," he repeated, "and assure him I'll try and move mountains to help him." Chapman hung up and grasped Linda by the shoulders. "I know what you're going to say, but this is important. Varley's gotten—"

"I heard," she said tartly.

"Then you understand why I have to go up there. Look, I'll be back in an hour or two. I owe these people."

"What about me? This hasn't exactly been my best day, and it's going to get worse if I come in second to some bonehead."

"I know what you've been through." He reached down and squeezed her hands. The diplomat was back in charge, and Linda knew that the battle was lost. "But I have to ask you to give a little or Laojiu to give a little. What would you do? He's got no one here, and people are walking all over him."

"Who have I got? Mother? Mrs. Griffin?"

Chapman craned his head around to make certain the neighbor hadn't heard. "You'll have me back," he promised, "just as soon as I take care of my obligation to Laojiu. People will be coming by the apartment tonight; you'll be okay here. The only thing that can knock you down is letting yourself get knocked down."

"Well, if Grant Chapman says so, then it must be true."

"Stop that."

"After all, it was he who felled mighty Tarlo with a blast of his nostrils."

"I said cut it out. I don't like this one bit better than you!"

"But you're going."

"I have to."

Linda didn't care to debate the point further, and Chapman hadn't the time. As she turned from him, her mouth set and her eyes hard, he spun with a huff of annoyance from the kitchen. Without another word he was gone, she brooding and swearing she never wanted to see him again.

The five-minute closing announcement drew most of the crowd to the doors, those who lingered belonging to the three types Chapman had identified to a guard on opening day: the event nuts, who intended to wring every last glimpse from the experience; the exodus haters, those scowling few who did not like bottlenecks of any kind; and the individualists, people who simply would not be told what to do. Tepper watched the thinning mass without making distinctions, simply tapping his foot impatiently beside Laojiu's desk as he waited for Chapman to arrive.

When the tenacious stragglers finally were ushered politely into the night and the guards had slid shut the iron gates on the two open sides of the hallway, Tepper sucked up his courage and pivoted to face Laojiu. The archaeologist had risen; Yu did not stand and looked away from the curator.

"Traffic," Tepper confirmed as his eyes bounced back and forth between the clock and the Chinese, like a man awaiting a stay of execution. "Grant said he'll be here, so he'll be here—with a *plan*. You have to understand, this is my first major exhibit, and I've had no experience with these kinds of politics."

"No one has accused you of infidelity," Laojiu asserted, no less eager than Tepper for Chapman to arrive. "Nor is there any need for you to defend your actions. You are not a frivolous man, and I trust that you have done nothing from selfish motives."

"Naturally not. The museum and the statues are all I care about, and right now the fate of each is intertwined."

"Both in the hands of fools," Yu opined.

Tepper nodded his agreement as the luminous clock ticked off 5:04. The drumming of the curator's shoe filled the empty hall until Chapman appeared moments later.

No one moved as he approached. "Good evening," he said, dipping his head toward the archaeologist and Yu. "What's the timetable?"

Tepper's thick throat rattled with anger. "Varley will be arriving at six o'clock to escort our guests to the airport. He offered, assuming that your evening was already accounted for. Einar's shuttle should be landing about now, and there's a limousine waiting to bring him here. Tomorrow morning," the portly man continued with a shudder, "we issue a press release which states that due to overwhelming interest generated by the statues, and because of the limited time they are on loan to our country, it has been decided to tour the exhibit rather than tie it to one institution exclusively. A simultaneous release from the State Department will list the museums, starting with Los Angeles and continuing on through the Smithsonian, the Field in Chicago, and so on." He shook his fists. "It's ghastly, Grant, and you must do something to prevent it."

Chapman turned to the Chinese. "Before I say anything else, I want you to recognize that I have no authority in this.

For what it's worth, if I could overrule part of the edict, I would. I want to see you returned to your dig, although closing the exhibit does serve a sensible purpose."

"Grant," Tepper gurgled with rage. "What are you saying?"

Chapman answered without looking at the curator. "There has got to be a link between the exhibit and the killings—even if it's only some maniac whose mother was once frightened by a statue. What I oppose is the diplomatic double-dealing that takes advantage of Laojiu's good intentions. I stopped at the reception desk to place a phone call," he revealed. "Doug Reedy is on the way over." He could feel Tepper cringe but couldn't care less. If he could stand the reporter, so could Tepper. "The government is never the final arbiter in any matter. It may be a little hackneyed, but let's see what the public has to say when they learn about promises made to you and then broken, about the threats used to get you here in the first place."

"Grant," Tepper roared. "Grant, forget the exhibit. You're going to start a third world war with us as ground zero! The government is the final arbiter where that's concerned."

"No," Laojiu said, "there will not be a war." His gaze fell respectfully on Chapman. "They will have a scapegoat, is that not so?"

After a moment's thought, Chapman nodded.

"The threats will be attributed to you, by virtue of your having arranged for the tour."

"I can only answer for what I do, not what will be done to me." Chapman hadn't intended his statement to ring like a phrase from *The Iliad*, though it seemed oddly appropriate in this setting.

Laojiu took a step toward his benefactor. "I feel no differently, which is why I must turn aside your offer to help. I can wage my own offensive, and then there is the reality of these heinous crimes. Your associate, Mr. Varley, suspects us of having committed them, and nothing but our departure will change his mind. My anger will pass, as it always does. This is but one more brief diversion."

Tepper raged, "Don't be an ass, Grant, listen to the man! We've had enough martyrs because of this exhibit. I won't have another."

"You both miss my point," Chapman said. "If you were my worst enemies, I couldn't do any differently from what I've planned. There is a principle at stake here, and no one person or government is above being reminded of that."

"Yes, but for Christ's sake, leave my museum out of it!"

Laojiu walked from the gathering, lost in thought. After a moment, his queue shook behind him. "No. I will go to California before I permit this." He turned around, his eyes moist. "If I have learned one thing in this past quarter century, it is that no statue is worth a human life. This will destroy you. There is no choice to make."

Yu shot up then, looking with disgust from Chapman to her father. "You talk as though you were old friends. Father, this man's government is toying with you! He must answer for their actions!" Her gaze softened as she regarded Chapman, whose hurt was quickly tucked behind his official demeanor. "It is unfortunate," she said softly, "but he is responsible for your welfare."

Laojiu wrested his eyes from the government representative to his daughter. "I do not believe that to be so. Yet if it is, there is nonetheless a matter at issue which transcends us."

"What is more important than our pride? Haven't you taught me never to put anything before it?"

"No," Laojiu replied. "I raised you to be proud, it is true, but never insensitive. More important than one's own dignity is the honor of a person who puts you before all else. It is a curious synergy that—"

"It is hypocrisy!" Yu interrupted. "These people created this trouble, and it is his responsibility to find a solution. Come to the Consulate, you will be safe there; this is not your affair."

There was a sudden commotion from the hallway, and everyone's eyes were drawn to it. A loud, familiar voice boomed, "Clear out you pipsqueak, I've nothin' to say!"

"Yeah, well, Chapman tells me otherwise. He says that they dragged you from D.C. for this, and U.S. Air confirms it. How do you explain that?"

"Reedy, you wart, I don't have to explain a friggin' thing to you. Now get off my tail before I throw you through the bleedin' wall!"

Einar Björkman burst into the room a pace ahead of the eager reporter. His bare arms were rope twists of muscle, and he shook them both at Chapman. Reedy, also spotting the official, hurried over ahead of the Swede.

Yu watched the display and then snarled at her father. "You may demean yourself if you like. I cannot bear to watch you commit such folly." She trained her wrath on Chapman. "I admire you, if you can believe that. I might one day have felt more. But you move and think in petty, deceitful ways!" Without another word she stormed toward the exit and was gone, past Reedy, who had paused to scratch out the quote in his note pad.

"She's grown more uppity," Einar observed as she breezed by. "Never thought it would be possible."

Chapman just stood there, his features blank, his wits upended, and his soul battered.

Tepper shook his head in defeat, confident that Chapman had managed to make a desperate situation worse. The Chinese left the hall, silently passing Laojiu, whose distant eyes revealed a man wrestling with allegiances. He opened his mouth as though to speak; suddenly, as if that very action had cracked some emotional dam, his face slid from determination to fear. He murmured aloud the thought that gripped him: "Dear Lord, she mustn't be alone!"

Chapman caught on at once. Without waiting for the elderly archaeologist, he snapped up the desk phone and ordered the waiting limousine not to take Yu away. The driver reported that he had not seen her.

Running to the exit, Chapman stared down Central Park West and then into the bleak, dark park. "Did she have cash for cab fare?" he called back. Laojiu informed him that she hadn't.

The early evening blackness was pierced by streetlights up and down the avenue. Under none of them did he see the girl.

Laojiu came up beside him, with Reedy tagging behind.

"Take the limousine," Chapman told the archaeologist. "Drive west, back and forth between here and the Consulate. Reedy," he said, "you go round the block starting on Seventy-ninth."

"Why?" the reporter asked with a hungry glint.

"Because if you don't find her, you don't get your story." The journalist was off like a cannonball. Chapman lingered a moment longer. "I'll go east through the park. If I find her, I'll call the car."

Chapman started toward the steps, but Laojiu grabbed a fistful of shirt-sleeve and held him tightly. The archaeologist walked around to face him. "Chapman, she believes in the Madjan. I do not, but I dread what we all will face if she is right and I am wrong. If anything has happened to her, hurry back. We will have much to prepare for."

"I'll be back with Yu," he promised, and then ran off, taking three steps at a time. He waited for a bus to rumble by and then, weaving along the maze of congested traffic, vanished into the pitch-dark, silent park.

Linda was wrathfully cramming the last of the dishes into the dishwasher when the phone rang. Expecting it to be Grant, she ignored the first half dozen rings. With a guttural rumbling of disgust, she gave in and answered only when she realized that it just as easily could be someone calling to pay his or her respects. Linda was quite surprised when it was neither.

"I know this is a terrible time to be calling," the bullish voice acknowledged, "but is there any way you could find some time to come up to the museum?"

Even if she hadn't recognized the voice, Linda knew only one soul on earth who was single-minded enough to beg a favor before offering his condolences. "Dr. Tepper, you sound upset. That must mean Grant is there."

"Oh, is he ever. Not content with destroying himself, your friend plans to bring down the museum's reputation as well. Someone has got to stop him, and you're the only person I can think of who even has a chance."

"What's he done?" Linda asked. As Tepper summarized the events that had followed Chapman's arrival, Linda found herself gripped with mounting apprehension.

"A scandal like this will ruin the museum's ability to land a first-rate exhibit for many years," the curator concluded, "but it will also ruin your boy friend for *good*. He's playing with the real giants now, not the dottish ogres of the toy industry whose powers are limited to that realm."

"I understand," Linda said, "and I'm on my way. Till I get there, lock Grant in the bathroom if you have to, only keep him away from that idiot muckraker he gave the Tarlo story to. After he's heard it, there'll be no turning back."

Tepper said he'd try and hung up; Linda cursed herself for caring about that hopeless saint of hers. She hurried to get her coat and some money while she explained the emergency briefly to Mrs. Griffin. The older woman promised to apologize to the few family members and neighbors who were expected to come by, though Linda barely heard her as she dashed out the door and down the hallway.

The blood lust that empowered him detected a presence that was stronger than all the others. He had sensed it before and had sought it, failing; now she was near, and she was vulnerable. This time he would have her, and when he had done with the woman, his regeneration would be complete.

With his spirit poised on the threshold they had provided between his world and the mortal sphere, the Madjan reached out for the Woman of Peace who had heretofore eluded him...

Yu stopped running when she could no longer hear the traffic, when the monolithic buildings were nothing but lighted silhouettes against the navy night sky. New York was gone, even if she was not yet gone from the city. Here she would be able to think clearly.

The woman sat down behind a large, moss-covered boulder and let the cool night air play about her sweaty face. She had never spoken so disrespectfully to her father. Behind all the resolve she had shown, Yu felt guilty about that. *It was for his own benefit that I spoke out. These people are not fit to host him let alone to order—*

Yu heard feet clap past. Peeking furtively around the rock, she noticed Chapman hurrying down the asphalt path, his head swinging this way and that as he peered through the park. He did not call her name, but Yu assumed he was searching for her. When he had passed, she rose and moved stealthily in the opposite direction.

Yu soon reached a plot of young grass in the shadow of a large bronze. The figure was that of the Spanish explorer Cortez, his sword held high above the head of his rearing steed. She'd not be seen here by Chapman or by the American thugs about whom she had been warned by employees at the museum, before the museum itself became more dangerous than any city street.

Yu considered the Madjan and her theory about him. She

recognized a perverse quality in her thinking as she sat back against the statue's pedestal.

If he exists, I may well die. Yet I want to know that he is, that he was more than just a fragment of nightmare. What has my life been but the quest for knowledge, and when have I shied from learning something new? And if it were possible to communicate—

This spot was not as cool as the last one, and even as she sat there, Yu found herself growing warm. She snaked a finger beneath her collar as she looked beyond the walk, at a small lake. A mist seemed to crawl from beneath a stone bridge that spanned it; the fog did not spread as much as roll and swell, gray-white as though possessing its own luminescence.

As the earthbound cloud surged forward, a cushion of hot air rushed before it. The warm bubble struck Yu with more than just heat. It carried an odor she'd smelled before at the Consulate. After the passing of the humid envelope, the cloud became a tawny hue, like the windblown sands of the basin. It began to spread higher than wider now. Yu was all but transfixed by the billowing mist.

Somewhere nearby she heard a din like the clattering of a jeep she and her father once had owned. The faint clanging seemed to ride the fog, growing in volume as the increasingly bilious mass rode forth. It was like the other night in every way but one: She knew that she was fully awake.

Yu didn't move from beneath the shadow of the bearded Cortez except to pant involuntarily from the heat. Then the fog rolled from the lake. It continued toward her, and her throat closed with fear and the hand of something unseen pressing on her chest, making it difficult to draw breath. She inched from the shadow as the fog collected its stray wisps into a great mass. The thing pressed ahead even as it formed, becoming vaguely human in shape though vastly larger. She started to rise at last but fell back or was pushed; she scurried aside crablike even as her legs grew leaden and the paralysis spread to her torso. Although she couldn't move, she could feel; because she could do nothing but fight for breath, there was no scream.

The ringing of metal was fierce now, and the cloud began to take on a distinct shape. It was the likeness of the Madjan, though to Yu's stunned bewilderment and sudden understanding, it was not the one to which they had become accustomed. This entity was vivid with the colors of the third century B.C., its mouth pulled into a sardonic grin, its eyes flaming red. The god had come to reclaim his kingdom.

The living Madjan floated toward the woman on its carpet of amber mist, with a halo of black death and the clash of weapons behind it. She felt the weight of something terrible upon her pelvis then and knew that she had been marked as a Woman of Peace, with no soldier to claim her. With the realization came a final mustering of defiance. She lurched back, shutting her eyes.

The pressure vanished so suddenly that Yu arched upward as though she were weightless. She opened her eyes and saw that the Madjan had gone, leaving the night as still as before.

Savoring the sweet taste of the clean air and the returning sensation in her limbs, Yu sat up. She looked ahead and listened, expecting to find Chapman nearby. There was no one, yet a man would have to have claimed her for the Madjan to retreat.

"Only once battle has been declared would he cast aside the protocol of his time," Yu reminded herself with tentative calm. In any case, the woman decided that she had learned all she cared to. She would go to the museum and persuade the authorities that it would take more than closing the exhibit to avert a holocaust now that the Madjan had tasted blood. "Perhaps there is an answer in Kuo, an incantation," she mused aloud as she rose from her knees and scuttled quickly toward the path.

Something struck the earth before her. Yu gasped and jumped back a step. A great sword lay on the ground, and the sickly squeaking that followed told her whence it came. Yu turned slowly, in time to witness the impossible destruction of her mute, inadvertent protector.

The upraised arm of Cortez was glowing and bending as though torched by an unseen furnace. The metal began to run then; as heat rippled over the entire statue, huge chunks of bronze flew off and vanished as balls of sparkling vapor. The fog spun like two great arms from inside the torn statue, coalescing above the ruin in the awesome shape of the demigod.

Yu thought of the dead girls bursting, of the fires that

burned at the command of the deity. The lake seemed the only place that might offer any sanctuary from the Madjan's fury, and she ran for it. As Yu waded quickly into the water, the first tendrils of mist snaked toward her, bearing the renewed Madjan on their back; a bench burst into flaming splinters as the giant approached and then passed the water's edge. She knew then that he would not be stopped, yet there was no turning back. Opting to cross the lake as directly as possible, she dove beneath the water.

The depths made a dull but deafening roar of the resumed clanging, which Yu knew now to be an echo of the age-old battle that had been dedicated to the Madjan and had ensured final victory for Ch'en. She felt a stabbing bolt of terror as she realized that the god might well be commanding an army of the dead, hellish hordes before whom the mortal world would be helpless.

A swell punched down on Yu, knocking the air from her in a string of bubbles. She tried to rise, but her struggles were useless. The paralysis of the Madjan's weight set in, and like a speared fish she twisted helplessly toward the yellow silt of the lake bottom.

Her brain hazy from the shock and loss of air, Yu recognized the stone foundation of the bridge several strokes ahead. Clawing along the floor of the pond, her mind spinning like the sands, she was able to move only because of the buoyant quality of the water. Yu was unafraid; there was room in her mind for nothing but preoccupation with survival.

The woman's fingers extended straight ahead, the tips quavering as they strained for the blocks. When she knew that there were only moments of consciousness left to her, Yu looked around desperately for something to help pull her toward her goal. She saw a rusted bicycle within hand's reach to the left; grasping it, she tugged herself ahead and upward, scratching at the blocks and pulling her head above the water.

Yu gulped down a hearty breath, which was simultaneously pushed from her by the Madjan. Moaning, Yu was forced underwater along the arcing leg of the bridge. Without breaking the surface, she was lifted and turned, the inside of her head all but bursting from the lack of air and the shattering sounds of combat. Her spine was pressed harshly to the stone, her legs forced apart as she suffered the needs of the evil presence. Her hands broke the surface of the water with a final marshaling of strength as she reached with futility for a handhold.

Staring with disgust at the lights of the buildings and traffic along Fifth Avenue, Chapman knew that there was nothing to do but double back. Yu could not have reached here much ahead of him, and nowhere did he see a sign of her. None of the pedestrians passing from the north or south had seen her, he learned. Experiencing an uncharacteristic feeling of helplessness, he turned and jogged slowly in the direction he had come. In the center of the park was a road that split it perpendicularly to the way he had come. He would follow that route, heading first toward the lake.

There was a young couple looking fearfully at the melted statue. Seeing it, Chapman called to them; they ran off, not as if they had done the deed but as though he had. Swearing, Chapman looked around.

A swill of red circled thinly toward the surface of the lake; he could see it in the stark light of the surrounding streetlamps. Then the hands erupted from its midst, and he could vaguely see a figure struggling within the murky water. Even before he was aware of whatever was amiss, Chapman had begun racing toward the lake.

As he neared, he saw that the figure was Yu. Although she appeared to be drowning, having tumbled or thrown herself in, he knew there was a chance of reaching her before it was too late.

"Don't give up," he cried as he closed the distance between them with long-legged strides. Inexplicably, her head and shoulders popped to the surface, and she stayed afloat with weak strokes. There was blood pulsing from her mouth, and her face twisted with pain as she swallowed air.

The fog rose like a plume beside her as Chapman skidded to a stop. Next to her, the bridge trembled for its entire length and then disintegrated, sending a rain of granules sprinkling over the lake. In the midst of the wreckage a smoky figure formed, materializing from the mist. Chapman recognized it as a lavish version of the statue in the museum.

"My God," he said respectfully as the stone particles from the quietly decimated bridge snowed down. Those which passed directly before the glowing eyes of the enormous statue puffed into tiny comets and sizzled to the lake. Even as the last of them came to rest, the giant began moving forward, toward Chapman. Yu, freed of her burden, sloshed weakly toward the far end of the lake; Chapman just stared, not knowing whether to run or confront what had to be an illusion, a mirage of some kind.

From across the lake, Yu rasped, "Behind you—the sword!"

Chapman turned and saw the fallen weapon several paces off. "You're mad. I'm not going to fight this thing!"

"You *can't* fight him. Surrender and beg clemency, it's your only chance!"

"What?"

"*Kneel*," she pleaded, "with the blade pointed down."

"What are you going to do?"

"Warn them," she declared. "Get back to the museum and warn them!"

Yu had climbed to her feet as she spoke and began to run. The statue did not turn but came ashore and continued toward Chapman as though intent on trying its powers on a warrior, on someone other than a young girl.

Feeling utterly ridiculous but recognizing that mirages don't destroy bridges, Chapman scrambled for the sword. Dropping to his knees and driving the point of the weapon into the ground, he grasped the hilt and bowed. For a moment, the only sound he heard was the wisping of his strained breath in the aftermath of his sprint. Then he improvised soberly: "Great Madjan, allow me to share in your glory by—"

"Hold 'em where you got 'em, pal."

Chapman looked up and saw a pair of police pistols trained squarely on him. Moments later, a squad car screeched to a halt where the Madjan had been. Its roof lights were flaring, and its headlights revealed the presence of another car from which these two men must have come. Another pair of officers hurried out.

"What the fuck hit this place?" asked one of the newcomers. His eyes settled on Chapman after passing over the war zone. "Just this fruitcake with some nitro?"

The officer's assessment telegraphed what was to come. Chapman threw aside the sword and saw the policemen's trigger fingers tense. "Listen," he said calmly, hoping that his manner would calm them where his actions had not. "I know this will be difficult to believe, but I'm with the State Department, and this all ties in to the exhibit we have at the museum now, the treasures of—"

"Take him," the same officer advised, leaving to examine the statue.

"On what charge?" his partner asked.

"Possession of a dangerous weapon, Wadapoulis, and suspicion of unlawful use of explosives."

"This is insane," Chapman wailed. "I'm trying to prevent a crime, not cause one!"

The officers kept their guns level on Chapman while the youthful Wadapoulis droned, "In accordance with the Miranda rulings, I am obliged to inform you of your rights, that anything you say or do may be held against you in a court of—"

"I *know* what my rights are. They keep the Constitution near my Washington office! Look, did you hear any kind of explosion? Do you think I melted that statue with a flamethrower or that maybe I just flicked a lighter?"

"Sergeant Diver," called Wadapoulis, "I think you should look and see if there's a torch of any kind hidden in the bushes."

"Jesus," Chapman declared, rising, "I've had enough of this. You saw that girl who was here? I'm going after her before she's torn to pieces like the other six girls who've died these past few—"

"Six?" gulped one of the armed officers.

"Come *on*! There was one in China that only a few people—"

"Shit, this must be the man; and he's after another one. Wadapoulis, someone ought to get Detective Varley on the horn. This is his baby."

"Yes," Chapman urged, "that's a fine idea. Get Varley and tell him you've got a gun on Grant Chapman, who is trying to save the life of Yu Laojiu. Tell him that!"

Wadapoulis looked hesitantly from Chapman to the other pair of officers to the destroyed statue. "All right," he said. "I'll call him." The gangly policeman ran to the car, though he didn't quite know whose order he was following.

Varley had been on his way uptown to the museum when the call was piped through. As he drove to the park, he could have kicked himself over and over; he might yet before he had the son of a bitch's confession. He'd all but discounted Chapman as the killer, and he still couldn't believe it. Not that he didn't want to. Whoever the butcher was, the detective wanted him in a cage.

I'm usually so good at seeing alibis for the crock they are, he said, chastising himself as he sped up Park Avenue and swung west on Fifty-ninth Street, siren blaring. *But he took me in. Damn it, I've got to hand Chapman that.*

Varley couldn't wait to grill the prisoner, a feeling that peaked as he rolled up Central Park West. He squealed into the park, nearly hitting a shabby-looking woman who staggered by, and continued until he saw Chapman. They had him, hands against the hood of one of the cars; a smile broke the detective's taut features.

Yeah, I can see it now. He looks like a friggin' killer. Man, is that crud going to pay for what he did to those girls and for the way he jerked me around. He's going to pay in spades!

He didn't need one cowering warrior. As he had proved with the bronze idol and the span over the lake, he did not require more than the scant blood he had drawn from this Woman of Peace.

Drifting through the ether, he returned to the shell Ch'en had made for him, thence to ride forth with his army and begin his crusade through this foreign place . . .

Chapter Thirteen

Linda was angry by the time the cab had reached the planetarium entrance, her initial fear for Grant now significantly displaced. It wasn't only Grant's self-destructive bent with which she was annoyed. It was the fact that she needed a role model who wasn't as self-neglectful as she tended to be—and he certainly wasn't that. Jon had been an unmitigated bastard, but she'd welcomed the swagger for a time. She was beginning to realize that only when it reduced her to a subordinate figure rather than freed her from her desire to please others did she rebel. Linda didn't want Grant to go that far into self-indulgence, but for him occasionally to monopolize his own time and attention and wrap it around her would be a pleasant change.

Sergeant Hall, the burly night guard, admitted Linda, and she passed quickly through the silent, darkened corridors. As she neared the Asian hallway, she heard Einar grumbling. She passed him as he and two muscular aides emerged from the service elevator.

"Watch it, girl," the Swede exclaimed as they wheeled out a pair of hefty carts laden with wood slats stacked in a pyramid. Linda followed as they proceeded to the display room, the casing boards in tow. "You here to observe or to nag? I may as well tell you now, I'm in no mood for an ass pain."

"Where's Grant?" Linda asked peremptorily.

"Where's Grant? Let's see, last I saw, he was runnin' out

the door with Laojiu and that reporter worm, chasin' down the Chinese girl."

"Why? What happened?"

"Well might you ask. If it were up to me, I'd have let her become a bag lady."

"Einar, please!"

"Oh, she got her nose all out of joint when her old man refused to let *your* old man put his butt on the line for him."

"Why, that miserable bitch," Linda decided. She looked imploringly toward the heavens and shook her white-knuckled fists. "God, Grant, when are you going to learn who matters and who isn't even worth the fuel to drive them off a cliff?"

"Probably never." Einar chuckled. "That's something I love about him." As they rolled into the Asian hall, he added, "Your boy friend's a sucker for distress situations, no matter who's in them or why. He'd feed the dog that gives him rabies!"

Of the four, Linda was the only one facing into the chamber when they arrived; the three men were all walking backward to make certain that the carts stayed on course. As a result, she was the first to see the noxious shadow. Upright, it stood where the statue of the Madjan had been. Matte black, it had neither depth nor dimension, was a mere silhouette of the idol. Flat from whatever angle she viewed it, the outline neither reflected the overhead lights nor created the impression of substance, yet it was there, occupying space as an absence of light and matter.

In the moment it took Linda to identify what she was seeing, Einar's black assistant turned to scout his path and also saw the hellish shade. He stopped in his tracks, and the other aide, pressing onward, stumbled against his slowed cart.

"Raymond, you dumb turd! What're you doing stopping like—"

"Shut up, Einar, and just tell me what the hell I'm lookin' at here."

Einar twisted his massive shoulders around as he braked the cart with the sole of his boot. "What is it, a shroud? Linda, did you do that?"

"That ain't no shroud," Raymond assured him. He stepped around the third man, Juarez, squinting as he walked ahead.

"I'll tell ya what else it ain't: spray paint. Must be—" Juarez followed his gaze "—yeah, must be one of those illusion things like I saw them do at the planetarium. Remember when they did that show on the black hole?"

"You sayin' that's a laser trick?" Raymond sniffed. "Can't be. Lasers are lights; this is black."

"You'd know?" Juarez asked.

"Hey, man, I know black when I see it."

"I'm talkin' about lasers." The Hispanic paused and looked up and around. "They got to be comin' from somewhere."

Frightened, Linda turned, hoping against reason that Juarez was right, expecting to see Tepper roll in from the staircase with some satisfactory explanation. Instead, what she saw behind her was a mist slithering along the floor, rolling up onto the walls, and curling in on itself to form a vertical fist of smoke. It seemed to be churning from the air itself at the foot of the stairs, with no flame or other source in sight.

"Einar, look," she said fearfully as the cloud began to billow taller, yellow-amber streaks infusing the creeping tones of the grave. Slowly, behind powerful eruptive surges, the fog sculpted itself into a vaguely human form. The yellows became gold; the amber turned red and fell into patterns of sashes and sheaths. The gray shaded slowly to blue and became a body of armor on a figure whose features were otherwise still indistinct.

"Big trouble," Raymond averred as four pairs of eyes were transfixed by the larger than life figure being created from thin air.

Juarez nodded blankly, intuitively backing away from the solidifying mass. As he walked on wobbly legs, he heard a sibilant whine from behind. Turning, he stared into a face that was the stuff of nightmares. Behind him was a figure in decayed armor, a creature at once evil and dead. Its flesh was white but as immaterial as the statue behind it; the pasty face beneath clumps of rotted hair was unrounded, insubstantial, given identity only by the eyes and nostrils and the scowling gash of a mouth that pierced it, each as black as the imposter shape of the Madjan.

All of this Juarez drank down in the space of his last heartbeat. The hellish thing hissed again and, drawing back a pale arm, drove its sword through the belly of the young man. A groan gurgled pitifully in his throat, and the others turned just as Juarez slid off the rusted sword. Only Einar noticed that to one side of them another statue had vanished, an infantryman, replaced by the same lightless void as the Madjan.

Raymond swore as his friend collapsed to the floor, fear supplanted by outrage at the assault. Without bothering to reflect on what had happened, he launched himself at the demonic figure. The warrior did not move, nor did Raymond reach him; there was a sharp crack, and the black man jerked backward, his hands shooting to his throat. There was a length of dull leather around his neck, and as his stunned companions allowed their eyes to follow it, they saw the thing vanish into the murky shadows where two cavalry figures had been placed. Yet another wraith emerged then from that dark corner, holding the whip on which Raymond was painfully leashed. The statue that this wraith and its empty black mount had been was now a dark outline beside him; even as they watched, Linda and Einar saw the mounted warrior beside this other give up its texture and mass to become a blank black profile cut in space. Linda's head was turned to the side by the clopping of hooves as the fourth specter appeared across the room.

"Holy Christ, we're surrounded," Einar announced. He looked from the newest arrival to Raymond, who was squealing and struggling to remove the strap from his torn flesh. The Swede began to edge toward him.

"Surrounded by *what*?" Linda asked as her gaze returned to the first figure, clearly that of the Madjan. It hovered on a carpet of mist, massive yet weightless, looking over their heads into the center of the room, where the rest of his sculpted army stood waiting. "These things, what can they be? Illusions? Are we sharing some kind of nightmare?"

"Juarez is definitely dead and Raymond is bleedin' for real," Einar said, edging toward him. He watched as the black eye sockets of the cavalryman remained fixed on the ensnared Raymond. "What I want to do," Einar continued quietly, "is not worry about what these are but just get us out of here. Linda, if I happen to draw their fire, run like the dickens, okay?"

Linda nodded nervously, her eyes flitting from the Madjan to the cavalry rider to Raymond. The black man was writhing helplessly, gasping now as his fingers clawed desperately between the noose and his raw flesh.

Einar licked his lips as he stole one last look at the second cavalryman, who stood rock still at his post. The infantryman was the liveliest of them all, his shoulders weaving to and fro, unearthly gasps rising from his putty-white throat. Einar paused; when he had worked his courage to its peak, he lurched at the taut length of leather, grasping at it with both fists to pull toward Raymond and loosen the pressure on his throat. His hands passed right through it, and he staggered ahead from sheer momentum.

The cavalryman tugged, and the coil tightened around Raymond's windpipe. The big man wheezed more painfully, his eyes and tongue bulging. Einar swung back and made a second grab at the whip. He looked hopelessly at Linda an instant before the stubby shaft of an arrow pierced his temple and flung him against one of the easels displaying her illustrations. The bristleboard was stained with red as the corpse pumped blood from the grisly wound. A second arrow followed even as Einar fell, this one driving itself through Raymond's heart from behind. The black man dropped forward as Linda's panicked eyes left him and spotted the crossbowman a few paces behind her. The warrior appeared not to see her.

"No," the woman moaned, trembling. But before she could begin to digest what had happened or think about what to do next, Linda felt a hot hand brush her shoulder.

"It is to be a new empire," came the familiar voice, soft but hollow. "I have been wondering when our lord would make you a part of it."

Linda turned and against all good sense saw Tally standing beside her. She recognized Tally's voice and general features; but this was not the same girl who had been murdered days before. This figure had pieces missing; it was a relief of Tally McGraw sculpted in blood but visible only where blood had stained her corpse. This was all of Tally that mattered to the Madjan and therefore all that was permitted to exist.

As Linda stared in horror, half a mouth and both of the devil's red eyes smiled. Aware of nothing but the need to get away from Tally—or whatever grim thing she had become— Linda turned and ran toward the arch that opened into the next hall. The whip-wielding warrior moved a few paces to bar her way; Linda flung herself frantically askew, toward the staircase. She neared, and the Madjan's eyes began to glow. Linda slowed then, panting with terror as he began to float toward her.

"Let him take you," Tally said soothingly. "It will be quicker that way, less painful. How I covet the role and the honor which fate has given you!"

Linda shook her head as if to drive out the dead sounds. She turned from the Madjan in time to see a partial red hand emerge from the void of the Madjan's black shell. Cara Thomas stepped from within, her bloody features fixing themselves on Linda.

Tally softly declared, "We shall attend to the rite of souling," as she and her ghastly companion wafted forward. Linda tore her eyes from Cara, who was missing a huge wedge from her thigh and torso. She backed away, shaking her head and denying that any of this was real. After a few paces, her back was against a showcase of ancient Chinese weapons; behind it was the wall; she could go no farther.

"Please don't do this. Tally, please let me go."

The sword-bearing infantryman hissed at Linda's plea and by slashing once at the air indicated that he stood ready to hold her for the Madjan's purpose should she elect to resist.

"Oh, God," Linda moaned as the Madjan approached. Her hands scurried nervously at either side, along the length of the glass display case. Just then, she remembered that the showcases were wired to the central alarm system; pivoting, she raised both arms above her and smashed her fists down hard through the glass.

Varley had Chapman alone by the hood of the car. The detective's gun was drawn, and Diver and Wadapoulis loitered nearby. The other two officers searched for the incendiary device they suspected had been responsible for razing the statue and the bridge.

"Sick," Varley was saying. "You're a real sick man. Damn shame they don't have the death penalty in New York. Damn shame. I'd have loved to see you sizzle, you friggin' nut case."

"I tell you I'm innocent, and I'm going to prove it."

"Oh?" Varley seemed amused. "While we wait for them to give me a shred of evidence to lock you up on, why don't you tell me how you're going to prove anything."

"Yu is probably dead by now."

Varley called over the lounging officers, Diver and Wadapoulis. "Spread out, look for a corpse. Female, Oriental, five-one. Unless—" his eyes jerked to Chapman "—unless you care to tell us where you dumped her?"

Chapman shook his head. "I don't believe this. I just *saved* her life. She ran off, back to the—"

The radio beeped, and Varley motioned for Shooter to answer it. "Flimsy alibi, chum. Try and convince the court that a monster killed her while we had our little chat."

Shooter bolted from the car. "Sir, we've got a ten-thirty."

"Robbery in progress? Where?"

"At the museum. We're tied in to the silent alarm."

"Robbery, my ass," Chapman declared.

Varley sent Diver and Wadapoulis on their way, clapped handcuffs on Chapman, and pushed him into the car. "Yeah, right, your Madjan just got up and walked away." He slid in beside him while Quinn took the wheel. "Looks like you're going to get to see some action before we put you away. Enjoy it, pal, cause it's the last you'll see for about six hundred years."

The dectective's car peeled off hot on the fender of the other, and in just over a half minute the museum was in view on the other side of the park.

Webster Hall seldom saw any action at the museum. That was the ex-marine's one gripe about this assignment. He didn't need the money; a career man in the military, he had a handsome pension and disability pay for a wound he'd suffered in Cambodia. He'd wanted some serious responsibility at a bank or an embassy, but there were a lot of unemployed vets, and this was the best his service could land him. He'd covered two bums, a freaked laserium goer, and a bitchy Chink in seventeen months of duty. To him, the flashing silent alarm on the planetarium wall was like a red flag waved before a bull. Whipping his gun from its holster, Hall rolled from his cubicle outside the museum and hustled toward the Asian chamber.

Coupla punks, he decided as he walked along the empty corridors. *A pro woulda seen the electronic eyes.*

Nearing the room, Hall went stiff-spined against the wall as he edged forward. His eyes on the threshold, he was almost upon it when he was distracted by a hiss to the rear. It sounded like his son's two-wheeler losing air, and he looked back in time to see the sword arcing toward him. Without thinking, Hall dropped flat, as he hadn't done since basic training; the rusted blade missed him, and by the backswing he had simultaneously backed out of range, risen, and swung his gun around. He unloaded two rounds, which pinged the wall behind the white-faced figure.

There was a sharp crack, and Hall felt a burning pain in his ankle. His left foot was tugged from beneath him, and he spilled face forward at the feet of the frowning figure. The fiend made no move to strike, and so Hall squirmed to get a look behind him. There was a thin length of leather around the ankle, held taut by a mounted figure as grisly as the first.

"I don't know what fag party you escaped from, but you're chewin' on the wrong prick!"

Hall pointed his gun at this new assailant and emptied the weapon. When the bullets proved no more effective than they had a moment before, Hall growled, "Fuckin' armor," and reached for the whip. His hands passed through it just as the rider gave a tug and jerked the guard to the open doorway. The expressionless cavalryman backed into the hall and yanked again. Still on his back, Hall slid forward.

Against the far wall, the guard saw Linda pinioned by two abominations. They looked back at him, and once more Hall tried to rise.

"Friggin' Manson loonies," he swore as he rolled onto his belly and scrambled to his knees. The shadow fell on him then, massive and ominous; his head shot around, and in that instant he exploded into flame. The Madjan, looming before him, played with the fires, causing them to rise like fingers of demons reaching from the pit. Hall's arms and head rose weakly within the inferno, before a blast of wind from the Madjan scattered him across the room like a collapsed pile of leaves.

The dozen-odd figures that now inhabited the room looked expectantly from the ashes to their god. The Madjan's eyes swirled bloody red, and an eerie outline appeared in the air before him: the contours of a man. Linda stared at it with shocked incomprehension. The figure was discernible as a displacement of everything behind it, as though the air had become defracted. Yet it wasn't an illusion; it had depth and breadth.

"Mortal to mortal," croaked the swordsman, who had moved between the Madjan statue and the warped image in the air. Linda recognized the museum guard as, dropping to one knee, he continued, "Subjects of the Madjan, guardians of his glory and servants of his will, the dead of Ch'en-shimm and battle-honored multitudes of its armies, rise! Mortal to mortal, the path is now laid."

From somewhere beyond the mirrorlike twist in space there

arose a clamor that Linda recognized at once: the din of metal striking metal she had heard before. Beside her, Tally said in an unpitying voice, "He doesn't need you now." A steaming red hand stroked Linda's cheek. "Time is short. The man's soul has been honored as a bridge between the worlds. Jiang will save you for the aftermath of battle." Her eyes stared toward the kneeling swordsman. "Jiang will take you in the name of the Madjan when the day is his."

Linda refused to consider what this creature had to say. She tried to put from her mind what was happening, to think of nothing but escape. That was the surest way to retain her sanity and survive whatever loathsome business was in the offing.

The clamor increased, swelling at uneven intervals as though unseen hills and chasms stopped or caught or echoed the sounds of things fast approaching. Hall—his shape, his soul, whatever the form was held trapped in the air—began to contort, throbbing and expanding as though pushed from behind and within. The head of the figure rolled as though suffering incomparable agony; its mouth was wide with silent pain when it fell into profile.

A wave of blood exploded from within the misshapen form, and from the frothing crest of it burst a red hand swinging a sword round and round. The crimson head of a rearing stallion crashed from the wave, followed by a demon rider made from the ancient blood. He rode the air, galloping skyward and shrieking hideously as a second red mount and a trio of bowmen rose from the roiling sea of blood.

The cascading army flew from the hall. Linda had no idea where they were headed, nor did she have the time to consider it. What held her attention was the daze into which the warriors as well as Tally and Cara seemed to have slipped. It was as if the Madjan, his attention on the summoning of the army, was not yet powerful enough to animate all the lifeless evil that was to serve him. And if blood were the source of his strength, she dared not even imagine the mission on which the vast new army was being sent.

Linda lurched free of her captors, who neither moved nor spoke as the woman ran toward the staircase and the exit nearest her.

Got to call for help . . . the police, a priest, someone. Her thoughts were erratic beyond the focused objective of getting to a telephone. Linda alternately ran and crawled up the stairs in a mad effort to put as much distance as possible between herself and the hell below. She cried as she struggled up the stairs, her mind losing its battle to block out the horror of what was happening a flight below her. Yet her haunted thoughts were nothing compared with the unbridled terror she experienced as a howl ripped the air from below. She turned in time to see one of the Madjan's devil warriors slip a rope from around the neck of a blood-red wolf.

Yu ran into the museum's side entrance, surprised to find it open and unguarded. Breathless from her flight but clear witted, she was at once aware of the changed atmosphere. It was home, the desert, yet what she felt was more than heat and endless horizons of waste; the air reeked of something tart, metallic, and foul. The Madjan was here and with him something dragged from whatever infamous realm he inhabited.

A woman's scream pulled her toward the corridor that bordered the west side of the Asian hall. Coming at the staircase from behind, Yu saw the four-legged apparition bound up the stairs before she could see the victim. Ignoring both, she raced through her memory and said to the human shape, *"Madjan itzi, hasheana. Onnana ho."*

The phantom creature looked at her, and the rope in its hand rose of its own volition; the wolf jumped back and slid into the leash, and the two unearthly creatures ran off trailing a vaporous veil of blood.

Yu swung round the steps and found Linda cowering behind her arms, her legs tucked up in a fetal position. She had sustained a few slashes, all superficial. Yu hurried to her side.

"Come, we must get upstairs."

"The—those *things*! Where?" She knew what she wanted to say, but the words would not come. Yu, helping her to her feet, offered what she thought Linda wanted to hear.

"I told them that the earth dragon had come to destroy the Madjan. I do not know what will happen when they learn that I have lied. I suspect there is nowhere these creatures cannot go, though we may be safer away from the hall."

"I was trying to escape. Yu, Tally is back there, and so is Cara. And the statues, they're *alive*."

"They are not alive. What you saw are shadows of another era, another dimension, not physical beings but energy which has somehow taken shape and consciousness."

"Shadows don't do what I just saw these monsters do."

Linda staggered from the steps to the landing, supported by

Yu. They continued upstairs in silence, pausing only when they heard the whoosh of a figure approaching from above. Ducking behind a case of prehistoric eggs, they watched wide-eyed as a horse and spectral rider rode along the stairwell several feet above the steps. The dim glow of the overhead lights did not immediately reveal what the oncoming wraith bore behind him. When at last he passed and Linda recognized the hulk being dragged along the marble steps as the butchered corpse of Dr. Tepper, she screamed as though she would never stop.

The rider reined to a halt as Yu pulled Linda to her feet and began to run. Heaving the curator's thick carcass down the stairs to the Asian hall, the cavalryman unhitched his whip and then turned to pursue the women.

The two police cars screeched into the parking lot an instant before Laojiu's limousine rolled slowly in. Reedy, reclining impatiently on a park bench, was up and over to Varley's car like a line drive.

"Picked yerself up a mighty distinguished escort, Grant! Who's in trouble?"

Chapman did not answer but sat in the car while Varley and Diver piled out. "Watch the prisoner," the detective ordered Wadapoulis as he and the other officer joined the second pair. The four men rushed inside the museum.

"Son of a bitch," Reedy said as he peered into the car, "*you're* slammer-bound? Jesus, Grant, what in God's name did you do?"

Chapman turned from the reporter and looked out the other window. He saw Laojiu emerge from his car. The Chinese approached quickly, casting concerned looks at the policemen as they passed.

"Mr. Laojiu, what do you know about any of this?" Reedy fished his note pad and pen from behind a crushed pack of cigarettes in his shirt pocket. Thoughts of the morning's headline, an exclusive, danced before his world-weary eyes.

"I know nothing," Laojiu admitted as he bent beside Wadapoulis's open window. "Chapman, what is it?"

"They think I'm the killer, but never mind that. Yu and I saw the Madjan in the park. He tore up a bridge, almost killed your daughter. She said she was coming back here to warn you."

Laojiu stood up and stared over at the museum. After a second in which his breathing quickened nervously, he turned back to the car. "Come with me, Chapman, please. I may need your help."

"Sorry," Wadapoulis finally interrupted. He seemed a trifle smug in his authority, denying the wishes of a statesman and an international scholar in a single easy negation. "This man's a suspected killer. He stays with me."

"A killer!" Reedy laughed as he scribbled down the quote. "And I'm a concert pianist, ambulance chasing for a lark. Boy, are there going to be some red faces downtown."

"Don't give me a pain," the policeman warned. "This job is tough enough without the snide comments."

Without wasting further words, Laojiu picked up a rock and drove it hard against the window. Before Wadapoulis could stop him, the Chinese had reached through the shattered pane and unlocked the door.

The officer drew his pistol as Chapman climbed out; Reedy, standing behind the officer, grabbed his wrist and easily twisted the weapon away.

"They don't train 'em like they did for WW II," he said, looking up at Chapman while he held the revolver on a stunned Wadapoulis. "Now then, Grant, old pal. I want the book rights. I'll write 'em in prison, but I *want* 'em. I want my shot at the Pulitzer goddam Prize."

Chapman nodded. "I owe you," he said as he pulled the key ring from the ignition and undid his handcuffs. He latched the officer to the steering wheel, flipped Reedy the keys. "All right, you can tell the world all about Tarlo, but I want the gun."

"God," Wadapoulis shouted, "don't!"

"Aw, shut up," Reedy complained as he turned over the gun. "You're wasting our time."

Chapman rushed into the museum, with Laojiu running alongside.

Wadapoulis turned and stared at Reedy; the reporter only shook his head and snickered as he slid into the back seat of the police car and lit a cigarette.

The sound of gunfire reached Chapman as they piled past Hall's post. The shots spurred the two men to a run. What they saw as they entered the Asian chamber could have been culled only from insanity's most tainted vision. From a giant, amebic displacement of space in the center of the chamber poured a clawing mob of shrilling soldiers and banshee women, filling the air with the sights and sounds of pestilence. Diver lay dead and Shooter lay dying on opposite sides of the room, gutted like cattle and being dragged by white-faced soldiers to the growing mound of dead bodies heaped at the Madjan's feet. Varley and Quinn were nowhere to be seen, and Chapman, even as he picked out Tepper from among the slain, found solace in the fact that Yu was not one of them. He could see from Laojiu's searching expression that the same thought had been on the archaeologist's mind.

"They're going to rethink a lot of theology after this," Chapman said, "assuming any of us are left to tell about it, that is."

"The dead of Ch'en-shimm," the archaeologist said reverently. "The people, the warriors, the honor guard, and their god. Stored, preserved over the millennia, somehow unleashed to perpetuate the beliefs they held in life. It is unthinkable, yet it's here before us."

"Those black shapes?" Chapman asked.

"Bodies somehow emptied of their living spirits. The statues were so much more than we know, filled by the intense faith of these people with energy—actually the focus and vessel of their worship."

Chapman understood, though his brain revolted against the evidence of his senses. He accepted this all purely for the sake of survival.

"I'm going upstairs," he informed the archaeologist. "I want to find the others and get the hell out of here. I suggest you leave before they see us."

"I'll go with you," he responded. "I may be of some use in the metaphysics of this. Not that there appears to be any protection against the issue of the Madjan."

The men turned back into the darkness and went upstairs. Chapman did not know if Laojiu had noticed it, but he had counted only seven animate statues for the thirteen empty shells. His chest tightened with fear, and his mind drew an utter blank as he considered what he would do if they met one of the demons.

The shrieking chilled them as it filtered upstairs, at the same time distracting them. They elected to continue on to the fifth floor, suspecting that the cluttered cubicles of the executive offices would offer Yu and the others more places to hide, if indeed there was any hiding from these seemingly omnipotent creatures. Chapman was glad that Linda was at home. He felt he could face death easier knowing that she was safe.

As they cleared the third floor, the archaeologist said at last, "I believe that if it were possible to reach the statues and destroy them, the Madjan would be unable to remain in our world."

"Don't ignore the possibility that in doing so we could just as easily trap him here."

"I don't think so, Chapman, for I don't believe these things are real. They appeared to Yu and to the other girls as visions; that is why there was never a physical trace in those crimes, why even people in the immediate proximity saw and heard nothing. By feeding on human life, which is, after all, electrical impulses, they have now become visible to more than the victim."

"Strengthening the broadcast signal, as it were?"

"In a manner of speaking. What they turn against people is that energy. They use it to maim or to kill, yet they themselves cannot be touched or countered. The ancients spilled untold seas of blood, never knowing that it was actually the life force which nourished their gods."

"Interesting theory, but I'm afraid it's just a trifle cabalist." Chapman's words were choked off by a whimper from just above them. The younger man bolted ahead.

On the fourth-floor landing lay Officer Quinn, his legs crushed and his arms pulled across the opposite shoulder blades. His blue uniform was stained liberally with red. He was squirming wormlike to the stairs in what was apparently an effort to escape.

Chapman dropped to his knees two steps below. Quinn's face trembled as he tried to speak. "Left . . . me . . . here . . . went t-to . . . kill . . . others."

"What others?" Chapman urged gently.

"Varley . . . two girls."

"Two?"

"Chinese . . . other one said warn y-you."

Quinn had gasped out the last word, dead before his face slid forward into Chapman's hands. Gripped with renewed alarm, Chapman laid the man's head down softly and then rose.

"Come on," he snapped at the Chinese, and leaped to the landing. Before he was firmly on it, a snorting red stallion flew between the two men, its rider reaching out and scooping up the body. Corpse in hand, the cavalryman executed a sliding about-face in the air; its red eyes burning with fury, the creature hesitated for a moment and then dove straight down the stairs.

Reading Chapman's mind, Laojiu offered quickly, "Before the life energy dissipates, the Madjan must have him. But this man, this creature, will return. He was Li, the Emperor's gift to the Madjan, an assassin."

Chapman wasted no time thinking about the soldier who had left them. Faced with the realization that Linda might be there, he ran onto the dark fourth floor.

Glancing at the elevator, he noticed that the dials on the three carriages all read four. Anyone who had gone to the fifth floor had returned. Chapman looked along the cavernous hallway.

"There are two large halls on this floor," he advised Laojiu. "Cretaceious and Jurassic dinosaurs. Right now I'd rather be facing one of them with just a popgun. Tell me," he asked with resignation, "just what the hell do we do when we meet one of these ghouls."

"Until we can destroy the statues, there is nothing to do but outmaneuver them."

Shaking his head at their plight, Chapman stirred himself into a brisk walk. They hadn't gone more than a half dozen paces when their heads were turned by a burbling shout from behind.

"There. They are ahead. New ones, new ones!"

Chapman thought his bowels would turn to cork as he saw a red, incomplete figure of Dr. Tepper walk toward them with dead languor. The oval face was tipped to one side on the partial neck; the arms were stiff at his torn sides.

A dull thrumming to the rear turned them again, and Chapman saw the crossbowman before Laojiu did; the shaft struck the Chinese in the shoulder and spilled him backward to the tile floor. Chapman fired at the unmounted creature, but the bullets passed ineffectively through him.

"Bad news," Chapman informed the wounded archaeologist as he scooped him in his arms.

"Not me. Save the women."

"It's not just nobility, friend. I may *need* some ideas, like right about now." The archer strung a second arrow and let it fly. Chapman hurled himself to one side, and the projectile slipped through Tepper.

"They are *my* find," Tepper shrieked, "the Emperor must be told that!"

"Even dead he's a bastard," Chapman said, staring at Tepper, whose voice and inexorable approach were the only animate qualities about him.

The demon loaded a third arrow. Looking up, Chapman decided that there was no sense making an easy target. Shifting the slight Chinese to his shoulder, he raised his pistol and shot out the two overhead lights with the remaining four bullets. From behind the archer, the light of the two great chambers shone cones of yellow luminance into the hallway; otherwise, it was dark. Chapman appeared a hazy smear in the grainy dark, and the bowman lowered his weapon.

Chapman was about to congratulate himself for buying precious moments, when a hollow clomping broke in back of them. He turned and saw the assassin charge from the stairwell. The crimson steed reared near the ceiling and then swooped down at the mortals. Chapman saw the rider's sword swinging, and he dropped to the floor with his frail bundle. Shielded by the dark, they survived the first pass. Chapman glanced up but could barely see the horse reined around and, snorting, driven into a fresh assault.

"How do you fight a ghost?" he cried as, watching the blurred figure, he pushed Laojiu to one side of the corridor and then rolled to the other as the horse arced overhead. An arrow struck the tile where they had been, and the bowman, perilously near, fixed a new one.

"Professor! If you've got any ideas, this is your last chance!"

"Fire with fire," he snarled, his voice weak from loss of blood. There was a four-legged showcase just behind him, and he inched toward it. "Use Tepper."

"Christ, of course! Dr. Tepper." He craned back at the curator. "The assassin wants us *and* the glor—"

"Quiet!" Laojiu snapped as he saw the archer level his crossbow in the direction of the voice. Chapman bellied down, and the arrow flew overhead.

"Want you, want the Emperor's favor," Tepper droned.

Chapman noticed the rider pulling around for yet another charge. "Then *stop* him," he insisted. "They wouldn't hesitate to stop you!"

The thing that was Tepper stopped and seemed to consider this, pivoting slowly as the horse flew down. Reaching over his head like a player in an astral circus, he grabbed the steed's forelegs; the animal somersaulted, turning over in the air several times and immobilizing Tepper and the assassin in an inertial tangle.

While the capsized pair tumbled toward the bowman, Chapman pulled Laojiu from under the showcase. The demon was momentarily disoriented.

"No, you will go faster alone. Locate the women, then find a way to destroy the statue. Nothing else can make a permanent end to this."

"Will fire work? Can I burn it?"

Laojiu shook his head. "The clay was oven-fired. It must be shattered."

Chapman considered this as he patted the older man's hand. "I understand. I'll be back for you later." He hopped to his feet and, dashing around the still-distracted bowman, ran into the Cretaceous chamber.

The room was dominated by the massive skeletons of two prehistoric animals, a long-necked sauropod and the upright meat-eater tyrannosaurus. Exhibit cases and stands of skulls and bones lined the walls. It was quiet enough in the chamber for Chapman to hear his echoing footsteps; there was not a specter in sight, nor did the bowman show any inclination of entering. He stared through the entrance for a minute and then looked toward the Chinese; after a moment, he continued slowly in the old man's direction. Chapman thought to go back and bring him into the chamber but was distracted by a scuffling nearby.

"Psssst! Grant!"

Chapman looked across the hall and saw Varley waving briskly from behind the pedestaled head of a horned dinosaur. The State Department official jogged over.

"I believe you, Grant, I really do." The detective shook Chapman by the shoulders. "I don't know how you made it up here in one piece! But God, you were right. There are all kinds of things that shouldn't be but *are*. It's like running around inside Pandor—"

"Detective," Chapman interrupted, "Quinn said there are two women here. Yu and who else?"

"Quinn? He's alive?" Chapman shook his head. "Shit, I'm surprised. Horsemen had him by either arm, ran him hard into a wall, over and over!"

"The *girls*, Varley! Is Linda one of them?"

"Afraid so."

"Where are they?"

"Upstairs. I found them there, but we got separated while we were looking for small explosives, the kind they use to move rock at digs. Yu said we've got to blast the statues. That's when something that looked like Shooter and one of those cavalry creatures found us. We were supposed to meet here—for some reason Yu thought we'd be safe."

"You *left* them?"

"There was nothing I could *do*, damn it. Matter of fact, they were in better shape than I was. They were in a niche with vending machines, where the horse couldn't fit. I was out in the open. Ran my ass off to reach the elevator before Shooter."

Chapman stood gnawing his lower lip. He looked around as he wondered aloud, "How did she know you'd be safe in here?"

"Beats me. We didn't really have time for long good-byes."

"Doesn't matter," Chapman said after a beat. "Right now our priority is to get upstairs. Those dead things may not be too bright, but it won't take long before a couple of infantrymen go upstairs or one of the horsemen thinks to dismount."

"Look, Grant, if you don't mind, I'll pass on this little adventure. I've got my family to think about, and besides, the women are probably dead by now. Even if they're not, *you'll* be once you step outside."

"You've got to show me where they are."

"Two doors beyond Tepper's office, stockroom with picks and shovels and cartons full of bones." Varley dipped his head toward the south entrance. "Elevator's right down the hall."

"Did you at least call for help?"

"Tried to get the bomb squad here, but the phones are full of static. Me? Grant, I'm going to sit here until sunrise, when maybe these vampire-ghost-werewolf types will go back to their coffins. If you had any smarts, you'd do the same."

Chapman hadn't the time or inclination to argue. With a sneer of disgust, he set off on his own.

CHAPTER FOURTEEN

THE DISMOUNTED CAVALRYMAN stared at his comrade, who by his relaxed posture and lowered sword arm clearly had made the kill. Although the girls' bodies were gone, there was blood on the floor of the alcove. There was nothing left for the warrior to do but rejoin the Madjan for the taking of an empire.

No other soldier came after the rider had gone, and after several tense minutes, Yu dared to look out. Poking her forehead over the mirror, she saw no one else present.

"Never thought I'd owe my life to Acme Vendors and Motts," Linda admitted, staring down at the seven cans of tomato juice she'd taken from the machine and spilled on the floor. "Dumb fucking ghost!"

"We still have much to do," Yu countered, leaning the mirror against the dispenser from which she'd pried it. "I believe that it is now but a matter of organization before they leave the museum, their new temple, for a war on the modern world. Against them," she said with a shudder, "not one of us stands a chance. As long as the Madjan remains behind to protect the statues, they are virtually invulnerable."

Linda offered practically, "If it came down to that, the army could always roll in some tanks and level the museum."

"Only if that is done soon. Once a spirit becomes oriented, each death gives the Madjan a new subject, a new ally. The army will swell, and if this building is not razed soon, none will be able to get past the guards that are certain to be posted for miles above and around."

"Hell, you make this sound like doomsday," Linda said anxiously.

Yu looked soberly to her companion. "Had Ch'en-shimm not fallen in the earthquake, the war machine which Ch'en had assembled in the Madjan's name might well have overrun the continent. History would have been radically altered. Consider that potential and add to it the evil occult power they now possess. I fear to contemplate where it will lead."

"Then let's not," Linda suggested as she used a rag that had plugged a leak in the machine's cooling system to wipe blotches of juice from her knees. The women walked cautiously from their haven, resuming their search for the explosives.

After a few minutes of fruitless exploration that saw Yu grow perceptibly more anxious, Linda perched her hands on her hips and sighed.

"I'll bet the charges are in the safe. As a matter of fact, I'd stake my life on it."

"Is the safe accessible?"

"It's a few doors down in the security office. I'm sure they wouldn't take a chance leaving explosives out in the open where someone could steal them."

"Do you happen to know the combination?"

"Webster Hall would have, but I don't. Still, it may not be hopeless. I remember someone from the lock company was up here the other day. Maybe it's busted."

Yu's fixed features didn't reflect the desperation she felt. "Let's have a look. There may be some way of getting inside, and it appears to be our only hope."

Linda led the way down the hall. As they finished their careful trek and entered the tiny security office, the women were startled to see Webster Hall standing dumbly beside an infantryman, guarding the safe. Without wasting an instant once they realized the dilemma, Yu and Linda retreated. They ran flush into the crimson figure of Laojiu, who gripped each girl powerfully by the arm, though he stared past them with lifeless eyes.

Yu screamed, her wail resounding through the whole of the uninhabited floor.

• • •

Chapman was reconnoitering the path to the elevator when he heard the woman's scream. Cursing himself because his caution may have cost a life, he dashed to the elevator. Chapman shut the gate, and the door closed automatically. It took a few seconds more for him to figure out how to operate the attendant-run carriage, but he finally got it in motion.

When the elevator creaked to a stop after the one-story climb, Chapman heard a faint hissing beyond the door.

They must have heard the cables and are waiting for me. Reaching up and knocking open the ceiling panel, Chapman pulled himself to the roof of the carriage just as the door slid back. He saw an arm covered with ancient and tarnished armor burst through the gate reaching for him. The arm froze as its bearer apparently scanned the empty lift. After a moment, the arm was withdrawn, and Chapman heard the whooshing sound of the soldier's departure.

Feeling his heart throbbing just under his chin, Chapman poked his head into the carriage and looked outside. The way was clear, and he lowered himself quietly from his perch. It took an eternal minute more to slide back the squeaky metal gate, after which he hastened toward the executive offices. He stopped just short of the bend in the corridor when he heard several pairs of scuffling feet.

"The women honor the men by nourishing their god," droned a vaguely familiar male voice from along the hall. "The hand too fair for battle, the limb too weak to lead. The bosom which flows with milk rather than sinew."

The chant was accompanied by grunting and women's voices bitterly protesting. Chapman was relieved to hear them.

The chant must mean there's a ritual involved with killing women, probably done in the Madjan's presence. That gives me four floors to get Yu and Linda away from whatever's got them.

He stayed board-rigid against the shadowed wall, waiting for the party to pass. Moments later, a horseman plied grimly through the air, vanguard for the women and Laojiu.

Chapman shut his eyes as he fought down a rush of nausea and regret. Yet the feeling did not linger, for Laojiu was gone, and nothing would undo that. His attention must be given to those who still lived.

The unearthly procession continued to the elevator, where

Laojiu, still gripping the women, thrust them into the carriage, following them. With slow, deliberate movements, he adjusted the lever that worked the elevator, never once looking at it. As the door began to grind shut, Chapman made his move.

Kicking off against the wall, he dove past the horseman into the carriage. The door closed before the cavalryman could strike; Linda gasped as Chapman braced himself between Laojiu and the women.

The ghoul did not move. He simply looked past the threesome blankly as the carriage groaned and lurched into motion. Chapman eased curiously when it became apparent that no attack would be forthcoming; then, aware in a flash of understanding what was afoot, he burst into a grin.

The archaeologist's red eyes vanished; actually, his lids folded into his brow. He looked from one to the other of the passengers and then fell forward, staining Chapman's shirt with red as the younger man caught him.

"Father?" Yu moved toward him, her manner suddenly excited. She took his face gently between her hands and saw his coloring smear.

Linda's nose crinkled. "Wait a minute! He's not one of them. I recognize that smell; it's my number 37B poster paint!"

"I . . . I heard the scream," Laojiu said weakly, "went upstairs when they thought me dead. I passed your studio."

Chapman cradled the fainting archaeologist, simultaneously informing Yu about the wound. Hidden in the coat of color, the broken shaft of the arrow was visible now that attention had been called to it.

Yu began to weep, and Linda put her arm around her. But as the carriage slowed to a stop on the fourth floor, Chapman reminded them that they were far from secure. Laojiu insisted on standing and leading them until they were past any of the demon warriors and safely inside the Cretaceous hall. Yu protested, but Chapman reluctantly agreed. He stood the scientist up and told him to retain a firm grip on the women's arms for support.

"You'll have to fend for yourself," the wizened man reluctantly advised Chapman. "If they see me with a live male, they'll pierce our charade."

"I understand," Chapman said, and unscrewed the light in

the elevator, lingering in the dark while the threesome made their way into the corridor.

The women wept convincingly while Laojiu proceeded with deliberate slowness, even as the thwarted bowman appeared with Tepper and the ruddy specter of Einar Björkman. The archer eyed the group with the hovering stance peculiar to these creatures, while Tepper and the Swede shuffled dumbly ahead.

Unexpectedly, the shade that was Einar stopped and searched the hallway, its dead eyes rolling over and over. What was still residually human in him seemed to be fighting forth. He said at last, "I feel him . . . always knew when he was near . . . aura . . . unique."

In the carriage, Chapman thought, *Fe fi fo fum to you, my stinking buddy!* Sweat running down his brow and sleeve, he reached out stealthily to shut the door.

The specter waited a moment longer, said, "He is mine," and lurched ahead.

Just within the door to the dinosaur hall, Linda turned and saw the Swede head for the elevator. Wrenching her arm from Laojiu, she ran to the elevator and jumped in.

"Beat it, Grant, they know you're here!"

Chapman was startled and tried to push Linda out. "Are you crazy? Get back in the room while you still can!"

"No. People with rocky times ahead shouldn't go them alone. My father didn't, and I sure as hell won't let you."

"You're a pain," Chapman declared as he slammed the gate shut moments before Einar arrived. The Swede didn't miss a beat as he gripped the grate and ripped it away; Chapman used that diversion to slip the carriage into a hasty descent.

"Where are we going?"

"Third floor. God only knows how, but we've got to find a way to smash the statue of the Madjan." He tortured his mind for a scenario as the numbers marked off their descent. "When Yu told Varley that the soldiers wouldn't attack him in that exhibit hall, did she happen to mention why?"

"Something about the earth dragon," Linda offered. "When Yu first found me, she drove one of those things away by telling him that the earth dragon was coming. Scared the ass off him."

Chapman considered this. "According to legend, that's the

monster that brought the temple down. I wonder." He tapped his lower lip. "Just could be they think the hall upstairs is the temple of the earth dragon."

"You mean the skeletons?"

Chapman nodded. "The idol of the Madjan is the portal which he used to enter this world. Destroy it and you imprison the spirit. If we could somehow get the Madjan to turn his power loose on the earth dragon's sanctuary—"

"You mean bring down the house?"

"Right on his own head," Chapman said with rising hope. "But we need him to collapse the floor, not just the statue. And if his hatred and fear of the earth dragon is as strong as I suspect, he just might do it."

"Only one problem with your plan," Linda said as the lift settled down on the Madjan's level. "How're we going to get our friend to come upstairs?"

"When Yu spoke to the warrior, do you remember what words she used?"

"Jesus, Grant, why don't you come up with something simple, like asking me to name the capital city of Rwanda?"

"Kigali," Chapman shot back. "Think, because if we blow this, we're dead."

Linda scratched her head furiously and then shook it. "Grant, I'm sorry. I just don't remember."

"A word," he implored. "A sound—something!"

"Sorry."

Chapman punched his open palm as the door opened. "Well, I hope your old man's watching over us if these antiques don't understand English. In which case—" he swiveled to one side and embraced the woman "—it's been great." He stepped from the elevator, with Linda gliding right behind him. He gave her a look to insist that she stay behind. She scowled back an equally insistent refusal. Sighing, Chapman pressed silently toward the Asian hall.

The ululating wails, running up and down the scale, shivered the small of Chapman's back. He found it odd that facing death, he was not so much frightened of dying as he was at the thought of chugging around as one of those bloody specters. He wished he hadn't used all his bullets, for he'd have killed himself before letting the Madjan or his evil issue have him.

"Itchy," Linda murmured as they all but tiptoed through

the arctic hall toward the exhibit. "One of the words was *'itchy. Madjan itchy hasho,'* something like that. No, not *'hasho,' 'hasheo,'* I think. That's about the first half of what Yu said."

"Okay, we'll lead with that."

"Yeah, best foot forward," Linda said nervously.

The couple froze as a mad human cry sounded from the adjoining Asian hall. Dashing forward, they arrived to see Officer Wadapoulis all but cleaved in two, his intestines spilling from the hacked side of his body. One of the riders was baying in triumph, holding the policeman by the heel and bearing him, dangling, toward the mounting pile of dead. Behind the rider, Reedy, his legs churning madly, was racing through the chamber trying to escape an archer who was poised behind him.

Linda watched the bowman, and when he raised his weapon, she shouted, "Doug, hit the dirt!" The reporter looked at her, reacting a split instant before the projectile was released. It passed harmlessly above him as Chapman ran in. He pulled at the journalist's arm.

"Got you a real page turner here," Chapman joked, his eye on the bowman. Linda screamed for them to watch out for two riders approaching from opposite directions. Chapman fell on top of Reedy and looked quickly for the Madjan. "Stay put," he ordered, scurrying crablike toward the floating god. Throwing himself to his knees he hollered, *"Madjan itchy hasheo,"* viscerally distrustful of Linda's enunciation, adding protectively, "This is the temple of the earth dragon! He is above us, great Madjan. He has sent me to order you to leave, sent *me*, for he saw me surrender to you by the lake, knows me to be one of the faithful."

It was a good improvisation, Chapman felt, and he only prayed the deity knew what he had said. The giant's eyes burned scarlet, and after a moment the great head turned.

Buy it, damn you, buy it!

The supplicant watched as the idol's head moved slowly, surveying the suddenly stilled multitude. The god's eyes rested momentarily on Reedy and then passed over him. Beneath the Madjan's feet, the swirling cloud surged forward. The great hands opened slowly and came to rest on his golden weapons. The gauntlet appeared to have been claimed.

• • •

Varley ran forward, stooped, and followed a serpentine course as though he were evading gunfire. He had not fired when Laojiu appeared, whole and not decimated like the other spirits; it was then that he saw the whites of his eyes and the smudged paint and suspected a fraud.

"Good work," he exclaimed as he ducked under the archaeologist's free arm and helped support the sagging figure. "I don't know how you did it, but I salute you!"

"He's wounded," Yu cut in. "Help me get him to the bench."

"What happened to Linda? She buy it?"

"Linda is with Chapman, Detective. Lord protect them, they're trying to reach the statue."

"God help them is right, lady. Jesus Christ himself couldn't make it in and out of that room in one piece. Somebody's going to have a lot of explaining to do when we finally get this mess cleared up."

Yu did not respond. Her mind was filled with visions of the desolation that would ensue if Chapman failed, yet she knew that it was worse than she could conceive even on the verge of surrendering the planet to madness.

As she laid her father out, a familiar gust of warmth blew over her, wringing moisture from her flesh and causing it to dry in the same hot draft. She fired off a backward glance in time to see a gray fog twist and billow into the hall.

Yu rose slowly. "We had better seek shelter," she warned. "There is about to be a showdown."

"What are you talking about?" Varley carped, tugging his gun from his belt and following her gaze. "We're going to shoot it out with a cloud? This a new wrinkle or something?"

Instead of answering, Yu helped her barely conscious father back to his feet. "He's coming," she informed the archaeologist. "Somehow they must have succeeded. The Madjan is coming!"

"The Madjan?" Varley squawked. "No thanks!" Shoving his arms around Laojiu's midriff, he waited until Yu had taken up his feet. Then they carried him toward the relative haven of the ceratopsian skull and pedestal.

The smoke folded over and over on itself, building as it rolled into the hall. There were flashes of light from within the smoky block. Watching from around the pedestal, Yu suspected that the Madjan was actually trying to create a dramatic entrance, rattling its saber impressively in the holy sanctum of its dire foe. Varley did not watch, though as he sat on his haunches, he felt the floor begin to rumble and heard the air fill with thunder.

The face of the foggy monolith vanished in a burst of brilliance, which burned on the remaining sides until the mist had gone black and swirled up and behind the Madjan in plaguelike tendrils. The god stood glistening white and gold just inside the room, its crimson eyes livid with eons of hatred and humiliation.

The idol's sword dipped slowly in the direction of the gaunt giant whose huge posture and ferocious skull looked down on him. The god's eyes flared, and radiant heat rushed from its eyes to the sword. The weapon burned but was not consumed, and as the Madjan raised its head, a spray of flame shot in all directions from the blade. These mighty fingers of fire were like the Madjan's own hand, burning and crushing the earth dragon in their grasp.

Chapman, Linda, and Reedy arrived then, unmolested by the inanimate demons, trapped in their spectral limbo while the Madjan's power was channeled elsewhere. Chapman slid to a halt in the doorway in time to see white-hot fireballs fly from the Madjan and the ancient fossils flame and crumple.

"He's only hitting the goddam skeleton," Linda swore as ivory and gray ash fell to the floor in bulging clouds. "Grant, if this doesn't work—"

"I know," he interrupted, "we go back and try to destroy the statue. Three of us against three of them. Some odds."

"Yu will come; she understands the danger."

"Sure, but it'll take at least two of us to tip that figure while the other two try to distract a trio of airborne monsters. Like I said, I don't like the odds."

"Grant the giant killer," Reedy put in. "These critters don't know who it is they're dealing with."

The talk ceased; all but the strained breathing of the onlookers was silenced. They watched as the last of the dusty tyrannosaur fell to powder, and the Madjan surveyed the ruin before turning his wrath on the lesser figures, the honor guard, the sauropod, and the fossils in their glass cases. Flame fanned in every direction while Yu barely managing to drag her father to a nearby bench before their protective skull was incinerated.

As the skeletons burned, the Madjan's head turned in a slow survey of the damage. With ponderous movements, he replaced his sword in its girdle sheath and let his arms fall straight by his sides. Chapman stared anxiously at the figure. Taking several steps back from the door, he prepared to race down the steps.

The Madjan stood rock still for a long moment. The battle was won, and animation seemed to go out of him; the fog began to cluster and reform about his feet, to bear him back to his own domain.

Chapman turned from the chamber and, pulling Reedy behind him, headed for the steps. Suddenly, the stairwell was filled with the onrushing army of the Madjan and the spirits of the dead. Chapman stood riveted with dismal resignation at the sight of the unearthly figures approaching, though Reedy turned and ran into a corridor. However, to Chapman's confusion, the creatures passed over and around him; not one so much as glanced at him. Even Reedy halted his retreat as the veil phalanx rode past him and Linda into the hall where their god had waged brief but victorious battle.

Spreading through the chamber, the hellish denizens lashed whips to pillars and bore fiery embers to the four corners of the room. Some of the creatures, bearing lengths of rusted chain, crashed through the banks of tall, high windows and looped the links around the arch-like stretches of wall between the panes. Whips brought sections of pillars crashing to the floor while fire chewed at whatever remained standing.

Chapman watched the holocaust with rising hope even as the Madjan began to rise his misty carpet from the room.

"It's not going to trap him," Reedy said.

"It doesn't have to if it falls. The Madjan is just a spirit; it's the statue we're after."

Just then, Chapman noticed Yu and Laojiu still inside, with Varley pinned nearby beneath a piece of masonry. Running over to them, Chapman rolled the stone from the detective's leg. When Varley was hobbling safely away, Chapman turned his attention to the Chinese. Gathering up the barely conscious archaeologist, Chapman scurried back to the hallway with Yu close behind. Moments after their sprint, Chapman watched as the warriors holding the free ends of the chain met in the air above the center of the room. Handing their lengths to the assassin, they saw him fuse the ends with fire. Below, the Madjan was about to leave the chamber. On the heels of a piercing war cry, the horsemen tugged the chains to make sure they were securely fastened to the arches, then rode forth in the wake of the triumphant god.

The century-old plaster and wood between the windows cracked, awesome chunks tumbled inward. They shattered harmlessly on the floor, and Chapman, looking on, once more began to fear a failure. There was a moment of utter quiet as the specters released the chains and turned their cruel eyes upon the humans.

Just then, beneath two resonant cracks, the inadequately supported ceiling fell in, spilling down the executive level and everything in the offices above: the desks and countless fossils, the building material itself, and even the safe. All dropped in an avalanche that struck the floor with a resounding crash. Chapman held his breath as he felt the superstructure of the Cretaceous hall shudder—and then creak visibly beneath the harsh concussion.

Handing Laojiu to Reedy, Chapman hurried Linda and Yu down the hallway to the stairwell while he slowed down to help the crawling Varley. His eyes drawn to the storming havoc in their wake, he saw the room fall downward, noting with profound satisfaction as the base of the tyrannosaur display crashed flat upon the black silhouette of the statue of the Madjan.

Even before the clamor of the debris had faded, a new tempest began. From their perch in the corridor, slanted precipitously toward the gaping chasm in the display hall, Chapman and Varley lingered to witness the cyclone of color, wind, and all manner of sound that rose from the destruction of the idol.

It was as though a dimension that lurks barely beneath the skin of our own had blistered and exploded. Chapman thought it must be what a volcano looks like from the inside. A spinning tumult of air grew from a point where the heart of the Madjan had been into a disk, sucking the crimson spirits into it and dissipating them in its ever-growing, spiraling diameter. The demons clutched at thin air as they were drawn to their demise, but not one survived. At the same time, the Madjan's dozen warriors looked to their own flight, many of them caught as they rose from the whirling vortex into the cretaceous chamber. Their white flesh and black features ran together, and their motions slowed and stiffened. They became the gray figures they once had been, solidifying in their paces and crashing to earth when the transformation had been completed.

As the whirling plasma whipped in its frenzy, material objects began to be drawn into its orbit and flung upward. Linda and the others who had fled stayed clear of the Asian hall, but the suction the storm created threatened to draw them in. There was one, however, who would not succumb to the expanding, darkening vortex. The Madjan ascended on a pillar of black smoke while he fought to work free of its pull. The clash of the opposing forces filled the level and punched Chapman backward in a series of somersaults; Varley, caught in the ricochet of those same powers, was drawn to the Madjan as though in a whirlpool.

The detective scratched at the uprooted floor tiles and torn wire supports on which the dinosaurs had been mounted, but the buffeting knocked him inexorably toward the abyss. The spectral chains left by the demons taunted him, hanging just overhead but intangible.

Beyond the pull of the maelstrom, Chapman felt helpless as he saw the wounded detective drawn in. He ventured as close to this awesome gravity as he dared, extending his arms to their utmost in an effort to reach Varley. But he could not, and so he withdrew to the entrance of the hall when his own endeavors threatened to become suicidal. Chapman even tugged on one of the skeletal coils in the hope of dislodging it and extending it to the detective, but the wire would not be wrested from the wall.

As Chapman prepared to launch himself again at the slipping figure, there was an unexpected change in the tenor of the storm. The Madjan ceased to resist; the winds stopped churning in the devastated upper floor, and the black cloud on which the Madjan stood swirled darkly around him, blown and attenuated by the powerful force whirling below it.

It's like he simply shut down, Chapman thought as the god gave up every vestige of life and motion.

Varley lolled face down on the edge of the gaping pit, and Chapman darted over to retrieve him.

"We're going to make it now," he said as he hooked his neck under the detective's arm. "I think our friend's giving up."

"Oh yeah?" Varley blurted, turning his battered face toward the pit. Chapman followed his gaze. Below, beyond the vortex that had gone black after swallowing its refugee inhabitants, the display base that had crushed the idol was itself latticed with cracks. Beneath incalculable pressure, the wood and plaster stand collapsed inward and disintegrated, with the dust blossoming out and away from the shattered statue of the Madjan.

"Dear God," Chapman muttered as several of the smaller pieces of the idol rocked and began to move toward the larger chunks. As though each had a will of its own, the jagged shards fit themselves seamlessly into place, rebuilding the idol in deliberate order.

Buffered against the storm by its smoky cocoon, the Madjan was channeling all of its energy into the telekinetic healing. Chapman knew that there was no way he could get downstairs in time to impede the Madjan's progress; he looked desperately around for something to heave at it.

"The safe," Varley wheezed. "Over there."

Chapman followed the weak gesturing of his hand. "I don't get it—"

"Look," he implored. "Door's broken, go inside!"

The puzzled official ran over and saw at once what the detective had meant. There was a case of low-powered explosives earmarked by stencil "Summer: Mongolia." Chapman ripped off the lid and grabbed an armful of the cylindrical metal containers. He hurried back to the lip of the abyss.

"No fuses. Just pray that the pressure he's exerting is enough for a concussion."

Kneeling, Chapman was almost directly above the knitting idol. He had three containers. With a deep, calming breath he bunched them in his hands, and tossed them into the vortex. He stepped back and crouched beside Varley.

Chapman swore as he heard two of the cylinders clatter on the floor and roll away from the statue. There was no sound from the third and, anxious, Chapman ran forward. He looked into the vortex. There was a heart-stopping moment as the charge just sat there, suspended in light; then the casing was rent and the powder compressed. The resultant explosion sprayed particles of the statue in a thousand radii and up into the vortex; at the instant of contact, the consumption of the particles produced a reaction that took Chapman quite by surprise.

Through the Madjan's misty shroud, Chapman saw its eyes flare with a flourish of white heat and then die. Its energy spent on the ill-fated reconstitution, the Madjan could no longer resist the opposing force; the color, the golds and reds, drained from the figure into the vortex as the fog swirled thick with the residue of its dispersing master. Transfixed, Chapman had no sense of time passing. In what may have been a second or an hour, the Madjan vanished, the smoke at last collapsing inward and down, funneling into the all-encompassing whirlpool. When the last tenebrous wisps had been swallowed, the vortex itself swirled smaller until, irislike, it had winked into oblivion.

The silence was sweet.

Chapman looked down at the rubble, the tangible matter that was harmless now. None of it could have happened, it seemed now, yet in any direction one turned there was evidence that this had been more than just the delusion of a disordered soul.

Varley moaned and tried to shake away the stupor that threatened to overcome him. Chapman tore himself from the precipice to help Varley into a sitting position.

"You know the proverbial ton of bricks?" the detective beefed. "I could build a lighthouse with what hit me, which I may just do after I transfer from here to Phippsburg, Maine, in the morning."

"This could've happened anywhere, Detective."

"Wrongo. There's a real low Chink population in Phippsburg, I hear tell." Varley squinted as he slid back a few feet to prop himself against an overturned bench. "I think my leg's broken, so I'm not going anywhere, but I've still got my gun. And any moralizing you care to make will be silenced by a bullet. Jesus, Grant, I've had enough bullshit for one day without your platitudes."

Chapman, looking for wood to use as a splint, regarded this man who had arrested him earlier, who had refused to help him try to save the women, whose life he had risked his own to preserve. Chapman regarded the intolerant detective, whose smugness even a god had been unable to dispel. He smiled down at Varley.

"Okay, Varley, have it your way. No moralizing. If you'll excuse me, I'd like to see how the others made out."

"You're leaving me here? Grant, I'm in no condition to be by myself!"

"Oh, I'm sure someone's called your friends at Midtown South by now, and—hell, you can probably explain all of this as well as I can. Maybe even better, since you'll give them just the hard-nosed facts about what happened."

"What facts?" Varley protested. "That a Chinese god popped by to say hello and decided he liked our world so much that he'd conquer it?"

"Isn't that what happened?"

Varley laughed with pure disbelief. "Even if it is, I tell them that, and they'll pitch me in a padded playroom right next to your pal Teres."

Chapman shrugged. "Could be worse. Look at it this way, Varley. You'll get a few things with Teres that you'd never get up in Maine."

"Such as?"

"A hell of a tan."

Varley stared uncomprehendingly, which pleased Chapman enormously. Feeling an inexplicable, uncustomary sense of ego and personal worth, Chapman strutted off, leaving the shouting detective behind him.

EPILOGUE

IT WAS A QUEER SHUFFLE, a matter of careful planning and precise timing, but somehow Chapman had managed it. Because of his rope pulling at the State Department and at two boards of regents, Gretchen Whyler would become the new curator at the museum. Her departure left the Smithsonian without an assistant secretary or even another woman on the executive staff. The board was only too happy to consider Secretary of State Leumas's personal request to review Linda Bergen's credentials. They did, and after two weeks offered her a six-month trial period to give the post a chance; after less than a minute's consideration she accepted.

The Waterside apartment was a jungle of cartons and furniture through which Chapman and Linda maneuvered. Mrs. Bergeni was only too pleased to offer last-minute advice whenever she deigned to poke her head from the bathroom where she was getting ready for the train trip to the nation's capital.

"I haven't seen your mother this up in years," Chapman said after a contemplative silence. "She's got more spunk than the two of us combined."

"There's some novelty for her in this," Linda confessed. "My father always did the planning and packing whether they went on a trip or moved to a new apartment. This is an adventure in her book."

"She's never even been to Washington. How does she know she'll like it?"

Linda stopped jamming newspaper around a boxed lamp base and looked over at Grant where he was dismantling a standing shelf. "Mother dear is convinced that, like it or not, Washington is just a momentary thing. She thinks I'll fall on my ass and we'll be back before the six months are even out."

"No, she doesn't," Chapman protested. "She's not that small."

Linda pursed her lips. "I'm not supposed to know this, Grant, but she's put a security deposit on an apartment that's due to open in September, two floors above. That's quite a vote of confidence on her part, wouldn't you say?"

Chapman shook his head. "Don't let it spook you. You'll disappoint her, I'm sure."

"I'm going to try, just as I seem to disappoint everyone else in my circle of intimates."

"You referring to anyone else in this room?" Linda's silence answered his question. Chapman grinned. "As Varley would say, balls to that."

"You can't tell me you're not disappointed that I'm going. I mean, you went through the motions of helping me get the job, but your heart wasn't in it."

Chapman laid down his tools and shoved his hands into his pockets. "Sure it was. You wanted to work at the Smithsonian, and I want you to achieve your goals. Besides," he said, shrugging, "it fits right in with the martyr complex everyone tells me I have."

Linda came over and slipped her arms around Chapman's waist. She rested her head on his chest. "That's got nothing to do with it, and you know it."

"You're wrong."

"I'm not wrong. You're just afraid of having your patterns and habits changed."

"Oh really, Ms. Freud?"

"Why else did you turn down Teres's post? Deputy ambassador to China would have been a rather large career move for you. Lots of heavy-duty responsibility, doors opening around the world."

"I like the work I'm doing," Chapman answered, "and I like New York. You know how psychiatrists are always saying that once you've realized your childhood dream, everything else is an anticlimax? Well, I always wanted to be Perry Mason, and for a while I was. Now I'm just happy being me and doing work that I enjoy."

"You need new dreams," Linda suggested.

"I've become too unaggressive for you."

"It's not me I'm thinking about. I'm going to be a couple of hundred miles away, remember?"

Chapman did not disagree, but he added that in any event, China wasn't a nation of dreamers. "In the meantime," he pledged, "I'll live through your dreams, that is, if you're not too busy to keep in touch."

Linda smiled and cuddled closer, her possessive embrace telling him exactly what he had wanted to know.

Varley picked up Chapman at Penn Station and threw on his siren to escape the grip of evening rush-hour traffic.

"She gone?" the detective snickered. "Hopped on the ole four-fifty-five and left, just like that?"

"I put my brand on her shoulder," Chapman said dryly. "She won't get far."

"Never had a girl walk out on me, Grant. Bad for the male image."

"You threw them out before they got the chance, right?"

Varley told Chapman exactly what he could do with his tongue and then changed the subject. "I was in with the commissioner for an hour this afternoon after he had his meeting with your boss. Interested?"

Chapman said that he was, of course. Although he'd been waiting weeks for this matter to be resolved, he found himself cynical about the whole thing.

"Whitewash," Varley said succinctly, nodding self-righteously. "I mean, the department doesn't see it that way. They think there was a gas leak—though none of the pipes that was torn up carried anything except water—and that those three tiny little charges did all that damage."

"They don't really believe that," Chapman countered. "How do they explain the bodies?"

"We were all dazed. We dragged them together after the blast."

"I see. And the arrow in Laojiu's arm?"

"Fell on a weapon in the Asian hall. There were lots of 'em on display."

"The fact that we all gave the same testimony, independently, hooked to a polygraph?"

"A shared hallucination isn't without precedent, Grant. That's what we all had, y'see."

Chapman was silent as they plied onto the FDR Drive heading toward the airport. "We're not going to go public with the truth, then, I take it."

"Not unless you want to become Teres's neighbor. He told the truth, for all the good it did him."

"I don't know, Warren. This really goes against my grain."

"So? Am I twisting your arm to keep quiet? Reedy's writing a book about it, which they'll slam into the science fiction section; if you decide to corroborate his story, angle for Fairfield Hills. It'll give me an excuse to come visit you in Connecticut. I'm tired of this fucking city."

Chapman thought for a moment and then said, "I'll hear what Laojiu has to say. He tends to see things in a larger light than the rest of us."

"For which I'll be eternally grateful. If it weren't for his scientific vision, look at all the fun we would've missed."

Chapman did consider it as they made the hour trip in twenty-five minutes. He regretted the pain and the deaths and was not even sure that their impact were fully felt as yet. As Linda had said when she stoically boarded the train, "One night we'll all wake up screaming. A kind of reunion." She'd tried to be funny, though they both knew that they'd be lucky to be able to walk away from this psychologically.

Traffic flashed past as the siren cut a clear course to Long Island. Varley shut it off when they hit the airport entrance ramp, since he said that Nassau County police didn't like borough cops "noising it up" in their territory. Five minutes later, the men were in the VIP lounge of the commercial airline that would carry Laojiu and Yu home.

Since the mishap at the museum, Chapman had spent most of his time spinning red tape about the event in Washington, while the Chinese had recuperated from wounds and exhaustion at their mission. Their deputy ambassador had escorted them to JFK, and Varley dutifully engaged him at the bar while Chapman made his farewells.

Chapman felt foolish and sad. There was little to say after sharing what they all had, and he knew he'd miss his new-found friends. He said nothing at first as they stood together, drinking in their own doleful expressions. Then he hugged them warmly in turn. Embracing Yu, he was touched by a momentary feeling that transcended friendship and made him want to call Washington and take the embassy post; but the desire to look into other professional options was in this case stronger.

"We shall miss you, Chapman," Laojiu said at last. "You are a good man, and I will think of you often."

"It'll be difficult to put any of this from your mind when you get back to the dig."

"Association is not why either of us will remember you," Yu insisted. "I look forward to seeing you soon for more than official matters."

"I think you can safely rule out another exhibit, that's for certain. Even if the official story is devoid of supernatural trappings, the show has had what we call in the U.S. bad press. Not only the museum but all the women. Would you believe," he said incredulously, "that they've got Varley working on that case still. They're going to keep it open until the newspapers forget all about it or Varley turns up new evidence."

Laojiu nodded sagely. "You will continue at your post?" he inquired.

"This hasn't done my reputation any good, but the kind things you had to say about me and the fact that the Secretary of State likes me shouldn't leave any residual damage."

"I think you'll leave them soon, Chapman, regardless of circumstance."

"It's been my modus operandi," Chapman admitted.

"You will stand by the facts of this event—somehow they will come out—and the order will no longer accommodate you. You will be made to become as I am, a loner."

Chapman grinned. "I had a feeling you'd leave me with some maxim of that sort."

"Do you mind?"

"Not at all."

"In that case," Laojiu continued, "I hope you won't be offended if I add one thing more." His brow beetled as he sought the words to express himself most accurately. When they came, they came easily. "Never worry about a deed, only the motive. I think if ever we look back on these days and study them, we will find that this very principle is what felled a god."

"That plus a few firecrackers."

Laojiu clasped Chapman's hand. "That's the trouble with apothegms. For all the truth in them, they are pretentious. Still, I hold them to be worthy."

The flight was announced a moment later, and the government agent came over to gather up his charges. The good-byes were brief, with the Chinese leaving Varley with warm words and good wishes. He stood beside Chapman as they left.

"In a crazy way, I'm sorry to see 'em go. They're decent people." The detective stretched and looked toward the bar. "I've got an unfinished bottle of Scotch over there. Care to polish it off with me?"

Chapman sighed. "Social drink or are we planning to get drunk?"

"Will it make a difference?"

"No," Chapman answered, moving toward the bar. "Just trying to keep a handle on my motives these days."

Scratching his head, Varley followed Chapman to the bottle. He decided that he wanted to be very drunk before he asked Chapman what he meant by that. Halfway through his second glass, he decided that he didn't care.

The void shifted around him as the spade struck stone. He felt rather than saw the archaeologist sifting away the sands, carefully freeing his head from the hard earth, the grave of ancient Wan-shimm.

He knew that he had won, for the void had spilled briefly into their sphere, gone out to reclaim its stray members.

He would not be so careless as the now-broken god of war.

His serpentine hindquarters stirred after eons of rest, and the earth dragon's green eyes gazed through his earthly idol into the world that soon would be his . . .